ONCE UPON A NEW YORK SUMMER

ANYA LONDON

Chapter 1

The hooded stranger moved fast—a blur even in the glow of streetlights.

Emma Neely had just reached the front door of her building when he leaped the steps. The heavy body collided with hers, crushing her against the entrance of her Upper East Side walk-up, slamming her cheek against the glass-paned door. Pain shot from jaw to spine.

She didn't hear the purse drop from her hands. The clamor of blood in her ears drowned out the sound.

The stranger hooked a sinewy arm around her throat, confining her further. He reeked of cigarettes, booze, and sweat; she could almost taste the acrid smells on her tongue.

"Don't move," he hissed into her ear.

Oh my God oh my God oh my God! I'm being mugged. And no one is here to stop it.

Not even a rat scurried down the empty street. Most of Emma's neighbors had escaped for the Fourth of July weekend, driven from the city by the humid heat. The few who remained slept soundly behind tightly shut blinds.

She had never been mugged before.

Oh God, what if he meant to do worse?

Her knees trembled. Clammy sweat glued her dress to her body. She opened her mouth to scream, hoping at least someone was still awake on this empty, tree-lined block, but her attacker's forearm squeezed her neck, dug into her windpipe. Choked her. His other arm encircled her, and she caught a glint of a knife.

Why didn't I take a cab home from Lizzy's birthday party? Why did I choose to walk? She hadn't stayed out this late in years. A sensible thirty-two-year-old should be long asleep by now, which was what Emma would normally be doing this late into a Friday night.

But no, she just had to give in to Lizzy's cajoling to join her for a night out. She had chugged a strong coffee, looked longingly at the summer read on her nightstand, braced herself, and went to Lizzy's party. Now here she was, being assaulted.

The man behind her shifted. The heat of his body radiated uncomfortably along her back, a terrifying reminder of his closeness. "Get into your building. Now."

I know better than that.

Her mind raced. She could stay here and hope a car drove by, but New Yorkers kept their noses planted firmly in their own business. No one would stop. She could go inside the building and scream, but were *any* of her neighbors home?

"No." *We stay outside.* Going indoors with an attacker could not end well.

Glimpses of the self-defense course she took flashed across her mind. She had been a regular in those classes after what happened to Riley. But now, without the safe confines of her instructor's directions, the images were vague.

Instinct took over more than muscle memory. She dug into his flexed forearms, struggling as she pulled them away from her neck. Twisting her head to the left helped her escape the pressure on her trachea. She planted her feet for purchase and squatted, trying to escape his tightening grip. She made herself as heavy as she could—

Not heavy enough.

He was stronger. He jerked her up in the air, and her legs kicked out. She struck back at him with her feet. He twisted, avoiding her flaying limbs, and pressed the knife deep into her neck. The sharp sting meant he pierced skin.

"Inside, bitch."

"No." Her voice stayed strong, but her entire body trembled.

What the heck do I do now?

He had constrained her movements. Emma bucked against him, trying to extricate herself from the oily clasp of his limbs, but he held tight.

She felt and heard the grunt. The attacker's arms closed tighter around her—then slackened. His body seemed to be jolted back by some unknown force. She stumbled as he released her, catching herself against the door pane.

A passerby must have seen them. Came to help, she prayed. The new stranger—tall, massive shoulders, wearing all black—jerked her putrid attacker away. He threw him down the front steps and tackled him to the ground.

"He has a knife!" she yelled out.

As the two men struggled, clasped together on the pavement, she caught a glimpse of her attacker's face. Older. Leathery. He fought back with the desperation of a man with something to lose.

A punch. A grunt. Another. Three in close succession.

She dove into her purse for her phone. *Need to call 911.*

The older man shoved her savior away, crawled out from under him—stumbled. Caught himself. Turned, and ran as quickly as his limping gait allowed.

She rushed down the steps to the stranger. He lay on his back, breathing heavily.

"Are you okay?" She leaned over him. "I'm calling nine-one-one right now." The phone shook in her hand. "Are you hurt—oh my God!" Blood pooled around him. "Hold on. I'll call for help."

"Stop." He grabbed for her phone, snatching it quickly from her grasp. The move was so fast and efficient, she didn't even have time to yelp.

"No police. No ambulance."

"You're bleeding. A lot. He had a knife. He *stabbed* you."

"I'll survive. Go inside."

She scanned his injured frame. "I'm not leaving you. You need a doctor. A medical professional. You could bleed to death. Maybe he punctured an organ."

"Go. Lock your door. Give me five minutes, then call the cops."

"Five minutes for what?"

"To leave." His eyes were closed, his face contorted in pain.

He had sharp features—a prominent square chin, a wide forehead, high cheekbones. The attacker had caught him in one of said cheekbones, causing it to swell and bleed. From the looks of it, he'd have a black eye soon, too. Sweat, from the exertion of the fight and the humidity of the evening, beaded at his temples and across his forehead.

"You're not going anywhere. If you don't want me to call anyone, that's fine. But come upstairs. I'm not leaving you here alone. Injured."

His eyes slid open. "Go inside."

"Not without you. Come on, let me help you up. Here, slowly." She moved to help him sit.

Her rescuer grunted out a frustrated exhale. "What will it take to get you out of this street?"

"You coming with me."

He struggled up, releasing her phone back to her. "Fine. Let's go."

"There's so much blood," she whispered.

The stranger took a step forward and stumbled, and Emma rushed to his side.

"Lean against me. I'm two flights up."

She could tell that he didn't want her help, but the injuries made him flag. His arm caped around her, an iron weight across her shoulders. She flexed every muscle in her body to not tumble backward. Even then, she tottered. They traversed the stoop steps to the building door.

"I have to find the keys."

He shifted his weight to the brick wall as she stuck her hand in her purse and blindly searched. The stress churned the blood in her veins, made her movements jerky.

Her fingers closed around cool metal. The keys jangled as she yanked them out and combed for the right one on the keychain. *Get a grip, Emma.* Her hands continued to tremble.

She missed the metal slit on her first try, but managed to work the key blade into the lock and turn it on her second attempt.

When she pushed open the heavy door, he followed.

The coolness of the compact hallway clashed with the heat emanating from the stranger. The scent of his cologne—which reminded Emma of clean laundry and cool, cotton sheets—mixed with the metallic tang of his blood.

Emma took a step toward the stairwell. "Up the stairs, two flights." She placed an unsteady foot on the first step.

The stranger didn't lag, despite his labored breathing. He trailed closely behind her, his hand pressed to his side. His strained panting sounded like a stormy sea in her ear, his warm breath sending a shiver skimming up her spine.

She hurried to unlock her front door.

He stumbled as soon as they walked in, pressed his back against the closest wall for purchase, and slid down with a groan.

Emma flipped the light switches.

Bright light illuminated him, propped against the wall, and the blood around him. She gasped at the sight.

"You're bleeding a whole lot." She dropped to her knees near him, and pulled up his black shirt enough to get a look at the injuries.

He gritted his teeth at her sudden tugging.

Blood ran down the left side of his torso from multiple deep stab wounds, saturating his shirt and pants. Crimson rivulets bled into one another, making it impossible to see the exact number of cuts on his side. The knife had also sliced through his wide bicep, where the split skin gushed profusely. The lacerations needed immediate medical attention—something she could not provide.

"We need to call an ambulance."

His dark eyes focused on her. "No ambulance."

She repeated her mantra from the street. "You'll bleed to death. We need to call nine-one-one. We need a doctor. *You* need to be in a hospital. And we need to call the police."

Not again. This can't happen again. Images of bloodied, injured Riley overwhelmed her.

"No. No doctor. No ambulance. And no fucking police."

"You're going to die."

His eyes closed. "Not lucky enough. Only a few scratches."

A few scratches? He looked like he needed to go into surgery this instant. The blood continued to jet, spreading along the parquet. Her building had been built one hundred years ago. Age had given it a few unique quirks, like a floor that sloped down eastward. She had stopped noticing the slight slant years ago. The gradient caused the blood to spread even faster into her apartment, a crimson river emanating from the dark-haired stranger at her doorstep. "We have to stop the bleeding. Don't move. I'll be right back."

If he hadn't been on the street...
If he hadn't rescued me...
He came to my aid and now he's injured.
Emotions roiled through her.
Stab wounds.
Blood.
She didn't do well around blood ever since Riley—
No. Focus. He saved her. She'd do the same for him. There were no alternative options. She blocked out the nightmare from her past.

Emma grabbed a throw pillow from her linen sofa, tucking it between him and the wall. After helping him settle into the pillow, she ran to her living room closet and pulled out neatly stacked containers until she located her first-aid kit. She had been religious about keeping it well-stocked ever since that helpless moment she found Riley— *Not the time, Emma.*

She pried open the lid, grabbed an array of bandages, gauzes, and wraps, a tube of antibiotic ointment, and miscellaneous odds and ends. She left her treasures next to the bleeding man before heading to her bathroom to collect two bottles of hydrogen peroxide and a bottle of iodine from under the sink. Next, she needed scissors. Where had she put them?

Hurrying into her kitchenette, she tried to remember where they might be.

She pulled open one drawer. Not there. Tried another one. Bingo.

Her fluffy Himalayan cat, Dusty, who had followed her home one day a year ago and never left, jumped down from his perch on top of the fridge to investigate the unusual situation. He watched from a safe distance, nose twitching at the metallic scent of blood, as his human, armed with scissors, moved closer to the stranger.

"What's your name?" she asked, realizing that she knew nothing about the man in her living room.

"What's yours?" came the grumpy reply. His eyes were closed. His face very, very pale.

"Emma."

After a long pause, he gritted out, "Max."

"All right, Max." She exhaled. "I'm going to cut off your shirt—I don't think I can pull it off you otherwise."

His lips tightened. "No sudden moves."

She sank to her knees. "Okay."

"Okay."

Cutting through the cotton fabric proved challenging. The blades struggled against the soaked material. Sweat ran down her face, stung her eyes. She sliced through what she could and, muscles tight with adrenaline, ripped what she couldn't cut until his torso was bare.

"You're bleeding a *lot*," she repeated for what seemed like the hundredth time.

"Have bled worse."

She ignored him. "I need to rinse off the blood to see what we're dealing with. I can't believe he did this to you. If you hadn't helped me—if you hadn't been there—I owe you my life."

Her apartment felt stifling, even at one in the morning with all the windows open. She didn't have AC, and summers were rough in Manhattan without it.

"Let's use the peroxide first, so I can see what we are working with. Ready, Max?" Without waiting for his response, she gently tipped the bottle, drizzling the hydrogen peroxide over his wounds. As the peroxide reacted with the blood, it foamed and fizzed, further covering up the lesions. "Crap. I forgot it did that," she mumbled. "But at least it's disinfecting. Let me get some water and soap. I'll be right back."

She poured the warm water straight from her faucet into a bowl and pumped in a copious amount of her lavender-scented hand soap, before returning to the stranger.

"This may sting," she said, mostly to herself, as she sank down next to him.

Finding the thickest cotton pad her first-aid kit included, she tore open its sterile packaging. She soaked the gauze in the water and soap mixture, and washed the blood from his body to better see the extent of the damage. She tried to be as careful as she could, but it still must have stung to the bone. He didn't even wince.

He had old scars and fresh bruising across the wide

expanse of his muscled chest, but the knife wounds held her attention. Three deep ones in close succession on his side. The gash across his arm was superficial. "If the blade nicked an organ, you'll die," she warned. "Are you sure we can't call nine-one-one?"

"Positive."

"We need to disinfect these. It's going to burn."

"Do it."

Without letting herself back down, she tore open another sterile gauze pad. She doused it in the iodine and applied it to his injuries. Though his body jerked and tensed, he didn't make a sound. The strong scent of the iodine hit her nostrils and cleared the odor of blood and sweat briefly from her memory.

With shaking hands, she searched through the various gauzes, finding the clotting gauze. She scanned the directions on the wrapping. "I'm going to apply it to your wounds on your side. It says if it doesn't help stop the bleeding, we'll have to pack it inside. I really hope it won't come to that. Here goes."

"Don't pass out," he warned.

"Don't scream."

She drew a breath and, with unsteady hands, pressed the dressing to the bleeding cavities, applying as much pressure as she could to stench the flow. The stranger didn't make a sound.

Blood saturated the gauze, seeped through her fingers, stained her skin and nails. *I'm not sure this is helping.* She continued to press down.

After a few minutes, the bleeding tapered off. The blood on her fingers began to dry. She kept pressing, even though Max's whole body broke out in a sweat. *The pain must be unbearable.*

"I guess there's kaolin clay in this or something. It's working." He didn't respond to her observation, but talking out loud kept her thoughts from racing in a thousand directions to the most macabre of outcomes. "I also have a ton of bandages… I'll put the large butterfly ones over your side wounds. But I think we should apply some antibiotic ointment first."

She squeezed out the clear salve from the tube and applied it to his lesions, then reached for the large butterfly bandages.

As soon as she secured the first dressing, a sense of determined calm entered her body. Her hands stopped shaking; her palms ceased sweating. "You really lucked out today. Imagine if you had tried to stop an attack on someone without first-aid supplies."

"Yes," he responded dryly. "This right here is the definition of luck."

Once she finished with his side, she focused on the cut across his bicep. After disinfecting the gash and applying the antibiotic ointment, she pulled out a roll of stretching bandages. "This should work on your arm. More flexible. Has more give."

Emma twined the wrapping around his expansive bicep and tied it securely in place.

"You okay?" she asked. He hadn't made a single move or sound while she trussed him up like a stuffed chicken.

"Tired."

He didn't look too good. Actually, he looked like he was about to pass out. She remembered the time she donated blood and felt woozy afterward. The blood bank had given her sugar cookies and grape juice. She didn't have sugar cookies or grape juice, but she had orange juice. It would have to do.

She rushed back to her kitchenette, splashing a large serving of the juice into a Garfield mug someone had gifted her. She brought it over to him. "Here, drink this."

He didn't even argue, gulping down the contents.

"Can you move to my bed? You'll be more comfortable there."

"Floor's fine," he mumbled. His body began to tremble.

"Let's get you out of your pants. They're wet with blood." Her hands went for his belt buckle. "You'll be more comfortable without them."

He shook her off. "Later."

"Just a bit more effort, and then you can rest."

"Wait," he said as she reached for him again, stalling her progress. "Gotta get my knife."

"A knife?"

He reached behind himself and withdrew the weapon, handing it to her handle-first. The mean-looking blade, with its solid rubber grip, looked custom-made.

"Gonna take out my gun."

Gun? Who the heck was this man I brought into my apartment? Not many people walked around New York City armed to the teeth.

He had a knife and a gun on him, but he hadn't used either on the assailant downstairs. She tucked that observation away as he slid out the pistol. The firearm lay heavy in her hand, P226 engraved on the matte handle. He handed over an extra magazine and a complicated-looking holster.

She hated guns and knives and didn't want them in her apartment. Setting the weapons as far away from herself as possible, she returned to strip off his jeans.

He wasn't wearing underwear.

Her fingers collided with hot skin as she tried to undo his button and zipper. Trying not to focus on that part, she worked his blood-soaked pants over his hips until he was fully naked on her floor.

"At least you'll be warm and dry now. Can you move to my bed? No? What about the couch?"

Fast asleep, he did not respond.

Grabbing the duvet off her bed in the bedroom, she dragged the down-filled covering to his horizontal form still so near her front door. Pulling two throw blankets off the arm of her couch, she added them on top. "You'll warm up in no time."

She watched the enigmatic stranger, tucked under a mountain of blankets. His face appeared dangerously pale, the shadows beneath his eyes pronounced and dark.

Her dizziness and shakiness returned, an atmospheric river pummeling her, and she sank down to the ground. Bile burned at her throat.

She allowed herself a brief moment to break down, quietly, on the floor. Then she counted to three and dragged her body up to a standing position.

First, she needed to clean up the bloodied mess around her. Working quickly, she tossed out the soiled gauze, bleached the parquet floor, then stripped off her dress and threw it away.

In the kitchen, she helped herself to some orange juice too, holding the glass in her shaky, bloodstained hand. As the trembling slowed, she went back to the stranger, terrified that he was dead. Layers of blankets covering him made it hard to tell whether he was breathing. Slowly, she made herself reach out and check his pulse. *Thank God thank God thank God.* Still alive.

Call the police, a voice told her; *call an ambulance.*

But instinct screamed no. Something about the desperate plea in his eyes had burned into her every cell, and her gut told her to let him be for now.

She dragged herself into the bathroom to rinse the blood from her hands. A bloody reflection stared back at her. Streaks of the stranger's blood had dried on her brow, grimed her face, stained the beige fabric of her bra. The slice across her neck caused a trail of her own blood to crust on her skin.

Stripping, she hopped into the shower and let the scalding water and soap and shampoo rinse every iota of blood from her skin and hair.

As the crimson water ran down the drain, she sank to her butt in the shower and sobbed.

She didn't hear the stranger in the other room slowly move. Didn't see him make his way toward her cell phone. Didn't know that it only took him four tries to gain access to the device and to start hunting.

Chapter 2

Who the hell are you, Emma Neely? What do you know?

She had been in the shower a good while, giving him enough time to search her two phones—one work, one personal. He found nothing of note on either device.

Setting them down, he explored her apartment.

Plants occupied a good chunk of her living room. A massive fiddle leaf fig spread out next to one of the windows. Floating shelves rose up one wall all the way to her ceiling, plants draping down each one. She preferred simple furniture: a comfortable-looking couch, a low coffee table, two pink retro armchairs.

A gray granite-topped island separated her kitchen from her living room, flanked by four wood-and-tan leather barstools. He assumed that the desk in the corner, holding a large screen, served as her home office. No laptop. It must be in her bedroom. As her bathroom was attached to her bedroom, he couldn't press his luck.

He heard the water shut off and stumbled back to his spot on the floor. The pain in his side tore through him like molten metal. Bile burned at his gullet. One wrong move and he'd hurl all over himself. He couldn't remember the last time he felt this physically weak. Never intended to repeat the experience.

Max watched her come back into the dimmed living room through his one eye that hadn't swollen shut.

He knew the moment she realized he was awake. She froze, tucked her robe closer around her slim frame, and hastily padded across the room toward him. He shut his eyes against the pain ripping through his side.

A cool palm stroked over his forehead. He couldn't remember the last time someone had dared touch him.

"Your color looks a little better," she murmured. "How are you feeling? Can I get you anything? Water? Another blanket?" He didn't respond, kept his eyes closed. Her voice flowed over him like iridescent silk. "I can't believe what just happened. Seems so surreal. If you hadn't been there… *thank you for what you did*. I'm going to file a police report tomorrow. Don't worry, I'll leave you out of it, if that's your preference. I hope they can find that guy. Whoever he is."

Max knew exactly who it was, but he stayed silent. He couldn't tell her that the man who was paid to find and attack her today was his father.

Chapter 3

Blazing sunlight smarted his face, penetrated the darkness in which he found comfort. He hadn't meant to fall asleep—he had a job to complete—but he hadn't been able to fight it. The quiet oasis of her apartment had dragged him under, despite his best efforts to stay vigilant.

He squeezed his lids tighter, trying to jam out the light. He shifted his head, seeking shadow. His body felt pulverized. The stinging pain resonated with startling force.

Something light and wet touched his nose.

He lifted one heavy eyelid and looked straight into the clear, focused eyes of a cat. The creature studied him intently, nose to nose, gaze unwavering. After an evaluative moment, the fluffy animal butted Max's chin with its head, rubbing its fur against his stubbly shadow. Purring, it pressed closer.

"Dusty seems to like you," said the woman. "He doesn't usually take to strangers."

Her voice came from somewhere above him, but it hurt too much to track her specific location.

As she dropped to her knees in front of him, his nose caught the heady fragrance of white flowers. Her cool palm returned. She touched his forehead, brushed across his brow. "Thank God you're awake. How are you feeling?"

He fought the warm feeling her touch stirred. He didn't do feelings. *Must be thirsty.* "Water."

She floated away, leaving a subtle trace of her perfume behind. His fingers curled into a fist as he fought the desire to pull her back.

To his relief, she returned quickly, producing a glass of tepid liquid that she placed into his hand.

"Slow," she warned as he consumed it in two big gulps.

Finally, he braved the light. Blinked open one heavy eye. His swollen left one struggled.

He managed to open both eyelids on the second try.

And fully saw her.

Her eyes reflected the exact color of Loch Ness in the Scottish Highlands. Large. Gray. Mesmeric. Her pale skin looked flushed, like she'd recently spent too much time outside and got scalded by the sun. Her dark hair fell haphazardly around her face in a riot of waves.

His body tightened. His fingers flexed. Heat flashed.

She sat too close. One move, and he'd be above her. A few tugs, and he'd be inside her. His gaze skimmed down the buttons of her silky pajama top. Each one had been meticulously buttoned, but the opening dipped low enough for him to glimpse a sliver of high, pert breasts. He wondered whether her nipples were the same color as her lips. What they'd taste like if he put his mouth on them. How quickly they'd tighten as he sucked and tenderly bit them.

He jerked away.

Too sharply. The pain crashed through him.

"Careful," she gasped, leaning in closer, trying to help right him.

He could see the delicate shell of her ear now.

Wondered what she'd do if he'd close his teeth around the lobe.

He gritted his choppers and willed himself to stay statue-still. Held his breath. Kept his eyes closed. Readjusted himself under the heavy fall of the thick duvet covering him.

Don't look at her. Don't breathe her in. *Don't touch her.*

He cleared his throat. "How long have I been out?"

"Awhile. It's almost five p.m.," she replied, tucking a pillow behind him to better prop him up. She hovered over him for a beat too long, then moved away.

He released the breath he was holding, tried to inhale air not scented with her. The apartment smelled of baking, of vanilla and cinnamon and sugar. Homey smells. Foreign.

"I made soup while you were sleeping, and muffins. I'll bring them to you here, so you don't reopen your wounds by moving."

Watching her walk away, glide to the compact kitchen barely twenty feet away, left him with a profound sense of loss.

Dumbfounded, hot, achy, Max leaped off the floor. He welcomed the pain. It brought him back to reality. He tugged one of the blankets around him and slowly hobbled to one of the stools at the granite island. Emma stood at the stove, ladling broth into a bowl.

For a split second, her gaze darted to his, then moved back to the soup.

Her flushed skin glowed. She avoided eye contact like a madwoman, fussing with the soup, moving quickly to the coffeemaker at the counter behind her, then to the cabinet for two mugs. She reminded him of a nervous sparrow, flitting from perch to perch, too nervous to stop. He could almost see her pulse beating rapidly through the delicate skin of her neck as she placed the bowl of soup in front of him on the counter.

She shifted out of the way.

He wanted to follow her. To stalk closely behind her like a predatory cat. To lean close and bury his face in her hair, bite her neck, kiss the sensitive hollow at her shoulder. He wanted to wrap his hands around her waist and lift her to the counter and—the animalistic urge to take her right there raged through his veins. He'd never felt such a viscerally wild reaction to anyone before. Exhaling slowly, he forced himself to remain rooted in place. She seemed nervous enough as it was. Invading her personal space would not be appreciated.

Overheated, dizzy, and horny, he grabbed for the coffee and took a burning sip.

Why was his biological father paid to kill this creature? What had she done to Milo for him to want her dead? Did she have a connection to Mercury Marketplace?

"Do you live here alone?" he asked instead.

"I do." She started to plate the muffins. "I have whipped cream."

"Pardon?"

"I whipped some cream up for the muffins. Do you want some?"

"Uh. Sure."

With brisk movements, she placed the muffins and whipped cream next to his bowl of soup.

She flitted from subject to subject as she did around the small kitchen, now at the fridge, pulling out a basket of bright-red strawberries. "I bake for anxiety. It helps calm me down a little. Would you like milk for your coffee?"

"No. You married?"

"I'm not."

"Got a boyfriend?"

"What is this, twenty questions?" She came around his side of the island, reaching out to feel his brow again.

The movement seemed instinctive for her, natural. But not to him. No one touched him. He had to tense every muscle to hold still, to let her fuss over him for a moment.

"No fever. Good. I was researching while you were sleeping. It doesn't seem like you have internal injuries, but an infection is a real possibility. And a fever is a sure indicator, but so far, you're okay."

He watched her try to control her rapid breathing. He made her nervous, he could tell. Was he having the same effect on her as she was on him? Or was she realizing that she let a monster into her home?

Max hadn't realized how hungry he was until he tasted the chicken soup. Diving into the food, he polished off the soup and a couple of muffins, dunking them into the whipped cream.

"They didn't turn out too bad. It's a new recipe, so it still needs some work," observed Emma. "I make a mean chocolate cake, though. I don't make it often. Chocolate cake is my weakness, so I try not to keep it in the house too often."

She bit into a plump berry. He watched her lips close over the fruit.

"The muffins are good," he croaked out, forcing himself to look anywhere but at her mouth. He picked up his mug. Set it down.

She noticed his erratic movements. "More coffee?"

He couldn't prevent his gaze from traveling down

her body, pausing at her breasts. He wanted to bend her over the kitchen counter and take her from behind. To power into her over and over and over again until he came deep inside her and she screamed his name. His fingers tightened on his cup. He shook his head.

"Are you from New York?" His voice came out gravelly.

"Born in Manhattan, but my family moved to Cold Spring when I was a kid."

Even a few feet away, Max felt like she was too close to him. She smelled like flowers and warmth and light, and he wanted to pull her into his lap and drown out the dreary, empty darkness inside him.

"My brother and his wife and their two kids now live in Cold Spring too. I have a niece and a nephew—Janie and Finn. Janie is eight. Finn's a baby." She pointed to a photo on the fridge. "That's them right there. I'll probably go visit them next week."

He glanced briefly at the photo. The one next to it caught his interest more. "You run?"

Emma's brow furrowed for a second, then smoothed when she realized he was looking at another photo on her fridge. "I do. That's me doing my first half. The Brooklyn one. I'm slow, but I enjoy it. I like the snacks."

Emma's gaze dipped to his lips, and he could have sworn her eyes darkened.

Thud.

Thud.

Thud.

His blood pounded in his ears. The apartment was too hot. Too bright. Emma was too chatty. Too *cheerful.* It was too much.

He needed to go.

He craved to stay.

She drew him in, with her scent and her warmth and those happy eyes.

Impossible. He didn't do warm and happy. He had to leave this apartment that smelled like a bakery. It was messing with his head and making him want things he knew he could never have.

He had to figure out why someone would pay Otis to liquidate her.

Wet work was not his biological father's profession.

It was his.

Chapter 4

Emma hadn't had a man in her apartment, other than her relatives, in seven years. Yet here sat Max, naked except for the throw over his lap, at her counter.

He made her nervous. Anxious.

She didn't like surprises. Didn't trust strangers.

Unable to still her racing pulse, she wished she could say the pounding in her veins was the adrenaline from the attack downstairs. Or the anxiety of having a stabbed man recovering in her apartment. But she suspected that, instead, it was… lust.

Her gaze traced his sizeable biceps and broad chest, skimmed over his washboard abs. Even his thighs looked strong and powerful. He was huge all over. Her eyes strayed to his long, thick fingers encircling his mug of coffee. *What would it be like—* She didn't finish the thought. She wasn't going there.

She had called it quits on all men seven years ago.

One attractive stranger who had saved her life wasn't going to end her moratorium.

She couldn't trust her gut when it came to men. Couldn't read them. She had thought Austin was a standup guy—and then he stabbed her sister nineteen times, almost killing her.

So, she had gone into self-imposed exile. No dating. No sex.

She liked her life. It was quiet and safe and orderly and just how she wanted it. She'd had enough commotion seven years ago to last her a lifetime. She didn't intend to shake things up ever, much less now.

Max had to go.

Once she'd get him all better, she'd send him on his merry way. Men like him were dangerous to her safe little world. They made her yearn for things she couldn't have, which was unacceptable.

She cast his butterfly bandages a surreptitious glance. So far, so good. The bleeding had stopped.

I'll keep him here one more night, just to make certain he is okay—it's the least I can do. And then lock up behind him. Goodbye, mysterious stranger. Don't ever come back.

He sat preternaturally still, as though afraid to breathe. She bet his injuries were to blame. His dark-brown eyes studied her with alarming intensity.

"Do you live nearby?" she asked, wishing to lighten the moment.

Dusty decided to take that opportunity to welcome the stranger. He gracefully hopped on Max's lap and plunked himself down, content. Emma's tensed muscles relaxed as the stranger redirected his attention to the animal.

She watched as his fingers hovered over the cat's fluffy head before he rubbed gentle circles between his ears. "I'm not a cat person."

"Dusty knows that. I wasn't one either. He targets us dog people and converts us into cat enthusiasts." She smiled at the purring feline, eyes following Max's fingers as he stroked across Dusty's fur. "What brought you to this area so late at night? A date?"

"Not a date."

Talkative, he was not.

Emma reached for her coffee, took a sip. "I'd like to know something about you. I don't know anything about you at all. Do you live in Manhattan?"

He cleared his throat. "Yes."

"Did you grow up here?"

"Moved here awhile back."

An evasive answer. She pressed further. "Where did you grow up?"

"All over the place. Nevada, for a while. I don't talk about my childhood."

"I don't mean to pry. It's just… it's an unusual situation is all."

His eyes focused on hers, causing her pulse to race. His gaze trailed to her lips… then, ever so slowly, to her neck. Sharpened. Anger flashed in their dark depths. "He cut you."

Her hand flew to the bandage across her neck. She'd almost forgotten it was there. "Just a scratch. I'm absolutely fine. It's nothing compared to what he did to you."

"Does it hurt?"

"Just a little sting."

"He'll never hurt you again."

The statement, said with such finality, unsettled her. She waved her hand. "Please don't worry about it. It'll heal."

"I'll make sure of it." His eyes darted to the door. "I should go."

Good. Yes, he needed to leave. He didn't belong in her orderly, safe space. He was too out of place. Too unsettling. Too stimulating.

Scooping Dusty off his lap, he placed him on the counter. Dusty, insulted at being moved, scoffed at the stranger and made a dramatic exit for the bedroom.

Max slid off the stool, his face contorting as he tried to straighten his body while holding the shearling throw to his naked hips.

Emma inwardly sighed. As much as she wanted him gone, she couldn't send an injured man out into the wild. He had been adamant about her not going to the authorities, so it was safe to assume that he wouldn't seek out a hospital were he to get worse.

Despite her relief at his desire to leave, she found herself arguing. "Go where? You can barely move without groaning. Stay the night. You can sleep in my bed, and I'll sleep on the couch."

"I have something I need to do."

"Today?"

"Yes."

"You can't leave. You'll develop an infection if you aren't careful. I still need to change the gauze pads—out of the question."

"Are you holding me hostage?"

"If I have to. You can't even stand up straight." Her eyes followed his pained path to the living room. "I don't understand your rush."

"Trust me, you don't want me here." He sank into a corner of her couch with a heavy exhale.

"You saved my life." Pulling away from her spot at the counter, she skirted the island to return to the kitchenette. "I want to make sure you don't regret it."

"I'm regretting it already," she heard him mumble as she pulled a small bottle of ibuprofen from a cabinet.

Filling a glass with water, she took both to him. She

handed him the water, then shook out three ibuprofens and extended them to him on her open palm. "You should take these for the pain."

He watched her as warily as a wild animal would: stock-still, as though he were as uncomfortable with her as she was with him. Finally, he reached for the offering. His fingers grazed her skin as he scooped up the pills.

Even that small contact made her pulse race.

He swallowed the pills, setting the glass of water on the side table. He shifted under his throw. "Where are my pants? Or are you going to keep me naked and trapped here?"

"No one is trapping you." She went to her living room closet, which also housed her washer and dryer. "I washed and dried them for you. I was able to get all the blood out, since it was so fresh."

Pulling the folded pants from the shelf, she rifled through her closet for anything suitable as a substitute for his shredded shirt. *Bingo.*

She brought him the pants, tossing the jeans to a spot next to him on the couch, and her brother's shirt over them.

"Here are your pants. And that's my brother's shirt. He left it here awhile back. Feel free to have it. Might be a bit tight… but it's the only thing I've got."

Max didn't move, just eyed the two articles of clothing, looking grumpy.

"Let me check on your wounds, see if they're still bleeding."

"Why are you always fussing over me? I just want to be left alone."

Definitely grumpy. Her nephew got that way too, right before he needed a nap.

"The least I can do is fuss over you a little," Emma explained in a tone she'd use with Finn or Janie when they'd get a little tired and crabby. "You saved my life, after all. Will you let me look at your bandages now, or a little bit later?"

"Later."

"All right. Would you like more water?"

"I can get it myself."

"You can't even walk upright. I'll get it."

When she brought him the water, he took a long swallow without making eye contact.

"Do you want to nap a little?" she asked, eliminating any coaxing note from her voice. Just like she spoke to the kids.

"No."

So surly.

"Will you sit or are you going to keep fidgeting?"

She tilted her head. "Why are you suddenly so irate?"

"I don't need you hovering over me. I'm leaving. You'll forget you ever saw me. I am not here."

"Max—"

He moved quickly. One moment, he was on the couch; the next, he was in front of her, his fingers digging into her upper arms. As his eyes bored into hers, she could see the gold flecks in their tea-brown depths. His warm, coffee-scented breath rushed over her skin. A muscle in his jaw contracted and released, contracted and released in rapid succession. She should have been frightened by his sudden closeness.

Instead, she felt… hot.

Hot and bothered, being so near this stranger. She wanted to inhale deeply and hold the scent of his skin forever in her memory. He smelled of crisp cotton and warm male, even with the overlay of iodine that still clung to his skin.

"Never speak my name," he gritted out. "Ever. Do you understand?"

"Who are you?" She pushed at him gently, heedful of his injuries.

He released her immediately, backing up a good six feet.

The throw lay forgotten on the floor. It took every ounce of self-control in Emma's body to keep her gaze glued squarely to his face.

He winced. "Fuck."

She glanced down then. Gasped. Blood seeped from his wounds. "You're bleeding again. Let me see."

He backed away from her reach, raising his hands to stop her approach.

She batted away his protests so she could look at the bandaged injuries. "They've reopened. What in the world were you thinking?"

His fingers twitched at his sides as he grew increasingly agitated. "I was never here," he snarled. "Understand?"

She had a feeling that he wanted to frighten her, but the only thing her mind could focus on was his bleeding.

"I understand," she said to placate him, before he did anything else to make his injuries worse. She pushed him gently to the couch. "Here, sit. Let me see." Although she had many questions to ask this mystery man, she understood his reluctance to open up to a stranger.

To him, she was an unknown entity, just like he was to her. If he wanted to remain a mystery, she'd let it go.

Current top priority? Making sure he didn't die after saving her life. She owed him that.

"We need to rebandage these. It probably needs more clotting gauze. Let me peel this one back."

"You'll never tell anyone I was here," he insisted as she fretted over him.

If she didn't give him assurance, he'd leap around and reinjure himself again. She moved up his body until her eyes were level with his. "I won't say anything about you to anyone. I promise."

His gaze reflected urgent insistence. "And you'll never speak my name again."

"If that's what you wish. Now"—she shifted away—"hold right there. Let me get some more gauze."

He didn't want to share anything about himself with her? Fine. She couldn't get attached to him anyway. His presence was making her feel all sorts of things she hadn't felt in years. She'd patch him up. Make sure he didn't develop an infection. Then she'd send him on his way and return to her serene, tranquil life.

Chapter 5

Max couldn't understand why this woman was making him crazy. He felt hot, horny, bothered. He couldn't even breathe right. Every breath smelled of *her*—of white flowers and hope. He didn't do hope. Didn't do intimacy.

He came from a long line of violent men. Men who hurt women. Violent blood that enjoyed pleasure in others' pain ran through his veins too. He refused to succumb.

His entire family was fucked up. His ironclad control kept him from following in his relatives' footsteps.

That was why he hadn't fucked anyone in his thirty-six years of life. Letting go of that control would cost someone greatly, and he refused to bring a woman pain. Keeping the worst-case scenario in mind was as effective as a cold plunge for any amorous urges.

Until he met Emma. Now his control was slipping. He wanted her.

He wanted to sink his fingers into her hair and push her head down to his cock. He wanted to split her top in half and watch her breasts spill out, to palm them and squeeze, to suck on her nipples until she begged for more. He wanted to sink into her heat, to mark her as his, to pound into her until she spasmed around him and screamed his name.

His body responded to his dark thoughts, hardening

under the throw he had tossed over himself again as she ministered to his wounds.

"Oh."

He heard the gasp. His dick was impossible to miss.

"Ignore it," he told her. *I won't touch you*, he wanted to add, but he wasn't certain he could keep that promise.

She applied the last butterfly bandage and moved quickly away. Even though she kept her face averted, he noted the flush of red on her skin.

"All done," she said from the safety of the kitchenette. "But don't make any sudden moves. We're running out of bandages. I guess I could go get some."

His pulse began to hammer. A hit had been placed on her life. He wouldn't let her out of the apartment until he confronted his old man.

Surprised by the sudden feelings that gripped him, he found the half-empty glass of water on the side table and chugged.

He had to leave, to go back to Otis's rundown shack and get his answers. Even if he had to carve it out of his biological father himself.

"Out of the question."

He could tell she wasn't used to being told what to do. She looked ready to pounce on him.

"Out of the question?"

Did she not have any sense of self-preservation? "Yes. A man attacked you just hours ago. And you want to go run an errand? Alone?"

"Not an errand... *to go get you your bandages...*" Although she clearly wanted to argue further, her voice trailed off. She appeared to think about it. Sighed. The wrought tension left her body. Then, to his immeasurable relief, she acquiesced. "But I guess you could be right. I can order them for delivery, if we need them. But *you* don't do anything stupid—don't reopen your wounds for a third time. Got it?"

"Got it," he agreed. Anything to keep her here. Safe. With him.

He'd give himself another hour to let the Advil kick in. Then he'd go find his answers.

Time was running out. His adoptive father's life was at stake.

***

Emma hated being told what to do. Despised it. Even more after what happened to Riley. The lawyers. The police. The media. They all had opinions on what she should do. She loathed every moment of it. She was her own person, capable of making her own decisions. If she wanted to go get his bandages, she would. He wouldn't stop her—she was an independent woman. She was also a smart woman and understood that traipsing about town when her attacker was still out there was a bad idea. She'd remain in the safety of her apartment until the stranger left and she could involve the NYPD.

Suddenly, Emma felt drained. The events of the night before and the lack of sleep pulled at her like a whirlpool. She tended to get more direct when she grew tired, so she decided to address the elephant in the room. "Why are you so tense around me?"

She didn't expect him to answer, and was surprised when he did. His eyes met hers. Anger and uncertainty and vulnerability flashed in their depths.

"I'm not used to this."

"To being stabbed? I don't expect many people are."

"No, to *you*. You keep taking care of me… I don't need it."

Oh. Her heart broke a little. "Everyone needs someone to take care of them once in a while." She paused, unsure whether to share something personal with him. "Awhile back, something awful happened to my sister. It was a lot to process, mentally. We all need someone to take care of us sometimes." Even that statement was too much. She never spoke about Riley's attack to anyone. Trying to shake off the strange current running between her and this stranger, she shrugged, feigning indifference. "I'm just repaying the favor. Don't take it personally."

He watched her with unmistakable wariness. "Who took care of you?"

"My friends. My family. We all need someone to lean on occasionally. Consider me your temporary shoulder." She frowned in mock sternness, attempting to lighten the mood. "So, suck it up. I'm not letting you die from an infection under my watch. I don't need some stranger's ghost haunting my apartment."

Max grunted.

Emma took that for agreement. "Want to go rest in my bedroom?"

His eyes moved to the open door. His jaw tensed. "I'll rest in your bedroom," he repeated quietly, and strode into the room.

A frisson of unease tickled the back of her neck. For a man eager to escape her apartment, he had agreed too easily. She considered going inside the room to check on him, but stopped. It wasn't like she had state secrets in her bedroom. Maybe her passport somewhere on one of the shelves, but he didn't seem like an identity thief. Besides, he had left the door open.

Shaking off her gathering suspicions, she dropped to her sofa. Exhaustion tugged at her, but she refused to succumb. Turning on the television, she tried to focus on the local news.

***

She was out like a light. Max pressed himself into the furthest end of the couch, as far away from her as he could. She slept with her legs tucked under her, her feet and upper body twisted in opposite directions. Her head lay heavy on the couch arm. Her face didn't relax in sleep, the brow furrowed and tense. He wanted to stroke his thumb across the two vertical creases, release the tension there.

He wondered what she'd do if he moved closer… ran his fingers along the downy skin of her neck. Nuzzled the curve of her shoulder. Covered her breasts with his hands, squeezed. Would she press her nipples into his palms? Arch her back to get closer? Spread her legs, needing his touch there too? What would her pussy feel like clenching on his fingers? His cock?

She had let a monster into her home. A monster who came from a long line of monsters, each one worse than the next. Yet she slept so soundly, so trusting of a stranger, settled in this warm, happy apartment.

He had taken advantage of her offer to use her bedroom to search through her work and personal laptops while she slept. Both were clean. Not even a raunchy porn search. She watched, in his opinion, too many YouTube cooking videos, but other than that she appeared squeaky-clean. Never had she accessed the dark web. He'd bet good money she'd have absolutely no idea how to download Tor. She'd never opened or been even remotely linked to Mercury Marketplace. He couldn't trace a single connection between Milo and her on her devices. She had a few tangential links to Trevor, but so did most people.

The news station that Emma had left on reported on the body found in the East River last week.

"The remains have been identified as those of NYU admissions counselor Clifford Reuben. Reuben was last seen—"

Max clicked off the TV.

He stood quietly, careful not to wake her. Lingered as he studied the rise and fall of her chest. It was time to leave, to seek out his biological father, and get his answers.

Several minutes later, Max hobbled out of her apartment building, staying close to the shadows. Dammit, he could still smell her on him. He had to wipe her face, her voice, her scent from his memory. Something had shifted and moved inside him in her presence, and the change hurt more than all his wounds combined. He needed to escape her spell.

Yet he hadn't left empty-handed.

Max had never stolen in his life. Not even when he was a hungry kid with no money. He would burn in hell for countless sins that marred his time on earth, but stealing had never been one of his transgressions.

Until today.

He reached into his pocket and pulled out the first thing he had ever wanted badly enough to take.

Emma's smiling face reflected at him from the photo he had snatched from her fridge. He studied it closely, skimming over her glowing skin, over her huge, gray eyes crinkling at the camera. He focused on her smile, letting it drive away the agonizing pain that tore through his body.

"Fucking shit," he mumbled as he tucked the photo away and staggered to his vehicle. The pain stabbed at him as he slid behind the wheel. Finally settled into the familiar leather seat, he released a pent-up breath. He felt achy, to-the-marrow tired, and he wanted to go *home*.

This was not how last evening was supposed to go. The plan had been simple. Visit the man he never called Dad. Find out what he knew about his only sibling. It was a long shot, but Max needed to try. His adoptive father's life depended on it.

He had headed to the decrepit house in Hunts Point from which the old man dealt. Prowling along the side of the dilapidated shack, he stopped when he saw that Otis had company.

A stocky, bald man wanted a woman—Emma Neely—dead.

Max should have left it alone. Stayed focused on the search for his sibling. Yet his gut told him to pry. So he merged with the shadows and listened for details on the hit.

"Emma Neely caused Milo enough damage," said the stranger to his bio dad. "It needs to end." That was when Otis began to haggle over the price.

Max wasn't in the business of letting innocent people die. He probably would have found Emma anyway, prevented his biological father from hurting her. Yet when the stranger uttered his brother's name, Max knew that he'd stop at nothing to get to Emma first.

Otis may have beat him to her apartment, but Max had arrived in time to stop the hit.

How was Emma connected to his little brother?

What had she done to him to warrant death?

Sticking around and questioning Emma was out of the question. He didn't trust himself around her. The once-indestructible tethers of his self-control had unraveled, and he couldn't be near her when the remaining cables finally snapped. The only path forward was to confront Otis, eliminate the interim threat.

Max barely saw the red light. He braked just in time. The car jolted. Agony crashed through him, and he spat out a curse.

He focused on the road, on the pain burning through his body, on anything but Emma. As his car retraced his earlier path and approached his biological father's shack, his eyes zeroed in on the scene in front of him, barely visible in the pale glow of the sparse streetlamps. Charred planks and beams lay in a blackened mass where the house had once been.

Someone had burned the place to the ground.

***

Inky shadows bathed the room when Emma jolted awake a few hours later.

How long did I sleep?

She had barely slept Friday night, and exhaustion still pulled at her.

Where was Max? She reached for her cell phone—nine p.m. Fully awake now, she turned on the lights throughout her apartment.

She had fallen asleep with the television on, but someone had turned off the TV and the lights. Walking to her bedroom, she expected to find Max stretched out on her bed, but the bed was empty. She peeked into the bathroom. Nothing. She even checked in the closet.

The stranger had left, and he'd taken his weapons with him.

Chapter 6

Emma was still thinking about the mysterious stranger six days later. The morning after Max disappeared, she had reported the attack to the police, excluding any mention of Max. The young officer at the station took down her information, had her write out what happened, handed her a printout with her case number, and sent her on her way.

For the rest of the week, she tried not to think about what had transpired. She went to work, came home, went for her runs, and tried to put all thoughts of the attack—and, mostly, of Max—out of her mind. Yet she couldn't shake the eerie feeling of being followed.

She'd never felt this way even with all that insanity around Riley's attack, when reporters and journalists and amateur sleuths kept attempting to track her down. It was odd to suddenly feel as though she were being watched. She suspected it was all in her head, yet she still looked for Max in the shadows.

At least work kept her occupied. She had been with the Manhattan Foundation for seven years now, the last two as their VP of programs, but the hectic summers still surprised her. The layers of meetings and stacks of reports served as a welcome respite to her preoccupation with the mysterious stranger… for the most part.

She had just returned home from the office when her

intercom buzzed. The sharp sound stopped her midway to her kitchen.

Crossing the distance to the buzzer by the door, she pressed the receiver button. "Yes?"

"Miss Emma Neely?" said a voice she didn't recognize. "I'm Special Agent Lincoln Russo. I'm with the FBI. Might I be able to ask you a few questions?"

An FBI agent is at my door?

What is an FBI agent doing at my door?

She had filed the police report just a few days earlier—but why would the FBI be investigating her case? In the grand scheme of all New York City crime, hers was not at the level of FBI involvement. Unease hummed at the base of her skull. She buzzed him up.

The knock on her door came too soon. When she opened it, a blonde man in a nice suit flashed his FBI badge. He was handsome, with bright-blue eyes the color of an autumn sky. His hand felt warm and solid as he shook hers.

"May I come in?"

She had dealt with enough law enforcement when Riley had been attacked. Special Agent Russo brought back bad memories.

Emma motioned him inside. It's not like she could turn away a federal agent.

After wiping the soles of his shoes on the mat just outside her door, he stepped into her apartment.

"Would you like some coffee?"

"I don't do caffeine, but thank you." The agent smiled, flashing a row of perfect white teeth.

Taking a calming exhale, she waved toward her sofa. "Please sit."

The agent settled his tall, slim frame, glancing

around her apartment with mild interest before directing his attention back to Emma. "Miss Neely, I need to ask you a few questions. Is this a good time to talk?"

Why was he here?

"As good a time as any," she offered, her mind racing, "but call me Emma."

"Ma'am—erm, Emma, do you know why I'm here?"

Could be because of the stranger who attacked me? Or the stranger who rescued me.

"Not at all," she replied, joints tight with anxiety.

The agent dove right in. "Have you ever been to the Crescent?"

The Crescent? "The luxury apartment building on Second?"

"Yes."

Emma sank into her rose-colored wingback chair across from him. "I've never been inside… but I do walk past it pretty often."

"Does the name Adam Smith ring a bell?"

"No."

"What about Derek Harbor?"

"No. What is this about?"

"A man named Derek Harbor was murdered at the Crescent on Wednesday. We have been investigating a series of elite, hit-for-hire murders by a professional killer we call the Ghost. We think he assassinated Derek Harbor."

Her stomach roiled. She tried to breathe. "How am I involved?"

"The crime scene had been fully scrubbed. The security tapes were wiped clean. All devices taken. Fits the Ghost's pattern."

Why was he telling her all this? "I don't understand why you're here. I've never been there. I don't know Derek Harbor."

"A neighbor interrupted the crime. They didn't see anything—were incapacitated before they could—but they appeared to have run off the Ghost before he could destroy everything. The witness did see that the fireplace was blazing. It's the middle of summer. Unusual. We found something in the ashes. It didn't quite get incinerated. I'm going to show it to you, but please don't be alarmed."

Blood pounded in her head. "I can't promise you that. I'm already very alarmed."

The FBI agent pulled out a file folder from the folio he was carrying and handed it to Emma across the coffee table. "Take a look."

Emma reached for the folder, slowly opened it, not knowing what to expect. Inside, she found a Ziploc bag holding a very burned photograph.

Oh my God. She didn't realize she had said the thought out loud.

Her hand trembled as she carefully took out the clear bag, studying the charred image. "It's a photo of me." Although a lot of it had burned, her face remained intact.

It looked exactly like the snapshot from her fridge. *Could it be a copy?*

Holy crap. Is the photo still on my fridge?

How could she look and verify without raising even more questions? Her gaze shifted to her kitchenette, but she couldn't see the front of the refrigerator from her spot in the armchair. *What if the photo from the fridge door was gone? Did Max steal it?*

Lincoln nodded somberly. "One of the NYPD

officers on the scene recognized you from the news a few years ago."

Emma studied the image again, her emotions roiling. Definitely the one from her fridge.

"Do you have any idea why there was a burned photo of you in the victim's apartment?"

Emma shook her head.

"Do you recognize it? When and where was it taken?"

It took a bit for Emma to find her voice. "At the Brooklyn half marathon a few years back."

"Who took the photo?"

"My boyfriend at the time."

"His name?"

She told him. "But he isn't involved in any murders."

"I'll need his phone number and address nevertheless."

Emma couldn't rip her gaze away from the charred picture. Max had stolen it. *But how did it end up burned? And in the Crescent apartment?*

Oh God.

Max was clearly this Ghost killer that the FBI was after.

Have I been aiding and abetting the Ghost?

"Tell me more about this day."

Lincoln proceeded to ask countless questions, and Emma did her best to answer as clearly as she could, her mind sprinting in a thousand directions.

Finally, he said, "You filed a police report last week. Someone had tried to mug you."

"Yes. I don't know who it was. Didn't get a good look at his face. He ran off, spooked by a passerby."

He considered her response with shrewd eyes, but didn't press further. "Since then, have you seen any suspicious persons around? Anything at all out of the ordinary?"

Emma considered telling him about Max, but every cell in her body screamed at her to shut up. She needed to process this information first. "No, nothing that I can think of right now."

"The Ghost is a dangerous man. He's a cold-blooded killer responsible for dozens of deaths. He gets paid to kill people, and he doesn't stop until the job is done. He's never left a witness who's seen his face alive. I'm not trying to scare you—"

"Sounds like you are."

"I just want you to understand the gravity of the situation."

"I appreciate it, and thank you for the concern. I just can't explain how a photo of me, burned, was found in that apartment."

He continued to study her, as though trying to mine for thoughts she was not speaking aloud.

"By the way…" Emma tried to sound casual. "Do you have a photo of this Ghost? Or a description?"

"None. Like I said before, no one who's seen him has survived the encounter."

"Wow." Emma exhaled. "Okay then."

Lincoln rose and extended his card to Emma. "If you think of anything, please give me a call."

Emma nodded. "I will. And here." She reached for her purse and found her own business card. "These are my numbers. Just in case you need to reach me."

"Do you have any plans to be out of town?" asked the special agent.

"Nope. None."

"I'll check back in with you on Monday."

As soon as she shut the door behind him, Emma ran to her fridge.

The photo of her from the Brooklyn half was missing.

Max took it. Took it and burned it.

But why?

The injured stranger who saved her life was a hit man.

A killer for hire.

The Ghost assassin knew where she lived.

Chapter 7

A low growl startled Emma awake.

After Special Agent Russo had left, she had turned on Nick at Nite, cuddled up with Dusty on her couch, and let a 1960s sitcom lull her to sleep. The cat's unrest alerted her.

Dusty, his butt still pressed close to her hip, now sat fully awake, facing her window—the one leading out to the fire escape. He detected danger, fluffing out his tail to thrice its normal size. Ears back, he focused on a noise only he could hear and growled low in his throat.

She'd never heard him produce that sound before.

Her heart pounded against her rib cage like a trapped gorilla.

What was the cat hearing? Emma bit her lip and listened, trying to slow her racing heart. It was almost morning. She caught the faint din from passing cars on Second Avenue, which ran perpendicular to her street, but detected nothing that would cause Dusty such distress.

She had left the lights on, and they bathed her apartment in a bright glow. She could be brave, go pull back the curtains, and see who was outside her window, but that sounded like a dumb thing to do alone. Her cat had never growled like that before, and she wasn't about to go explore by herself.

What if the limping older man who'd attacked her had returned—and now sat out on her fire escape, waiting to finish the job?

Or, suppose it was Max causing Dusty's reaction?

Either possibility unnerved her.

She didn't want to be the person who called 911 for a foolish reason, like her cat hearing a strange noise, but Dusty was fully freaked out now and so was she.

Emma reached for Dusty and for her phone. She'd stay close to the door in case whoever sat out there tried to get in here. She would dial 911 quickly in that case and run. But what would happen if no one from the outside made a move? Would she just stand here by the front door until morning?

I would not be in this situation if I had just gone to Europe with my family. Hindsight was always twenty-twenty.

Emma grabbed her purse. If she had to make a break for it, she wanted her wallet and keys.

Dusty, still hyper-focused on her window and growling, sat tense in her arms as she inched closer to the door.

She heard it then.

Someone shifted out on the fire escape.

Dusty, on high alert, pushed away from her and sprinted toward the window, tail swishing as he ducked behind the curtains to investigate the source of the noise.

Her cat hissed—then again, even louder. Someone moved outside her window—the sound clear in the early morning stillness.

Time to go.

Her trembling fingers grasped for the lock.

Slipped.

Tried again.

Success.

Swinging open the door, she—*bam!*—collided with a solid male wall. She screamed.

"It's me."

Someone grasped her by her upper arms. His familiar scent engulfed her. *Max.*

"S-s-someone is outside my window—the fire escape—"

He set her aside. "Stay here. Don't move. Don't go outside. No cops."

Drawing his weapon, he strode into her apartment.

***

Getting to her window was like navigating an obstacle course. Max moved her massive fiddle leaf fig to gain access to the sill. He yanked open the curtains. More plants blocked the way. He shifted enough of them aside to reach the window, navigating around Dusty, who sat on the sill and growled into the darkness outside.

"Good boy, guarding your mistress," Max told him and popped the net screen free.

On a mission, Dusty jumped out, heading straight for the corner nearest the window to sniff. Max raised his Sig Sauer and followed the cat.

The air here smelled of stale cigarettes and booze. After the earlier attack, he'd recognize that combination anywhere. His birth father.

Otis had returned to do who knew what to Emma.

Max glanced up the expanse of the fire escape. Was he still nearby? Clenching his teeth against the pain in his side, he set his foot on the metal rung and began to climb.

By the time he returned, the Sig holstered, Emma

fidgeted on the fire escape platform, holding tight to her cat.

The woman never listens. What part of stay here *did she misunderstand?*

Her eyes widened at his return. Still clutching the cat, she stepped into him. Her arm closed about his waist and she tightened her hold, all soft and warm in his arms—*hugging* him.

The feeling was foreign. No one had ever dared to hug him before. A part of him wanted to shake her off. To run. To escape.

She smelled mouthwatering and felt light and fragile in his arms. Of their own volition, his arms closed about her form before he could stop them. The feeling was novel but not unpleasant. Actually, it felt excruciatingly pleasant. His blood pumped; his body tightened. He extricated himself quickly. "Tell me what happened."

Her nose crinkled. "That man from earlier was out here. I can smell him."

"Yes, but he's long gone now. Wasn't on the roof or on the roof of the next building over."

"Dusty alerted me—he heard something out here and kept growling until I woke up."

"A smart boy." He scratched behind Dusty's velvety ears. The cat tilted his head to give Max better access.

Emma's gaze narrowed. "What are you doing back?"

"I'm not back. I'm not—nor was I ever—here, remember?"

She scanned the fire escape. "What could that man possibly want from me?" With one last look around her, she set her cat back into her apartment and followed it inside through the window.

Max climbed in next. He reinstalled the net screen

he had popped out earlier and locked her window shut. "What do you think he wants?"

Emma arranged her plants back in place before drawing the curtains firmly closed. "I have no idea. My wallet? My jewelry?"

When she stepped toward the fiddle leaf, Max cut in front of her and moved the large potted plant back to its original spot himself. "Are you involved in any underground activities I should know about?"

Emma laughed. The sound sparked up every nerve ending in his body. "No underground activities. I go to work, I come home, I volunteer."

"Where do you work?"

He already knew her story, of course. Graduated NYU Law, top of her class. Had a cushy job lined up in a prestigious Manhattan law firm, but never started the role. Her sister had been attacked around that time. Emma took a year off, moved back home to be with her. When she returned to Manhattan, she went the nonprofit route and was hired as the programs officer at the Manhattan Foundation. With its twenty-billion-dollar endowment, the foundation was one of the largest nationally. Promoted several times, she was now the VP of programs. She had a big role in a big org.

Cynthia had sent him an extensive briefing on Miss Emma Neely within hours of his call to her last Saturday, but he'd ask her the basics anyway. If she lied to him, he'd know, and he'd figure out why.

"The Manhattan Foundation."

"And where do you volunteer?"

"The New York Stop Domestic Violence Project. I work with women who're trying to escape domestic abuse."

Pretty much what he already knew. His adoptive

father was a generous donor to the domestic violence nonprofit—Cynthia was attempting to run down a possible correlation.

"Any unusual fetishes, perverse hobbies, or activities?"

Emma gave him a look. "No."

"Anything I should know about?"

"You're a stranger. You shouldn't know anything."

She studied him from beneath her lashes, and he could tell her emotions warred with each other. He wanted her back in his arms, her body pressing into his. He wanted to inhale her fragrance, to wrap his arms around her slim frame, to hold her to him. He wanted to crowd her up against the wall, spread open her thighs, and taste her.

He wanted too much.

As if reading his thoughts, she stepped back, far away from his reach.

Good. She didn't belong so close to him.

He couldn't believe he had returned to her apartment. The last place he wanted to be was back in front of Emma Neely.

But with his biological father's house incinerated and the old man at the moment not pinned down, Emma was his last remaining clue—a clue his brother wanted dispatched. Max couldn't let that happen.

"Are your wounds healing okay? Are they hurting?" Emma looked as if she wanted to come examine them for herself.

"They're fine." He didn't tell her that scaling up the fire escape was excruciatingly painful, or that he had reopened his injuries and felt them bleeding into the dressings under his black shirt, or that being in her vicinity again, so close yet unable to touch her, was the most all-consuming pain of all.

Chapter 8

The Ghost had returned. She should be screaming and yelling and contacting Special Agent Russo. Instead, she wanted to bury her nose in his chest and inhale.

Having an assassin for hire in her apartment in the middle of the night topped perilous. Yet, illogically, she felt safe with him here, locked together in her apartment.

The gimpy assailant had been moments away from breaking into her home. If Dusty hadn't alerted her…

Why had her attacker come back?

How did he know which apartment was hers?

What did he want from her?

How did Max know to return at that very moment? Were the two colluding? Was it some twisted game for them?

She had so many questions, so many accusations for Max. "Where the *heck* have you been?" was the first thing that came out of her mouth instead.

"Nowhere worth mentioning."

His eye, which had been swelling shut a week ago, still sported a shadow of a bruise, but his cut cheek looked much better. A bandage peeked from underneath the sleeve of his simple black tee. She remembered the deep, bloody lesions she had patched up just days earlier, now mostly hidden by the cotton. Although seriously injured less than a week ago, here he was, more or less hale and whole. He had survived the slashes that the attacker had ripped through him and was here, in her apartment, with her.

She craved to lift his shirt and check on how the injuries on his side were healing, to make sure he was truly okay.

Not the time or the place. Besides, he is a cold-blooded assassin. A dangerous criminal wanted by the FBI. The Ghost killer had returned to her apartment, and she had no idea why.

Emma tore her gaze away from his wide chest. "What brought you back?"

Max shrugged. "Found myself in the area."

"Tonight of all nights, while Gimpy was out on my fire escape?"

His lips twitched. "Gimpy?"

Emma pinned him with her gaze. "Have you been following me this past week?"

"Yes."

"Why? What do you want from me?"

Max didn't reply to that.

Of course not.

Emma huffed in exasperation. "You stalk me, and you don't have anything to say?" She made an attempt to walk past him, to head to the safety of her kitchenette, but he stepped in front of her, impeding her progress. Confusion and frustration radiated from his heavily muscled, coiled body.

"I… needed to see you," he finally bit out, as though he had to fight just to say the words.

Why?

"Why?" Her heart beat in her throat.

Silence. Then a growl. "I don't know."

She made an attempt at humor. "Did you miss my baking?"

An explosion of emotions flitted across his face. She couldn't name a single one, but he didn't find her comment funny. His gaze turned impenetrable.

Should I confront him about being the Ghost? Does he know the FBI came to my house? Does he know that I know, or should I pretend like I know nothing?

"Did you tell the FBI agent anything?" he asked.

Well, that answers that question. He knows the agent was here. Her heart raced at the realization, but for some reason, she wasn't as terrified as she felt she should be.

"I didn't tell anyone anything."

"What did you tell him exactly?" He kept his voice low and studied her with eyes so dark they looked black.

"Nothing."

"You told him nothing?"

"I told him nothing," she reassured him. His intense gaze was making her nervous. She wanted to take a step backward, but stood her ground. "He showed me the photo you stole. Why did you take it?"

Something flashed in Max's eyes. His jaw ticced. "He had my photo of you?"

"Yes, *my* photo." Anxiety made her hot and sweaty. She knew what she had to ask him. "Did you kill someone in the Crescent?"

Max's response came quickly. Devoid of any emotion. "Yes."

Oh God. Her stomach knotted. "Are you going to kill me?"

"Of course not." The reply was vehement.

"The FBI agent thinks you will."

Max stalked toward her until he was close enough for her to see gold glimmer dangerously in his dark eyes. "What did you say about the photo?"

"That I don't know how it ended up at the Crescent. *Which I really don't know.* I know *you* took my photo, but I didn't tell him that."

"That's a good girl."

He stared down at her, not crowding her or pressing closer. Yet he was too big; he overwhelmed her. Warmth radiated from his body, and she fought the urge to step closer, to let his heat sear her.

Before he spoke, he seemed to weigh each word. "I am having trouble staying away from you."

Emma understood. She was having trouble staying away from him as well—a big problem, considering she knew nothing about this man except that the FBI called him the Ghost because *he left no witnesses.*

She couldn't take his proximity any longer or she'd do something stupid, like grab him and kiss him. Instead, she hurried into the shelter of her kitchenette, grateful when he didn't follow.

"I have to go."

That's all I ever wanted him to do. To leave. To leave me, and my quiet, safe space, alone.

But what would happen then? She knew his darkest secret—she knew what he was, and what he did. Could she let him disappear into the night and not tell the authorities?

"Max—"

He was so close to her so quickly, towering over her with six foot plus of pure, agitated male, that she gasped. His scent submerged her. Large hands engulfed her shoulders.

"*I told you not to say my name.*"

"What do you want from me?" she asked as his fingers tightened. He was so much larger than her, so much stronger. He could easily move his hands, encircle the column of her neck and squeeze, strangling his only witness and ensuring his continued anonymity.

"I want you to leave me alone." His hands stayed on her shoulders, their warmth branding her.

"*You* came to *me*," she pointed out, trying to grasp for logic amid the riot of sensations. A man hadn't touched her like this in more than seven years. A part of her wanted to shove him away, to run. A stronger part wanted to press closer and rub against him like a cat.

"I need to go." He didn't make a move to release her.

"All right…"

His hands moved along her shoulders until his fingers found her trapezius, the area where she carried all her stress. For a moment, they sank into the tense tissue, finding the knots clustered at the base of her neck and massaging.

Emma's chest rose as she inhaled at the exquisite pressure of his touch. His eyes went straight to her breasts, and she saw the need he couldn't bank. She didn't know whether it frightened or aroused her, knowing that he wanted her as badly as she wanted him.

His hands dropped away.

"I don't think he'll return tonight," he said, more to himself than to her, leaving the confines of her small kitchen.

Who was… oh yes. Gimpy. "I hope not."

Focus, Emma. You have questions to ask. One important question, specifically. She fought to emerge from the pleasurable trance his touch had induced. "M—" She thought better of using his name, as that seemed to be a trigger for him. She licked her lips.

His gaze followed the trail of her tongue.

"How did that agent get my photo?"

His eyes flashed. "I burned it. I don't know how it didn't burn to fucking ash or how in the fuck he got his hands on it."

The same question she had asked him earlier still bothered her. "Why did you take my photo?"

"I wanted—*needed*—something to remember you by."

Emma's heart pounded. "And yet you burned it?"

"I didn't need anything to remind me of you," he spat out.

He wasn't making much sense, but at least he was still here, talking to her. She had so many questions that she could have spent the rest of the day asking them. They felt like a lit sparkler inside her.

"Do you kill people for money?"

A pause. "Used to."

Used to kill people for money. Emma's vision blurred as blood pounded in her ears. *What am I doing? I'm lusting after a murderer currently in my apartment. A lethal fugitive had crashed into the safe confines of my home and instead of calling the cops, I am salivating at his cologne.*

This is why I can't date anyone. My gut is wonky. It can't tell the good from the bad.

Max looked like a wild creature now, barely contained in her apartment, fervently seeking escape. "You won't see me again."

That scenario didn't sit well with her. All she wanted this whole time was for him to leave the sheltered little world she had created for herself. Yet now that he was doing so for good, she hated the idea.

He used to be a hit man, this Ghost the FBI sought, but he had done nothing but protect her from the very moment they met. Hadn't he?

Last week, he had gotten stabbed multiple times while fighting off her attacker. He had almost bled out on the floor of her apartment because he had foiled Gimpy's assault. A cold-blooded killer would never have intervened—would have looked the other way. Instead, he had jumped right in and most likely saved her life.

She didn't want him to leave. At least not yet. The connection between them scared her, but she had to explore it.

"What if I want to see you again?" she asked, finding a boldness she didn't know she possessed.

He halted, turned to look at her. "Why?"

"I don't know. But you want to see me again too."

"I don't." He looked frustrated. Annoyed. "I'm just making sure you aren't snitching to the FBI."

"Oh really?" Challenging him, she stepped into his space. When he didn't counter, Emma shrugged. "Fine then. Have a nice life, *Max*."

"I told you not to call me that," he growled, reaching for her arm.

"Fuck you."

His fingers tightened. "Fuck *you*."

Although his grip wasn't tight enough to hurt, she felt it burn through her skin. She felt it even after he released her.

His scent surrounded her as he leaned a fraction closer. "You're going to be okay here tonight?"

Yes.

He continued to watch her, and she realized she hadn't actually spoken the word out loud. She tried again. "Yes."

"Want me to stay? Make sure you're safe tonight?"

Emma laughed. "I'm pretty sure the most dangerous thing here is you."

"No," he said soberly. "The most dangerous thing here is you."

Emma addressed the elephant in the room. "This." She motioned between them. "This is a problem, huh?"

He didn't hesitate. "Yes. And it needs to stop. This is where it ends."

"Does it?"

"You'll never see me again after tonight."

She should be relieved. She should be happy.

"Why?" Emma found herself asking instead.

"Because I don't do"—he motioned between them, imitating Emma—"this."

She tilted her chin up. "You're scared of me." The realization shook her. She expected him to deny it, to laugh in her face.

Instead, he agreed. "Yes. You frighten me to the depth of my very soul. That's why I'm going to leave. And you're going to forget you ever met me. And life will go on."

"Is that what you want?" Emma wondered, wanting so badly to touch him, to lay her hand against his cheek.

He stood there, silent.

Her heart hammered. The prudent thing to do was to let him walk out of her life. She inhaled deeply. The words tumbled out of her mouth. "Well. If this is goodbye, I want a goodbye kiss."

"What?" Max looked so shocked that Emma almost laughed.

"You don't have to appear appalled about it."

"*No,*" he finally spat out, and took several steps away from her.

Now that she had thrown down the gauntlet, she refused to back down. "Why not? I know you want to."

"Emma. Let this die."

"I will. I want one kiss. To know."

His eyes narrowed. "To know what?"

"To know that you're real."

Max closed the distance between them in one leap, sending Emma to take a heedful step back at his sudden proximity. Then another.

"Is this what you want?" He stalked toward her.

Emma walked backward until she hit her cream-colored wall.

When he realized she had nowhere left to go, his eyes darkened.

As he stopped a mere inch away, his scent encircled her, making her weak in so many places.

He settled his gaze on her lips, paused there. Staring. Considering.

He wanted to kiss her. She could feel it. She could see it. Then, snapping out of whatever held him so close to her, he shook his head and stepped away, moving until he had placed one of her two pink wingback chairs between them.

She eyed his freshly made barricade, tried to catch her breath. The smart thing to do was to leave it alone. Yet now that she had regained a semblance of personal space, she found herself taunting him. "Are you too chicken?"

Her goad had an effect. He sprang toward her like a beast of prey, grabbing her head and kissing her so fast that their teeth clanked. The heat from his lips jolted her like lightning in a summer storm. Spurred by her now electrified skin, she clambered to get closer, wrapping her arms around him. His fingers dove into her hair, tensed on her scalp. Their kiss deepened, so raw and charged and animalistic that Emma forgot to breathe. It was too much. Too fast.

"This was a mistake," she gasped, shifting away.

"Yes. Yes." He covered her mouth with his once again.

Although as electric as last time, this kiss was less forceful, softer, and the world fell away for just a few moments. It felt… right.

"Shit," he muttered, lifting his head, his eyes dark and glazed. "Shit."

Then he kissed her again, making Emma's every cell sizzle. His hardness rocked into her, and her body responded, demanding him even closer. He fitted his palm around her breast, kneading. When he grazed her nipple through the silky fabric of her pajama top, a moan left her throat.

He froze. His head lifted.

For a moment, his gaze met hers. She saw hunger and alarm in their brown depths. He watched her with a baffled expression, as though she were a puzzle he couldn't solve but his life depended on unscrambling her. Then his hand dropped away, skimming her waist and hip before he finally released his hold and stepped back.

She didn't know what to say—what to do—as he headed for the door, reached for the doorknob.

Wordlessly, he escaped, leaving her alone in her apartment, every pulse point in her body pounding.

Chapter 9

Fucking, fucking shit.

Two decades. *Two decades* of impeccable work. Ten years of being the premier killer for hire and being worth every penny of his seven-figure fee. Of eliminating the worst of the worst discreetly, flawlessly, and quickly. Ten more years of working with Cynthia and Trevor on identifying and eliminating the monsters that lurked on the dark web: child rapists and human traffickers and murderers, the ones authorities couldn't find or identify or stop. It all went to shit last week.

The Crescent job was supposed to be easy. That was why he took it, even with his still-smarting injuries, even feeling off his game. Derek Harbor had been a top producer of child abuse materials sold on Mercury Marketplace for years. He had to be stopped.

Mercury Marketplace had quickly become the largest marketplace on the dark web, selling every illegal service or product imaginable. It had twenty million users, billions in revenue, and the authorities of almost every country trying to shut it down. It'd been impossible to track down its administrator, no matter how hard Trevor, Cynthia, and he (and, frankly, law enforcement) had tried over the last few years. In the meantime, they did their best to stop the criminals lurking in supposed anonymity one at a time.

Derek Harbor's apartment spanned the entire thirty-eighth and thirty-ninth floors, the 360-degree views laying New York at his feet. The job was supposed to be quick. In, out. Make it seem an accident. Derek tripped down his too-artsy stairs. Take his devices—track down and help the victims, anonymously notify the authorities about the buyers of the disturbing material he produced.

It all went wrong from the beginning.

Max couldn't shake Emma's face from his mind, her scent from his brain. It made him fuzzy. Sloppy.

He had eliminated his mark. Found his collection of reprehensible photos and albums. Turned up the fire. Tossed in the prints, the videos, the memorabilia. Let it all burn. They had enough from his transaction history to track down his clients without letting the hard copies of his abuse live on.

Then he heard him. Derek's neighbor. Logic told him to eliminate the witness. Clear-cut. Textbook. But the neighbor hadn't seen him yet. Had he done anything that would justify death? It didn't sit right with Max, so he did the next best thing. Knocked him out and left him right there on the hallway floor.

Disgusted with himself for not being able to tie up the loose end, Max knew he had to eliminate his inconvenient crush on Emma once and for all. He extracted Emma's photo from his shirt pocket. The one he couldn't seem to leave behind. The one he'd kept close to his heart from the moment he had plucked it from her fridge. Ridiculous.

His crush was changing him, and he didn't like it. It was time to end his obsession.

He tossed the photo into the fire and, hearing the witness stir, got out of Dodge.

For the first time in his entire life, he had left a trail… and that trail took the FBI straight to Emma.

Chapter 10

With only a narrow wedge of time left until dawn, Emma couldn't bring herself to sleep. In an attempt to soothe her anxiety, she made chocolate ganache-topped brownies, but they hadn't helped much. She couldn't shake the foiled break-in, her conversation with Max, or that kiss from her mind.

That kiss…

That kiss scrambled her brain.

She should be calling Special Agent Russo bright and early this morning and telling him everything. Instead, she kept replaying the feel of Max's lips on hers… the taste of his tongue… the pressure of his palm against her breast. Had seven years of celibacy made her so horny that she'd welcome a hit man? Emma didn't think so. No, there was something about Max himself that drew her.

The cold-blooded assassin that Russo had painted just didn't fit. Granted, she hadn't known Max long, but he'd managed to save her life, interrupted a break-in, kissed her silly, and was kind to her cat.

Was that standard assassin behavior? Emma didn't think so.

Not that she was a great judge of character, of course. After all, she'd thought Austin was a standup guy—and then he almost murdered her sister.

Trusting her gut, which told her Max wasn't as evil as Russo made him out to be, couldn't lead anywhere good. Her gut had been devastatingly wrong before. It couldn't be trusted ever again.

Max was a killer. He himself had said he was a hit man—granted, a *former* one—but he couldn't be a former hit man if he had killed the man at the Crescent this week, could he? Nothing former about it. He was bad news.

But if he left no witnesses, why didn't he kill her? She was a witness. A live one, and she knew his name—one no one else seemed to know. Did he trust her to keep everything to herself that blindly? He didn't seem like the trusting type.

Yet he hadn't ended her life. In fact, he'd saved it. Twice.

How did he know to be at the right place at the right time—both times?

Emma didn't believe in coincidences. Who was Gimpy anyway? Why did he attack her once and try to break into her apartment a few days later? What did he want from her? How was he connected to Max?

She suspected that Max knew what her attacker wanted. Max wanted something from her as well. He wouldn't have stuck around otherwise, watching her this past week.

Bleary-eyed, confused, anxious, she glanced at the time. Six in the morning. She needed to wake herself up and to expend her nervous energy, or she'd spend the entire day in groggy anxiety.

She needed to go for a run.

Was it a smart thing to do with both an anonymous assailant and a hit man the FBI dubbed the Ghost out there? No. But she refused to hide. It brought back too many memories. Ones she refused to live through again.

She made sure all her windows were locked, put on her running clothes, grabbed her pepper spray, and exited her apartment.

The sun had risen a half hour ago, but the summer day had yet to turn hot and humid. As she stepped out of her building, refreshing morning air teased her ponytail. Joggers, out early to beat the heat, peppered the streets. They dodged sleepy-looking, pajama-clad dog owners tethered to their pups.

Being surrounded by people while holding on to her pepper spray gave Emma a sense of security. She'd head to Central Park, to Turtle Pond. It was only five blocks away, and watching the turtles play amid the duckweed there always calmed her nerves.

She made it a half block when a hand fastened around her elbow.

Max.

The man moved as silently as a glimmer. She hadn't even heard him approach, yet he got close enough to touch her.

His gaze lingered on her lips, or maybe she imagined it. The baseball cap shadowed his features. "What the hell are you doing out here? Don't you have any sense of self-preservation?"

She did have a sense of self-preservation. She'd been in self-protection mode for the last seven years.

"You know," she shook off his hold, "I'm starting to think that I'm imagining you. That you don't really exist."

"I don't exist."

Emma wanted to smack him. "You're so frustrating. You live in the shadows. That can't be a very nice life."

"I have a very nice life. Independent."

"Independence isn't all it's cut out to be."

His gaze scanned their surroundings. "You shouldn't be out alone like this."

"Why? In case Gimpy returns? He is probably some junkie needing a fix… I doubt he'd try again. I refuse to cower in fear because of him."

Emma felt hot even in the crisp morning, claustrophobic. She needed oxygen. Max's body invaded her space. "You're still watching me. Why? What do you want from me?"

He offered up nothing. Frustrated with him for his taciturnity, she resumed her path to the park. She suspected Max would follow her, and he did—as closely and hotly as a fever. He fell in alongside her, his steps measured.

"What will it take for you to go home?" he demanded at the next intersection. "I have places to be today. I don't have time to babysit you."

"I never asked you to babysit me in the first place." She tilted her head. "I have a feeling you somehow know everything about me."

He didn't deny it. "I do."

"But I don't know anything about you."

"You don't."

"Stop that!" Emma exclaimed, frustrated. "I hate your stupid short answers. Give me something. *Anything.*"

"Like what?"

"I don't know…" She thought about it. What did she want to know about the Ghost assassin that was safe to discuss out in public? "Tell me about your childhood."

"Okay," he agreed too easily. "I grew up in Arizona. Three brothers, one sister. We get along great. Nice parents. I had a dog."

"That's all a lie." Emma rolled her eyes at him.

No hesitation. "Yes."

Emma sped up her stride in frustration. "You're impossible."

As they ventured closer to the park, the streets grew more crowded. Emma waited for a jogging couple to pass them before she spoke. "Tell me something about yourself—something *real*."

Max considered her question. "My stab wounds really itch."

That made her laugh. "All right," she allowed. "Progress. What was your best childhood memory?"

"I didn't have many." He didn't offer more for a while.

Emma couldn't tell whether he was trying to think of one, or whether that was his final response. She kept quiet, hoping he'd continue. When it felt like the silence stretched for too long, he finally spoke.

"There was an ice cream shop a few blocks from where my fos—from where I lived. A bunch of us kids would save up money to get ice cream cones. Mint chip was my favorite. Best mint chip I ever had. It was always scorching out there in the summers. We'd run down the road to get ice cream, through air so hot and dry it burned. Always worth it." A pause. "That was my favorite childhood memory."

"You ever go back?"

"For ice cream? No."

"Why not?"

"I burned that shack down. What was your favorite childhood memory?"

Whoa, whoa, whoa. What? Emma stopped. Nothing about Max should surprise her anymore. He was a paid assassin. The fact that he was an arsonist too shouldn't come as a shock. Yet for some reason it did. Max didn't seem like the type to burn down places of business. To be fair, he didn't seem like the type to murder people either. Yet that's what Max did, so what did she know?

Her streak of not being able to read men continued, she thought glumly, angrier at that than at anything else. Just like she hadn't seen Austin for what he was then, she still couldn't tell bad guys from good now. No, no more adventure for her. She'd send Max away and go back to her safe, comfortable life.

That possibility didn't seem as appealing as it had just a week before, though.

"Wait—you *burned it down*?"

Max kept walking.

When he didn't halt, she rushed to catch up to him. "What do you mean, *you burned it down*?"

"Owner turned out to be a creep."

Words escaped her.

"What was *your* favorite childhood memory?" he pressed, as though he hadn't revealed something that shook her to her core.

"Um…" Emma tried to recover. To focus. *They needed to come back to his childhood memory later. But soon later.* "I don't know…" she replied because she owed him a response after what he had shared. "I guess I have many… I feel very fortunate. My favorite, I guess, would be being in the tree house in our yard in the summers. My brother Tim, my sister Riley, and me. Sometimes, we'd drag the cat up there. We spent so much time in that tree house as kids. Some evenings, my parents would project a movie on the back of our house, and we'd watch it from the tree house."

"That sounds like a good summer."

"It really was. Tim is going to build his kids a tree—never mind. I'm not revealing any more about my life. You already know too much."

Max chuckled. "Fair enough."

"So why was the owner a creep?" she asked, but he walked beside her in silence. "Fine. Don't tell me. I'm going to get to the bottom of who you are, Max."

"I advise against that."

***

She was so naïve to think that she was safe with him when she was in more danger next to him than she was next to anyone else. Appalling instincts ran in his blood. Couldn't she tell that he was hanging on by a thread? Every cell in his body screamed at him to take her.

It was only a matter of time before he'd snap and turn into a monster like all his male relatives. Not even his little brother had escaped the curse.

He had to stop the hit on her and on his adoptive father; then he could walk away from her for good.

Why did Milo want her dead? Cynthia had hacked into Emma's Wi-Fi and continued to monitor her activity. There was no link to Milo or to Trevor or to Mercury Marketplace that they could see. Yet Max knew a connection existed. He needed to solve the conundrum so he could be rid of Emma, and the urges she stirred in him.

Emma turned to face him, halting their walk. The breeze stirred her hair, sending a gossamer strand to tease her cheek. His fingertips itched to brush the hair away, to graze her downy skin. He kept his hands firmly at his sides.

Don't come any closer.

He didn't know whether he was cautioning himself or Emma. This close, he could see the faint freckles peppering the bridge of her nose.

When she opened her mouth to say something, he interrupted. "You should go home."

She had no business being out here with a monster. She should be tucked away in her apartment, baking and streaming her YouTube, safe in the confines of her space. He'd watch over her from afar.

Expecting her to protest, to skewer him with her gaze and object, he waited.

Instead, she acquiesced. Too easily. "Fine. I guess this is goodbye."

He hadn't expected her to agree so quickly. Had wanted her to argue and debate his request. This ready assent rankled for reasons he did not understand.

The right thing to do was to let her go on home, to surveil her from a distance. Instead, his brain flipped through reasons to keep her next to him a little longer. "Let me walk you home. Make sure Gimpy isn't around."

She didn't argue, just walked right past him and headed back toward her apartment.

Inwardly relieved at her pliability that morning, he followed her, his eyes fixed on her pert ass as she moved.

He was spending more time in her building than he was in his own place, he realized as they entered her walk-up and she scaled the stairs ahead of him. Her running shorts revealed long, tanned legs—he couldn't look away. What would her legs feel like wrapped around him as he plunged into her? His fingers begged to sink into her ass cheeks, to lift her against the wall right here—

He almost tripped on the last step.

Emma's sudden stationary stance in front of her

apartment snapped Max out of his erotic thoughts. He forced his eyes away from Emma's frame, zeroing in on the small white envelope that had frozen her mid-stride.

***

Emma couldn't believe she was letting the hit man follow her back to her apartment. Whatever possible outcome could there be from letting this weird attraction continue? She should end it right here, right now, on the stairwell. To turn him away, to say goodbye.

She had fought hard to build the life that she led, and didn't need a man turning that topsy-turvy. The words directing him to leave never came.

A letter, leaning up against her doorjamb, muted her.

Not a USPS delivery. The mailman would not have had time to swing by that early in the morning, and the envelope had no stamp.

Emma knew the sender.

The very handwriting made her clamp her teeth together to prevent a furious scream from erupting.

Chapter 11

Skirting Emma, Max plucked the letter off the ground. "What is this?" he demanded, starting to tear open the flap.

"Don't—don't open it." Emma covered his hands with hers to stay him.

"Someone dropped this off for you."

She gave him a quick nod. "Yes."

"This happened before?"

"It happens constantly," she bit out, releasing her hold on him. "I usually toss them out in the lobby. I don't want that thing inside my house."

He turned over the envelope. "Do you know what it says?"

"Probably the same thing they always say. They're anonymous, but I know who writes them."

Max slid the envelope into his pocket as she unlocked the door, and he followed her inside. The familiar scent of her apartment—of warmth, of baking, of *her*—surrounded him. It was too warm. She was too close.

"All I wanted was peace and quiet. And now I'm being hounded by the FBI, some malicious drunk, and… and"—she gestured her hand at him—"you. On top of it all, the stupid letters keep coming." She turned for the kitchen. "I need tea. Tea and chocolate. Go sit. You might as well join me."

Dusty hopped down from his spot on the couch and twined around Max's legs in figure eights.

After petting the cat, Max sat at the counter just as he had before, when she had served him soup and muffins. No one had ever cooked just for him before that moment a week ago. It was a kind gesture he'd never forget.

Emma slammed a cup down in front of him. "You're having chamomile."

He didn't argue. She seemed in a mood. Although he didn't know her well, hadn't yet learned all her nuances and triggers, he recognized that this belligerence wasn't customary for her. The letter had genuinely made her upset. He wanted to make it better, but he didn't know how.

She set a plate of brownies and her own cup of tea on the counter with a bit more restraint.

Breath baited, he waited for her to come around the divide, to sit next to him, but she remained standing, the gray-topped island a safe boundary between them.

"Tell me who sent the letter." He broached the subject cautiously.

Emma's body seemed to empty fully on her sigh. "Seven years ago, my sister's boyfriend tried to stab her to death." She moved a brownie to her plate, eyes sad as she remembered. "She had so much internal damage. He pierced her liver, her stomach—she flatlined twice during surgery. You may remember the media circus around it. Every major news outlet covered the trial. It trended on social media. Some livestreams went on for hours, discussing every tiny detail of the case."

"I remember. Austin Skylar. He died in prison."

"Yep. Committed suicide. More than a year ago. The letters are from his sister, Leila. She attacked me in court one day. The letters started pretty soon after his death."

"She blame you?"

"Leila blames everyone, but she hates me specifically. Says I'm the one who set my sister against Austin, I'm the one who broke them up, I'm the one who spurred Austin to attack Riley, and I'm the reason he killed himself. All ridiculous, of course. Austin professed repentance in prison, and I'm the only family member who refused to forgive him."

"You take these to the authorities?"

"They haven't been able to do much. She claims it's not her. The letters are not threatening—just disturbing. Unsettling."

"They always arrive at your home?"

"Home and work. I toss them at home. My assistant at work knows to dispose of them before I even get a chance to see them. You can read it—just not in my apartment. They're weird poems, sometimes drawings… they're meant to scare me. I refuse to be scared."

Max reached for the ganache-topped brownie. "How'd Austin and your sister meet?"

"In college. A whirlwind romance. Funnily enough, I really liked him for her—thought he was a nice guy."

"But he wasn't."

"It started small… Riley didn't even notice herself, I don't think. Maybe she ignored it. He became increasingly controlling. I think she loved him so much, but couldn't do it after a while."

"She broke it off?"

"Yes. She didn't tell me how hard he took it. Or that he began following her around, coming by her office and yelling and begging. She didn't tell anyone. Didn't want to worry us."

"He tracked you guys down camping?"

She occupied herself with the kettle, set more water to boil. The memories were too raw, he could tell. Keeping herself busy helped her share them with him. "I had just graduated law school. She had the breakup. We decided to go camping with our friends in Fahnestock. She stepped away for a minute… a minute. When she didn't return, I went to look for her. I found her in the parking lot… that bastard had stabbed her nineteen times. It's a miracle she survived."

"Did he run?"

Emma returned to her spot across the counter from him. "Yes. The weasel. The police found him the next day, hiding out at his sister's house." Her gray eyes searched his. "What's it to you anyway? You want something from me. Or you know what Gimpy wants from me."

"I'm pretty sure Gimpy wants you dead."

He shouldn't have told her that. Her face paled, her eyes rounded. She fought myriad emotions before adamantly shaking her head.

"Stop saying that. No one wants me dead. A few crazies found me online during Austin's trial and sent me death threats… they didn't want me dead either. They were just crazy."

"Did those messages scare you?"

"Yes. Yes, they did. And I refuse to be scared like that again."

A rapid pulse beat in Emma's throat, and her teeth chewed her lip. As much as she protested, she was frightened. *Good.* She should be—of him.

He stood. "You should be scared." Although he walked

around the counter, he paused at the threshold of the small kitchen, not entering her safe space. "You're secluded in your apartment with me. No one to hear your scream."

"I doubt you'll do anything bad to me. You won't even let me jog to the park unescorted."

She really thought she was safe with him. The woman didn't realize how very wrong she was. A part of him wished he could be that man, the man who was honorable and decent, the one she had imprudently created in her mind. He knew better. All he would do was destroy her—hurt her in ways she couldn't even begin to fathom.

Angry with her for challenging the man he knew he was, furious with himself for being who he was, the last vestiges of his control snapped.

"Max?"

Before he registered what he was doing, he pulled her close to him and kissed her. A stupid thing to do. The kiss sparked as electric as last time, and it lit every part of him on fire.

Tugging up her shirt, he sought the heated skin of her midriff. The contact made her gasp, and he savored her reaction. She was always so responsive to him. So eager. Kissing her was a mistake. He needed to stop.

Inside, sanity battled with craving.

***

For Emma, sanity won. When she pushed at him, he let go.

"This can't happen."

He looked as breathless and confused and frustrated as Emma felt. In between drawing in massive gulps of air, he muttered, "I know."

Trying to regain control of her breathing, she stepped back. "I want to know more about you—I want to know about your past."

"Why? So you can justify my present? I don't need you making excuses for my choices."

"I want to know more about you, and I don't know why. I'm obsessing over you, and I don't want to be. I want you out of my head."

"I fucking want you out of mine." His pupils dilated as he reached for her again and crushed his mouth to hers. "Can't stop—have to taste you—"

She could scarcely comprehend the words he growled against her lips between hot, biting kisses.

When he lifted her shirt and his hot mouth closed over her breast, her legs almost buckled. He sucked on one nipple before switching to the other with a satisfied snarl, sending bright spots to dance behind her eyelids. As the world spun around her, her only constant was the wet heat of him tugging at her flesh, and she tangled her hands in his hair, seeking more.

"Don't stop," she whimpered as he skimmed up her chest, her neck, her jaw, nipped her lower lip. He kissed her ravenously, his palm gliding from her waist to her hip, tightening on her ass.

His glazed gaze found hers. "Don't move," he ordered, unerringly finding and undoing the ties of her running shorts.

She barely felt them hit the ground.

Emma hated being told what to do, but when he made the command in that low voice, her knees went weak. Why did this man cause such a response in her? She was already so wet that all she wanted was for him to touch the very core of her, yet he didn't.

Instead, his fingertips grazed the inside of one thigh, drawing teasing circles across her heated skin. With maddening leisure, he found the lace of her underwear, slid briefly over where she needed him most before retreating to run across her other thigh. She shifted in frustration.

"I said"—he pressed a palm to her sternum, emphasizing the command—"don't move."

He resumed skimming patterns across her sensitized inner thighs, the sensation making her core throb. Her eyelids fluttered open to see him watching her with a primal hunger, yet his hand was gentle as he teased her.

Two fingers finally found her center, stroked over the lace, ever so light as they grazed her folds through the fabric. He was driving her mad. She wanted to move, to lift into him, but his command held her still, captive to his ministrations.

"What a good girl," he whispered into her ear. "Following instructions."

When he cupped her, she rocked into him, needing him closer, but he retreated. Her head fell back against the wall in a frustrated groan, and she had to still herself from repositioning.

Sheer need thrummed through her. She hadn't felt such fathomless lust for anyone before, and the feeling frightened her.

Max's hand finally slid inside her panties, stroked through the liquid heat of her arousal. Emma wanted to press her pelvis into his teasing hand, increase the pressure. He found her swollen peak, grazed it, then retreated in a maddening glide.

She couldn't breathe.

He teased her for an excruciatingly long moment, finally returning to circle around her clit.

His head dipped to bite her earlobe, his clever fingers continuing their incessant teasing. "Do you want my finger inside?"

Emma nodded feverishly.

He slid just the tip into her wet opening, then retreated. Then returned to the first knuckle before ebbing again. He worked his finger slowly into her through the slick moisture, until Emma thought she'd collapse to the floor. One finger finally sank deep, then two. She felt unbelievably full as he worked in and out of her in a steady rhythm. Acute pleasure refracted through every nerve ending, drawing a moan from her as sparkles danced across her skin.

Suddenly, he stopped, his fingers stilling inside her.

"Max…" She needed him to continue.

His mouth plundered hers, tongue plunging as she wanted his fingers to do, but they held steady.

"Move on my fingers," he ordered.

Emma almost sobbed with relief as she started to rock herself on him, the pressure exquisitely intense as she set a cadence.

Her inner muscles quivered as the tension coiled. She thrust against him in a wild rhythm, the pleasure tautening as she ground into the heel of his hand. The sensation was too much. She came on his fingers, collapsing against him as a tsunami of sensation crashed over her.

He froze.

His heart beat so loudly that she could hear it clash with hers, but his body stood stock-still. He withdrew his fingers as if burned.

Stepped away.

Legs unsteady, she almost slid down to the ground without his solid form for support.

Whatever lust and passion she saw reflected in his face earlier was gone.

Cold indifference had replaced it.

The look chilled her.

She didn't recognize this Max, with his stony expression, almost mocking as he stared at her.

"You don't know the things I'm capable of," he bit out. "I don't frighten you only because you don't know the real me."

The front door shut quietly behind him.

He left her, shaken and confused and so very terrified of these feelings he could draw from her.

Chapter 12

Monday dawned busy for Emma. Waking up even earlier than usual, she ate a quick breakfast and headed to work. She hadn't left her apartment at all on Sunday, her thoughts consumed with Max despite her best efforts to shake him from her mind. After being indoors for almost a day and a half, she welcomed the refreshing morning air and the brisk walk to the subway.

As she got on the train at the Eighty-Sixth Street station, her shoulders sagged with relief. She had half expected Max to pop up somewhere along her jaunt, and she couldn't face him today.

Her cheeks flamed as memories of Saturday morning played through her brain. She came on Max's fingers, her juices all over his hand, and then he left her—walked out like the moment meant nothing to him.

Maybe it didn't.

She didn't know him, after all.

He could be juggling a harem. Oh God, *was he*? She'd have no way of knowing—who would she ask? The FBI?

She exited in Midtown, walking by Rockefeller Center to get to her building on Sixth Avenue. The Manhattan Foundation was housed on the forty-third floor of a forty-seven-story skyscraper on Avenue of the Americas, once known as the Time & Life Building.

Work had been her sanctuary for years, and she looked forward to being in the office, to putting all fears of Gimpy and all thoughts of Max out of her mind. Not that she could escape thinking about Max for that long.

At 8:30 that morning, she had a meeting with Special Agent Lincoln Russo. She had requested that they meet at the café near the high-rise—not at her work—to avoid any questions from colleagues, and he had agreed.

Emma stopped by her office prior to her meeting with the FBI agent so she could tick a few things off her to-do list. Her colleagues would not arrive for another hour, so she helped herself to a cup of coffee and slid behind her desk. The view outside spanned the Manhattan skyline. When Emma glanced at the traffic below, the bright-yellow taxis looked like Hot Wheel cars.

She skimmed down the *New York Times*—still nothing about the Crescent, but the death of NYU admissions counselor Clifford Reuben had been deemed a homicide.

A half hour later, she met Special Agent Russo at the café. While he got into the line to order, she grabbed a corner table away from the others. The line moved quickly, and it didn't take long for him to get their drinks. A sweat bead dripped down his cheek as he approached her with a steaming paper cup and a can of seltzer. Setting the drinks down, he shrugged out of his lined suit jacket before settling into the wooden chair across from Emma.

"How are you doing with all of this?" He slid the cup of coffee toward her.

"I'm fine. There's nothing to do, really. I maintain the photo was a fluke."

"We spoke to your ex, the one you said took the photo. He had no information for us either. Emma, let me ask you again. Do you have any idea or inkling about how that photo got there?"

Emma wished she could help him. "None whatso-ever."

"You seem a little nervous."

"Well, you're a trained interrogator asking me questions really early in the morning. You'll forgive me if I'm a little on edge."

"You shouldn't be if you have nothing to hide."

"What do you think I have to hide? You found a burned photo of me. One that I didn't even take. I can't begin to explain it, and I want to get back to work." She felt bad lying to the agent, but there was no alternative. At least, not yet.

His eyes flashed. "If you're hiding something, I'll get to the bottom of it."

Standing, Emma picked up her coffee. "Well, I wish you luck with your investigation. Truly. I hope you find the right lead to follow. I'm not that lead. And next time you need to speak to me, I think I'd like a lawyer present—because this didn't feel like a check-up visit."

"I need to show you one thing before you go." He tossed a manila folder on the table between them.

"What is it?"

"The contents are a little disturbing. These are photos of some of the murders that were committed by the Ghost. In case you recognize anything."

Emma laid her palm across the folder to keep it shut. "I don't need to see that. I don't know anything, and I really don't need any nightmares. But I hope you catch the guy."

"I know you know something, Emma. You've been much too calm. It's not safe for you to keep this to yourself. Your life *is* in danger."

"Thank you for your concern, but I must get back to work."

"Hey, do you want to grab lunch later?" he asked as Emma turned to go.

Confused by the question, she spun around. "Lunch?"

"Yeah. Or maybe dinner. Tonight? I feel like we got off on the wrong foot. I'd like to apologize."

"I don't think that's a good idea, Special Agent Russo. But I accept your apology."

"Call me Lincoln. If you change your mind, you have my number." He flashed a gorgeous smile, dimple and all.

Emma gave a nod. That dinner would not end well, she decided. Best to spare Lincoln. Yet as she attempted to leave the café, she hesitated at the door.

She knew almost nothing about Max. If she continued to romanticize him in her head, she'd never move on, never recover from him. She needed to return to the safe world she'd built around herself—and make sure Max would stop haunting her thoughts. Knowing what she had to do, she turned around.

Lincoln looked up in surprise when she strode back.

"Let me see the crime photos."

Lifting his brows, he slid the folder back toward her.

Emma sat down and pulled the folder closer. She flipped open the cover. "Oh God."

"Investment banker who used to work just a few blocks from here," he explained.

She turned the page.

"The next photo is a grandfather of four."

Next page.

"That is a twenty-two-year-old boy. Just graduated from college, had his whole life ahead of him."

Bile rose in her throat. Emma closed the folder. "How do you know that the same man did all this?"

"I know."

Her knees felt too weak to stand. Cold sweat seeped from her pores. "None of these ring any bell for me."

Lincoln popped the tab on his cold can of seltzer and handed the fizzing drink to Emma. "Here. Drink." When she did, he added, "I don't want you to be the next crime scene photo, Emma."

She wanted to throw up. "I should go."

Fleeing the café, she barely made it outside before vomiting under a tree.

Chapter 13

Emma's day picked up significantly from an already-busy morning, and she ran from meeting to meeting for the majority of the afternoon. The images in Special Agent Russo's folder stayed with her throughout the day, and she felt nauseated and dirty. She couldn't wait to leave the office, get home, and shower.

As her last meeting finally came to a drawn-out conclusion, she packed up and headed home, arriving at her apartment, exhausted and drained, just past eight o'clock.

The shower helped a little. She had just tugged on a pair of red-and-white striped pajamas when a knock on her door startled her. Whoever it was had already gotten inside her building. Grateful for her locks, she left her bedroom to see who it was.

Lincoln Russo stood on the other side of her peephole.

Ugh. The last person she wanted to see tonight.

Emma glanced down at her button-down pajamas and reluctantly swung open the door. "Lincoln… you found me again so soon."

His eyes skimmed down her body. "Is this a bad time?"

Yes. A terrible time. Go away. "I was about to go to bed."

"Those were some pretty disturbing photos you saw today."

"Yes. I don't think I'll ever be able to put them out of my head."

He shuffled from foot to foot. Emma could tell he expected an invitation, but she didn't want him in her apartment.

"I refuse to answer any more of your questions without an attorney," she told him. "I mentioned this earlier."

When Lincoln leaned toward her, she fought the urge to move away.

"I just wanted to check in… make sure you're okay."

"I'm fine." She studied the special agent. He seemed tense and restless, standing at her door. His eyes reflected deep exhaustion, emphasized by dark circles beneath. "Are *you* okay, Lincoln?"

His blue gaze narrowed. "What do you mean?"

"Don't you have other cases? It's late. Shouldn't you be home? Having a beer and getting ready for a long day of bureaucratic red tape?"

He considered her questions for a moment before he spoke. "I guess… I guess I've been a little more involved in this case."

"How come?"

"It's… personal."

"Personal how?" Emma sensed the change in his demeanor.

Lincoln hesitated before speaking. His voice lowered. "The kid? The twenty-two-year-old? That's my little brother. That was my little brother."

Emma gasped. "Oh my God. Lincoln, I'm so sorry." She meant every word.

"The Ghost bastard killed my little brother, Emma. He got paid to kill my brother. And I need to know why. My mom and stepdad need to know why."

The photograph flashed across Emma's mind. "That's horrible. I had no idea. And you're sure the Ghost did that?"

"Positive. His laptop, phone, all his devices were missing when we found him. That's how I discovered the other hits, identified the Ghost. I started to look for deaths in which the devices had gone missing, even if the death looked like an accident. I tracked some going back almost twenty years. Derek Harbor at the Crescent follows that exact pattern—apparent accident, all devices swiped. If the neighbor hadn't come around when they did, we'd have never found your photo."

Emma chewed her lip, absorbing the new information.

Lincoln leaned his body even closer forward. "What I don't understand is why you seem so blasé about the situation. The Ghost is a cold-blooded killer. Ruthless. Soulless. We found your photo in the murder victim's apartment. Yet you don't seem concerned."

"I don't have a reason to be concerned. No one wants me dead."

"No one wanted my little brother dead either."

"I wish I could be helpful."

"I know that you can be. You're not sharing something, Emma. Whatever you're hiding can help us. I don't know if you're scared, but we can protect you. *I* can protect you. I wouldn't let the Ghost do anything to you. Tell me what you know."

Emma got lost in his pleading eyes. She had almost lost Riley. If someone had senselessly killed Riley or

Tim, she'd have moved heaven and earth to find the perpetrator and bring them to justice.

She understood Lincoln, knew what drove him, and wanted to help. Yet she couldn't bring herself to share what she knew. Something inside her told her to keep the information to herself for now.

"If I think of anything, you'll be the first person I call."

Lincoln studied her for a prolonged moment. "Don't bite off more than you can chew."

After Russo left, she bolted every lock and poured herself a large glass of red wine.

"What am I doing?" she mumbled as Dusty jumped on the couch and made his way to her lap. "Dusty, did I just make a terrible mistake?"

The cat gave her a soulful look before settling himself down with a sigh.

After a quick dinner, she climbed in bed with her laptop, her mind still spinning. She needed to learn more about the mysterious Max, about the Ghost. He knew too much about her—and she knew next to nothing about him. The internet was the best way to learn information about a stranger, and she finally had the impetus to look.

Opening up a new browser on her personal laptop, she typed Adam Smith into the search bar, a name Russo had mentioned to her during their initial encounter. The first entry that came up was for a Scottish economist and philosopher from the 1700s, followed by too many contemporary names to stalk. Next, she typed in Derek Harbor, followed by the Crescent and New York.

She hit the News tab.

Several articles popped up about the man who died. Derek Harbor, a resident of the Crescent, was found dead in his apartment, cause unknown. He was last seen heading back to his apartment from the gym, according to neighbors. He had been an investment banker, had recently moved into the building. No persons of interest. Investigation ongoing.

She looked up Derek Harbor, his job website, his LinkedIn profile. No results connected Derek to Max.

Bracing herself, she decided to learn more about Lincoln's twenty-two-year-old brother. A number of articles popped up, most from a decade ago, and she read them all. Phillip Russo-Wellesley was alone on his sailboat the day he died. Foul play was suspected because all devices had been taken from aboard as well as from his Manhattan condo, where security cameras had been mysteriously disconnected. No witnesses. No known suspects. Absolutely no leads. His parents, devastated, had announced a five-million-dollar reward to anyone who would come forward with information that would lead to the capture of the killer.

She scanned article after article. Yet again, nothing signaled Max.

Emma wondered who had hired Max to kill these people. And why. Did a hit man even need a reason? Or just the right price? He had said he was retired… but Derek had been murdered last week.

She swallowed, remembering what Max had shared about his past. Irrationally feeling like she was betraying his trust, she typed in "ice cream shop burned down" into the search bar. An innumerable list of search results populated, pages upon pages of them. She deleted the wording and tried "ice cream shop arson" instead. Just as many results. She started to flip through the pages.

FENTON'S CREAMERY DESTROYED BY ARSON FIRE, 2001

THE HOUSTON YOGURT SHOP ARSON, COLD CASE, 1980

10 FACTS ABOUT THE GRUESOME, UNSOLVED MURDER OF 4 IN MICHIGAN, 2010

None sounded right. She tried "ice cream shop arson Nevada." He'd said he lived there for some of his childhood.

OLDEST ICE CREAM PARLOR IN NEVADA BURNS DOWN, KILLS OWNER INSIDE, 2003

Twenty-two years ago. Emma clicked on the link to an old newspaper article.

Vincent Vacanti, 40, was inside the Rose Falls, NV ice cream parlor when it went up in flames. Suspected arson. The fire started in the early hours of the morning and there were no witnesses. No one was arrested, although the police questioned several suspects. The crime remains unsolved.

There was no additional coverage.

Emma looked up the town next. Rose Falls, Nevada. Population 850. An hour northwest of Las Vegas.

She knew what she had to do.

"I'm going to find out who you are, Max," she told no one in particular.

It was a wild-goose chase. She barely had a lead. But something seemed to click. She cleared her search history and purchased a direct flight to Harry Reid International for early the next morning before she could change her mind.

Walking across the hall, she asked her neighbor to watch Dusty while she was away. The neighbor had a cat of her own, and she gladly took in the Himalayan. Emma packed lightly, set her work out of office message, and headed to bed. She had a 7:30 a.m. flight to catch.

Chapter 14

Waking up with the sun on Tuesday, Max rolled out of bed, feeling… strange. He felt fidgety and uncomfortable. Was he getting sick?

Stepping into the shower, he welcomed the sting of water he'd set to ice-cold.

He wished he could go see Emma before his day officially began, but would she welcome him back?

Oh fuck.

Nervous.

He was feeling *nervous.*

It took him a moment to realize the feeling that was so unfamiliar to him.

He had gone through his adult life not really feeling anything. Probably because he'd felt enough emotions in his childhood to shut off his body to them entirely now.

Why the hell did Emma Neely make the pesky feelings claw through a door he had sealed a long time ago?

How could this one person, this one woman, affect him so strongly? He needed to put an end to that for good and move on with his life.

He didn't get attached to anyone, and he wasn't going to get attached to her.

Saturday had been a major fuck-up, and he'd kept

his distance to avoid a repeat. He shouldn't have done that with her. He hadn't done that with anybody because he didn't trust himself to stop. Yet when it came to Emma, he couldn't control himself. It had taken every ounce of his strength to leave her apartment, to leave her.

He had wanted to frighten her, yet all he had succeeded in doing was terrifying himself.

They both needed a break. Unwilling to leave Emma unprotected, he had asked Cynthia to hire her an interim bodyguard while he figured his shit out. No one but Ezra, he had insisted. They'd contracted with Ezra now and again. He was a mean asshole, but dedicated to his job and trustworthy.

With Ezra watching Emma, Max would take today to visit Leila Skylar's last known address on Long Island.

Stepping out of the shower, he dried off and reached for his toothbrush when his phone rang. Ezra.

"What is it?"

Ezra got straight to the point. "She just went through airport security at JFK. I can't follow her further."

Where the hell was she going?

Cynthia was tracking her phone. He speed-dialed her next.

Chapter 15

Rose Falls, Nevada

The most beautiful thing about Rose Falls was its name, Emma decided as she turned down Main Street in her rental car. There were neither roses nor falls within miles of the small, ramshackle town.

Parallel lines of buildings in the Old West style flanked the main street. She drove past several pubs, a handful of restaurants, and a row of parking spots for the far-in-between visiting tourists. A few coats of paint would have improved the look of the town significantly. With its peeling paint and boarded-up storefronts, it looked almost abandoned, like a ghost town on its last breath in the desert.

The inn was easy to find. At four stories, it stood as the tallest building on the block. Emma pulled into a parking spot in front of the inn and killed the engine.

What was she doing here?

She wasn't a private investigator.

Now that she'd parked, she felt silly.

Maybe she should turn right back around for the Vegas airport and return to Manhattan before she made a fool of herself.

But she hadn't gone through a six-hour flight, a half

hour wait at the car rental, and an hour drive from the airport to Rose Falls just to turn back.

Resolute now, she grabbed her overnight bag from the trunk and went to check in.

Inside smelled of dry wood and chemical cleaners. The woman at the front desk glanced up and beamed in greeting. She looked to be in her mid-forties, her thick hair cut bluntly. "Welcome, welcome. I can check you in. Your full name, please."

Emma handed over her driver's license but insisted on paying in cash, sliding over the full amount in crisp bills.

A few minutes later, Emma took the stairs to her room on the second floor and unlocked the door. The space was meticulously clean, although in dire need of a thorough update. Emma's gaze ran over the queen-sized bed with a red quilt, a vanity in the corner, and a very spacious restroom that screamed the '80s. The room's windows looked down to the narrow back garden and out across the flat, open span of desert to a mountain range Emma couldn't name.

She glanced at her watch. Just past noon.

Sitting on the bed, she answered a handful of urgent work emails on her work cell before heading downstairs to explore.

"Would you like a recommendation for where to have lunch?" asked the woman at the front desk.

"Umm," Emma stalled, approaching. "Sure. Something local. Something that's a landmark."

The woman smiled. "That would be Jilliann's Place, just across the street. They have really good fries. Are you here for business or pleasure?"

"Just visiting. This town was the location of the oldest ice cream shop in Nevada at one point."

"Yes." The woman gave her an odd look. "It burned down."

"Was anyone hurt?"

Her brow furrowed. "The shop owner died in the fire."

"That's terrible." Emma tsked, leaned closer. "How did the fire start?"

The woman considered Emma before responding. "We don't know. Probably faulty wiring. Maybe he left an appliance on."

"Rumor has it some foster kids set it aflame," offered a young woman who pranced up to them. "Sorry I'm late for my shift," she added, gliding behind the front desk and leaving a waft of cotton candy-scented perfume in her wake. "Are we talking about the Vacanti ice cream shop?"

"Where was that ice cream shop before it burned down?" asked Emma.

"It was just off Main Street, down Grisley Road." The girl waved a hand in the general direction. "After it burned, it was never rebuilt. There's a small garden there now."

"Why did people think that foster kids burned it down?"

"I heard that no one liked that group home being here," said the newcomer.

"Just kids being kids," offered the older woman, "but you know how folk can be."

"Where was the group home?"

The younger employee shrugged. "Not sure."

After a long pause, her older colleague responded. "The Morgans had a bunch of foster kids in a rickety house on Cedar. They did a good thing giving those kids a home, but didn't care for them much. My little sister used to play with them, and boy, did our parents hate that. The Morgans moved away a long time ago, though."

"Where did they move to?"

The woman studied Emma. "You certainly ask a lot of questions."

"Just curious." Emma smiled. "Thank you for your time, Mrs...."

"Ms. Pepper. Leslie Pepper."

"And I'm Cassidy," offered the younger woman with a wide smile.

***

Emma strolled down the main street until she found Grisley Road. The path was barely paved here, with sandy plots of land on either side of the narrow street. The homes, with their boarded-up windows, falling siding, and patchy fences, looked abandoned. Colorful toys were scattered across one of the yards. A half-empty aquarium with live goldfish stood on the shaded porch in another. A dog barked from the third. People definitely lived in these houses.

She found the garden, guarded by a chain-link fence, where she assumed the ice cream shop once stood. Looking farther ahead, she saw a home in the distance. Although it was larger than the ones closer to the main street, it also looked significantly more decrepit.

Emma walked toward the house. This had to be the Morgans' home. Was this where Max grew up? She could almost envision him as a gangly little boy running to the ice cream shop just down the street. Or was she grasping at straws?

Graffiti marked the exterior walls, and the windows that had been intact once were now fully smashed. Tumbleweeds grew haphazardly along one side of the yard. A rusting truck occupied the other. Its windows had been broken a long time ago too, and curse words had been spray-painted across its matte exterior.

A shudder worked its way through her vertebrae, and she turned back toward the main street.

She picked up extra fries at Jilliann's and took them back with her to Ms. Pepper and Cassidy, who—between the two of them—seemed to be a font of information on the town.

Cassidy wasn't at the front desk, but Leslie looked up as Emma approached.

"I brought you some fries." Emma placed the bundle in front of the woman.

"That's very kind of you, sweetie."

"Can I ask you a question? Did you—or your little sister—happen to grow up with someone named Max?"

The woman shook her head. "No, not that I recall. No one named Max in this town."

"What about those foster kids? Do you remember their names?"

"I don't. It's been quite some time now that they all moved away. I hear one of them is a big shot restaurateur on the Las Vegas Strip now. Imagine that! Good for him."

"Do you remember his name?"

"I don't, but it could come to me a little later, I guess."

"What were the Morgans' first names?"

"Oh, I don't recall that. I was just a kid. Called them Mr. and Mrs. Morgan."

Emma wasn't done with her questions. "Do you know anyone named Adam Smith?"

Leslie mulled the name over in her head. "No one. How come?"

"Just curious."

She narrowed her eyes. "Are you with the police or a newspaper or something?"

"No, just wondering if you and I have a mutual acquaintance," Emma explained.

"I doubt it."

Emma wished there was a town library or a records office of some sort, but there wasn't much else to go on with just a first name—which might be fake. Feeling absolutely stupid, she thanked Leslie and went back up to her room.

Once inside, she perched on her bed and opened her work laptop. Maybe she could find the answers that Leslie Pepper wasn't providing online. She searched for Rose Falls foster care, Rose Falls foster home, Rose Falls Morgans.

Not finding anything, she typed in Rose Falls Morgan Vacanti.

An article snippet from the Rose Falls paper was one of the few entries that populated. She clicked to zoom in. The picture showed a man and four kids posing in front of the Rose Falls Creamery.

JUNE 2001. ROSE FALLS CREAMERY CELEBRATES ITS CENTENNIAL ANNIVERSARY, announced the heading.

Vincent Vacanti with customers Maximilian Clark, Jake Morgan, Chris Heyer, and Matilda Pepper, said the caption underneath. The four children, all of them around age ten—give or take a year or two—held overloaded ice cream cones and grinned for the camera.

Emma almost swallowed her own tongue. *This* she did not expect.

"I can't believe it," she whispered. "I found you, Max."

If Leslie Pepper's sister, Matilda, was photographed

having ice cream cones with Max, then Leslie should at least remember his first name. Either she had a terrible memory, or she was lying.

Emma went downstairs and plunked her laptop right in front of Leslie. "I was scrolling the web and, look, it looks like Maximilian Clark is next to your little sister. Do you remember him at all? Maybe he didn't go by Max then but by his full name? Does this photo of him look familiar to you?"

Leslie studied the image for a very long time. "I vaguely remember him, but… I don't know how to tell you this. Max Clark died. Twenty years ago."

Chapter 16

The floor dropped out from underneath her. *Impossible. Max wasn't dead.* Or, if he were, who was the hired hit man who had been following her around? Who in the world had she been kissing?

"You seem a little pale. Is everything okay?" asked Leslie.

No, nothing was okay. "Yes, yes, everything is fine, thank you."

"You don't look fine."

"I think I just… need to sit. And think."

"Here." Leslie exited from behind the counter. "Our inn bar won't open for another few hours, but let me make you a drink. This way."

Leslie crossed to the bar tucked away in a corner. Although it seemed small, with only enough stools to fit four people, it looked well-stocked. The shelves brimmed with a wide variety of liquors, arranged in a colorful pattern against the dark paneling.

"What can I make you?"

Emma pondered the question. "Gin. I think this is a gin kind of moment. How did Max die?"

Leslie plucked a bottle from the shelf. "He went exploring some caves out in the desert. Got lost, never came back out."

"How old was he?"

"Maybe around sixteen?"

"Are you sure he died?"

Leslie poured the liquid and added ice. She turned away with the glass to grab a lemon.

Emma glanced out the inn window to the desolate street outside. Its scorched emptiness reflected how she felt on the inside. Her one lead had fizzled.

Leslie turned back and slid the glass across the bar to Emma, the ice cubes clinking. "He's definitely dead. Why are you so interested in him anyway?"

"Doesn't matter anymore, I guess." Emma took a sip. The scents of juniper and lemon hit her nostrils. "Did he have any friends? Anyone who's still in this town who could tell me more about him?"

"Afraid not. The people who can tend to leave this town and never look back."

"What about your sister? Were they close?"

Leslie poured a shot of liquor into her own glass and downed it. "They were close."

"Is she around? May I speak to her?"

Leslie's face shuttered. "Matilda… died. Suicide."

Emma's mouth dropped open. "I'm *so sorry*," she whispered, covering Leslie's hand with hers.

"I think I should be getting back. Finish up your drink. It's on me."

Emma gulped down the rest of the cold liquid and grabbed her laptop. There was nothing more to do but collect her things from her room and go. She headed upstairs.

***

Just below her room, behind the oak reception desk, Leslie Pepper dialed a number. "Hey, it's me," she said into the phone. "There's someone here asking about you. Her name is Emma Neely."

Chapter 17

Max hung up the call as he exited the private plane into the familiar Nevada heat. Hopping on a flight to Rose Falls was the last thing he had expected to do that day, but at least he wasn't more than a couple of hours behind Emma's arrival at the Las Vegas airport.

She had learned more about his life in just a few days than law enforcement had in almost two decades. Max was impressed. That was his girl. Smart, resourceful. Fearless.

Dangerous.

It was his fucking fault. He never uttered his real name to anyone. Yet, when she had asked him for his name that cursed July night, he didn't use Adam or James or Walter or any of the infinite identities he swapped about like smartphone cases.

No.

"Max," he had told her.

Max.

His real name. The only remaining part of his past. Hell, he'd even told her he grew up in Nevada.

He wanted to attribute the slip to blood loss, to the shock of being stabbed by his biological father, to the realization that his own old man hadn't recognized him or known who he was.

That night, he had felt an ache deep in his soulless body. And for once, for once in his life, he wanted someone to know him—to say his name. His *real* name. Just once.

Max hadn't planned to ever see Emma again, yet he couldn't seem to stay away from her, like an addict who had discovered the most potent drug of all.

He craved her.

She had taken care of him, fought to stem his blood flow, argued with him to prevent an infection, fed him those cinnamon muffins, and checked him for a fever. No one had ever done that for him.

"I'm going to have to kill her now," he said to himself, a sucker punch of regret deep in his gut as he slid behind the wheel of the waiting car.

Max shook off the feeling.

Emma had to die.

Chapter 18

Emma didn't want to stay in the inn any longer. If Leslie Pepper hadn't lied to her, then Max was dead and the man she'd been groping was someone else altogether. If she had lied to her, then Leslie was covering for Max. Either way, she was in over her head.

She could connect the dots from the information she'd learned.

Vincent Vacanti's ice cream shop burned down, with him in it.

The Morgans' foster kids were the suspects.

Max (or, rather, the person who called himself Max) admitted to setting it on fire.

He was one of the foster kids.

Had he known Vincent was inside?

Of course he did.

He had been only a child when the creamery burned. Fourteen at most.

How many others had he killed since then?

Flashes of the crime scenes that the FBI agent had shared with her earlier multiplied in her mind.

The man was a cold-blooded killer, playing judge, jury, executioner and getting paid for it. He killed people for a living—as a business—and she had been so blinded by his pheromones that she hid the truth from the good guy, from the FBI agent trying to put a stop to the gruesome crimes.

Talk about ignoring red flags.

Nausea flooded her mouth. She wasn't disgusted with him as much as she was with herself. She could have put a stop to him, to any future murders, by simply telling Russo what she knew. Yet she hadn't. Instead, she had protected him. What a fool. Too mesmerized by him to see the obvious: he was a cold-blooded killer for hire. Whatever his real name was.

Now she knew better. He was a ruthless criminal, and she needed to tell Special Agent Russo everything.

Emma tossed her cell phones into her purse, shoved in her work laptop, grabbed her travel bag, and took the stairs to the lobby.

Leslie looked up when Emma walked past her. "Exploring the town some more?"

"No, I'm checking out, thank you," Emma called over her shoulder on her way to the exit, grateful that she had paid for her stay in full when she had checked in a couple of hours earlier.

She paused at the door, searching her purse for her car key—

A sharp pain exploded in her head, and then she felt nothing.

Chapter 19

"What did you do?"

A loud voice. Male. Angry. Familiar.

"She found out about you. I'm trying to protect you." This one belonged to a woman.

"Not like this. Jesus. Not like *this*."

She was lying on a bed in a dim room, but enough light seeped in through the curtains for her to make out the shapes around her. Random bed frames and mattresses leaned against one wall, their shadows only slightly pronounced in the grayness. The room seemed familiar. She was still at the inn. Maybe in an unused guest room now used for storage? Her arms were numb. She glanced up. They were tied to the bedframe. *No, no, no, no, no.*

She gasped for air. *Calm down, Emma. This isn't the time to hyperventilate.*

The conversation from somewhere beyond the room continued.

"What was I supposed to do? She asked so many questions."

"You shouldn't have done *that*. Just… go. I'll deal with this."

Max. The voice belonged to Max. Or to the man claiming to be Max.

The door creaked open. Even lit by the startlingly bright light from the hall, he looked as shadowy as a figment of her imagination when he sauntered inside. He went straight for the bed.

Emma caught the silvery flash of metal. She attempted to twist away from the blade in his hands, but the ties binding her wouldn't let her.

"Shh, you're safe." He lifted both palms up to show her—including the one with the knife. "I'm just going to release you—need to slice through the ties."

Whatever constrained her arms cut painfully into her wrists. She angled her head up to take a closer look. Plastic zip ties.

She thrashed her feet, kicking at him. "You get away from me. Don't come any closer. I regret ever meeting you."

Max stopped his approach. "I'm going to let you go. Let me come closer to cut the ties."

"You said your name is Max. *Max is dead.* Who are you?"

"My real name is Max. Max Clark. I left this town as a teen, and rumors spread that I got lost and died in the caves. Those weren't true. Leslie knows they were false. She was trying to protect me."

Her chest heaved. She was starting to hyperventilate.

"I don't like knives," she ground out.

"I know. But I have no idea how to get through those ties otherwise. May I cut them?"

She gave a nod of approval. Only then did he move closer.

When she was released, she crawled off the bed. Stars flashed across her vision, and nausea fought against her throat. Woozy, she plopped her butt back down on the mattress.

"Easy." He sat next to her.

She tried to move away again, but her head spun. His arm wrapped around her shoulders. As much as she wanted to fight him, she didn't have the strength. She was queasy, and she wanted to lie back down. She leaned against him. "Don't feel good."

"I think we should take you to the hospital. This looks like a concussion."

"Not going anywhere with you," she mumbled, resting her head against his solid shoulder.

"I know, sweetheart, this isn't ideal. But you'll be okay. I promise."

"Why should I believe you? You're a *killer*. I saw the photos… Agent Russo showed me." He smelled so good, and he was so warm and solid that she found herself snuggling closer. "So tired… just need to rest my eyes."

"Hey." He pulled back to study her face.

She heard the concern in his voice, refused to trust it.

"Don't sleep, okay? I'm going to take you to the doctor."

"Head hurts."

His hands skimmed her skull, and she winced when he grazed the wound. "That's a nasty bump. We need to get you checked out."

"Hate you," she mumbled, breathing in his familiar, comforting scent.

"I know, sweetheart, and you should. Just let's get you to the doctor."

"I'll tell them about you. I'll tell everyone about you. I'm not covering up for a criminal. I liked you. Ugh. I did it again. Can't trust my judgment when it comes to men. Can't read them to save my life."

Standing, he tugged her up with him. "Let's get you up. Oh, whoa, slow… here, lean against me."

"Go away." She pushed at him. "Leave me alone."

He caught her when she stumbled. "World's going to tilt." And he swung her up in his solid arms.

She threw up on his chest.

Chapter 20

Max carried her out of the darkened storage room and into the bright light of the hall. "I'm taking her to the hospital."

Leslie scurried up to him. "You can't take her to the hospital. She knows who you are."

"No alternative." Max eyed his friend. "She has a concussion."

"I didn't hit her *that* hard," Leslie argued, following them down the empty hall.

"She passed out and threw up. I'd say you hit her hard enough."

"I gave her a sedative with her drink. It's probably that. She'll be fine once she's hydrated and rests up."

"I'm not taking that chance."

He needed her alive long enough to find out why his brother wanted her dead. That was all. The panic that gripped him and only slightly eased when he had her in his arms stemmed from her being his only clue. Not from concern for her wellbeing. He had to remember that.

"I can't let you leave, Max. She'll tell everyone."

Emma didn't help the situation when she lifted her head from his shoulder. "Give me my phones back. I want to call Russo."

Max ignored her. "Which one is her room?"

Leslie pointed to a door.

"We both need to change our clothes. Got a spare shirt? Then we're heading out."

Leslie nodded. "I'll bring you one. But don't say I didn't warn you."

"Unlock her room, will you? That medical office still in business? I want a doctor to look at her." He hoped he wouldn't have to drive to the next closest medical facility, which was a good hour away.

"Yes. New doctor heads it up now. You don't know him, but you could be recognized around town." Leslie swung open the door to Emma's room. Through the drawn-back curtains, brilliant daylight warmed the space. "Are you sure going there is a good idea? Max Clark is supposed to be dead."

Max carried Emma inside and sat her on the edge of her bed. "Got no alternative. Where's her stuff?"

Leslie pointed to Emma's things in the corner. "These are her bags. I'll get you your shirt."

When Leslie disappeared down the hall, Max approached Emma's luggage and searched her purse for her phones. Finding the devices, he slid them into his pocket.

"Can you get me a clean dress out of there?" Emma waved toward the larger of her two bags.

Max unzipped it and found a few clothing items inside, one of them a dress. He pulled out the thin pink textile. "Need help?"

"Not from you. Or I'll throw up again."

He handed her the dress. "Here. Change fast."

Emma must have been too sick to argue. She stripped out of her soiled dress and tossed the dirty garment on the floor, heading to the bathroom covered in just the lace scrap of her underwear.

Max almost followed her, but Leslie returned.

"Here. This should fit." She handed him a T-shirt.

He pulled off his stained shirt and took the clean one from Leslie, tugging it on over his head. Returning to Emma's purse, he took out Emma's car key and passed it to Leslie. "Get her rental returned."

Leslie tucked the key into her pocket. "I will. Max… I'm sorry. I panicked. I didn't mean to hurt her."

He knew she'd never intend any harm. Resting his hand on her shoulder, he offered a reassuring squeeze. "She'll be fine. She's my only tangible connection to Milo. I can't let anything happen to her just yet."

"I trust that you know what you're doing."

Max didn't have the same level of trust in himself.

***

The lights seemed too bright. The sounds too loud. Emma brushed and rinsed her teeth. She was still nauseated, but felt marginally better.

Max spoke to Leslie just outside her door. Something about her being a connection to Milo. She didn't know any Milos, and she didn't intend to help him, so he could try all he wanted.

Even if it had ruined her favorite dress, she was glad she threw up on Max. He deserved it.

"Ready?" He appeared in a new shirt in front of her just as she zipped up her clean dress.

"For what?"

"The doctor. You may have a concussion. I want you looked at."

"Sure," she agreed, moving past him to exit the bathroom. "I'm going to tell the first person I see everything about you, so beware."

"You sure threatening me right now is the best idea?"

She met his gaze with a challenging one of her own. "What are you going to do? Kill me like you killed all those people? Like you killed Russo's *brother*?"

It was dumb to taunt him, but words were the only weapon she had at the moment.

He ignored her baiting. "I'll grab your stuff. Want me to carry you down the stairs to the lobby?"

"No. I want to push you down those stairs."

"Come on." Max motioned for her to go first. "It's probably best you lead the way then."

Emma didn't see anyone around as they made their way outside. Leslie must have sent her young assistant away and hid out of sight. Good. She didn't have it in her to give the woman a piece of her mind right now. As soon as her head stopped pounding and her stomach roiling and her vision doubling, she'd report Leslie Pepper to the Better Business Bureau.

They bypassed Emma's rental and headed for a white Highlander. Florida license plates. Max's rental, Emma deduced.

He held open her door, offering his hand to help her up. Although she took it despite herself, she released him as soon as she sat. The midday heat had left the vehicle sweltering, making dark spots swim in her eyes.

"You going to throw up again? Need a plastic bag?" He slid into the driver's seat and blasted the AC. Hot air escaped through the vents before it began to cool.

She swallowed back the nausea and blinked to clear her vision. "I'll be fine. The less I speak with you, the better I feel."

Max grinned. "If you can be this witty, I'm going to assume you don't have a concussion."

"Not witty. Deadly serious. I don't want to hear the sound of your voice ever again."

He directed the AC vents toward her. "And you won't have to. But I'm taking you to the doctor's office. Don't say anything to him that would get you in trouble. Got it?"

"What are you going to do to me if I do?" she challenged, letting the cool air restore her.

"Not you. Him."

She blanched.

"These are nice people, Emma. Don't screw them over."

Too focused on not throwing up, she bit back a response.

The small, square medical building stood on a compact lot smack in the middle of the dusty desert. Emma would have never assumed it was a medical office except for the sign indicating so.

The parking lot allowed for a handful of cars, and there were several open spaces. Max pulled into the one straight in front of the entrance. He came around to hold open Emma's car door, but she didn't budge.

"I don't want to go inside."

"You got no choice. The doctor is seeing you. You either walk or I'm hauling you in."

Emma weighed the options. She reached for her seat belt.

Max extended his hand, but she avoided it, gingerly hopping out of the tall SUV herself. The sharp contact with the ground stabbed her brain.

The hot desert wind ruffled her hair and tossed up the skirt of her dress. She grabbed handfuls of the material to hold it firmly at her thighs as she stalked to the medical office.

Max held open the door and motioned for her to go first.

A young receptionist glanced up from scrolling on her cell phone. "May I help you?"

"The doctor here?" Max asked the teen. "I'd like for him to see my friend."

"Erm…" The girl looked behind her. "He's finishing up a very late lunch. Let me check. Hey, Dad?" she called out. "You done with lunch yet? There're new patients here for ya."

Max and Emma exchanged a glance.

The doctor emerged from the back room, wiping his hands on his pants. "Hey, folks. I'm Dr. Ross. You new in town? How may I help?"

"My friend here hit her head pretty hard. We want to make sure she doesn't have a concussion."

"Oh no, you poor dear. Dangerous things, concussions. Glad you came in. Serena here will just grab your insurance information, and then we'll take a look."

Emma pulled out her insurance card and ID.

Max tensed next to her as she slid the cards across to Serena. She didn't bother wondering why; she no longer cared. As soon as she felt better, she'd go find the nearest police officer and tell them everything.

Serena ushered her and Max into a small, sterile room in the back, and waved Emma to the paper-lined exam table before prancing away. Emma pulled herself onto its high surface just as Dr. Ross walked in.

"All right, dear, tell me what happened."

Emma glanced at Max. She couldn't think of any explanation for how she could have a concussion, so she said the first thing that came to mind. "Fell off the bed."

Dr. Ross perched on a padded stool next to her.

"Let's take a look. I'm going to ask you some questions and it may seem like we are pedaling in sauerkraut, but we want to be sure on all fronts."

Her lips lifted upward. She had heard that expression before, and it had amused her then too.

The doctor proceeded to ask a plethora of questions to test her memory and cognition, then checked her reflexes and coordination, and advised that she rest for the next few days.

"What about a CT scan?" Max insisted, unsatisfied. He seemed to take up the majority of the exam room as he, arms crossed, watched the doctor like a hawk.

Dr. Ross glanced at him. "The nearest one is fifty minutes away. If symptoms get worse, do go, but I think a few days of rest should do the trick."

"I feel better, so I think we should be fine. Thank you, Doctor Ross."

Max prowled behind Emma as they exited the office.

"I'm taking you to a hotel," he said as she approached the passenger side of the car, his presence looming at her side.

"I'm not going back to your friend's murder house."

He opened the car door for her. "Leslie wouldn't have done anything to you—she was freaked out by your line of questioning."

Emma climbed into the roasting heat of the SUV. "I beg to differ. I'm going back home to New York. Give me my phones back so I can change my flight and call the cops."

"I'll give you your phones back as soon as we are in a nice, air-conditioned hotel room. You're not flying after a brain injury." He slammed her door shut. The desert wind whipped at him as he came around to the driver's side.

"People fly with concussions and it's perfectly safe—and I don't have a concussion. You heard the doctor. I need rest. I'll rest on the plane."

He started the car. The air-conditioning blew hot air inside the already-broiling vehicle, struggling in the three-digit heat. "I'm not arguing over this with you. One night in a hotel. You rest. If you feel better tomorrow, we fly back together."

A stream of cool air finally emerged from the vents.

"Are you going to be my shadow from now on? Why? What did I ever do to have you stalking me? Did you even save my life the July Fourth weekend? Or was it one big setup for some elaborate reason I can't begin to comprehend?"

"It wasn't a setup."

"How did you end up at my doorstep at that exact time? It wasn't a coincidence."

His face hardened. "I know the man who attacked you."

Processing the words, Emma frowned. "You do? How?"

"He's… he's my father."

Emma thought she'd misheard. "Gimpy is your dad? Your *dad* tried to attack me? Tried to break into my apartment?"

He looked grim when he responded. "He was trying to kill you."

The dizziness sucked her under again. "No one is trying to kill me."

"Someone took out a hit on you. They hired him to do it."

His voice took on a hollow ring as it reached her, and darkness danced in her eyes again. "Never mind. I don't feel better. I'm going to be sick."

She leaned her head against the headrest, careful of the smarting bump, and tried to breathe through her nose to control the nausea.

Max's fingers were gentle as he brushed the hair from her face. She knew that she should pull away, to not let him touch her, but his hand was soothing, so warm and familiar, that she let him do it even though she knew she shouldn't.

Max turned up the AC to full blast. He pulled out a bottle of water from one of the cup holders, uncapped it, and handed it to her. "Here, drink."

She took a sip of the warm liquid, glancing at the desert beyond the windows. The remote location didn't escape Emma. Max could do anything to her here. Sand, rocks, scraggly brush, and the occasional Joshua tree stretched out for miles around them, the perfect place to hide a body.

Max reversed the car, pulling out onto a narrow, empty road. "I'm taking you to get a CT."

"It's not a concussion. It's… this whole situation. My body can't handle something this stressful again."

"Because of your sister?"

"Yes." She took another gulp of water. "Did someone hire you to kill me?"

"No. Whoever is paying for your contract can't afford me."

He wasn't joking. "Excuse me? How much are they paying to… off me?"

Keeping his eyes on the road, he shook his head. "You don't want to know."

The whole conversation seemed surreal. Someone had actually offered money to someone else to kill her. What kind of mess was she in? "I do. Tell me. What is it?"

"Five grand, last I checked."

Emma blinked. Then outrage sparked. *"Five thousand measly dollars?"*

Max's voice stayed casual. "Yes. I charge two hundred times that."

It took her a good half minute to process his statement. "Your fee is one million?"

"Was. I'm retired. But yes, one million—starting. I wouldn't usually take anything for less than five."

The amount still didn't compute. "Million?"

He slanted her a glance. "Feel better knowing that I won't touch you?"

"Not really. I feel insulted someone would go out and try to murder me for five thousand bucks. Who would pay your dad to kill me? And why?"

Max's gaze sharpened on something in the rearview mirror.

"Everything okay?" Alarmed, she twisted her head to look behind them. A red pickup was closing in on them fast. "Think it's just a local rushing somewhere?"

Max sped up. When he hit ninety-five, she peeled her eyes away from the gauge to scan the uninhabited wilderness that surrounded them.

Stretches and stretches of desert as far as the eye could see bled into distant mountains. Not a building in sight.

The pickup ate up the distance. It was the only other car on the empty road and it was getting frighteningly close, its headlights growing larger and larger.

The Ford F150 reached them, then veered right, lining up to the Highlander.

For a split second, the driver was right next to Emma. Bald, with a round face she didn't recognize. Diving into the very recesses of her memory, she tried to mine for any recollection of him. Her mind came up blank. The stranger's head whipped to his left and they made unmistakable eye contact.

She knew that he was very much there for them.

He swerved left, smashing into their side. The impact of the hit threw their car to the left and the attacker's car to the right. The man struggled to get back on the road, back on track.

Max straightened out the Highlander, keeping them on the paved road. "Glove compartment. Gun. Get it."

Emma released the latch and opened the compartment. "Why is he after us?"

"Not us. You."

"Why? What did I ever do?" Emma's hand shook as she reached for the weapon. It was cold and heavy in her palm. She glanced back at the vehicle. It was almost on them now. A few more—*oof.*

Max veered into the gravelly desert, expertly maintaining control of the SUV even as it bounced across the sandy stretch of land.

The man caught up to them.

Rammed into them again. Hard.

Emma screamed at the force of the impact.

The two cars were now both in the sand. They kicked up dust around them in a thick, orange fog.

"What the hell is he doing?" She handed the weapon to Max, feeling infinitely relieved when his massive hand closed about the firearm.

Max gunned the Highlander, getting them back on the paved road.

The pickup followed, moving easily across the bumpy sand.

He was on their ass again.

This time, Max braked.

Their pursuer had two choices: crash head-on into them or go around. He sped around them, overcorrected, but righted the F150.

"He's trying to kill us."

"Not us. You," Max repeated, focused on the road. "Can you aim?"

"*No.*"

Max maneuvered their vehicle behind the pickup truck. He lowered his window and trained the weapon. "Cover your ears."

Before Emma could ask why, Max pulled the trigger.

A loud thunderclap exploded near her eardrum. Through the hollow ringing in her ears, she heard another shot. A bit belatedly, she covered her ears.

Max's aim was true. The back tire blew, but the pickup kept going. Their attacker veered right, then braked, positioning himself next to the Highlander.

Max lowered Emma's window. "Get down."

She ducked.

Max waited for the angle to be just right, fired again.

The truck's left front tire blew.

The driver lost control of the vehicle.

It started to flip like a tossed quarter, leaving a trail of debris in its wake. The pickup rolled off the road into the desert.

"You okay?" Max skimmed his hand down her arm.

His voice sounded faint in her ringing ears. She nodded. "Fine. Do you know who that is?"

Pulling over next to the Ford, he unbuckled his seat belt and sprinted toward the upside-down pickup, his gun drawn. Emma hurried after him. They both slowed as they approached.

The man had been ejected through the windshield. His body hung halfway out, sliced through with the glass. Blood mushroomed around him.

Max felt for a pulse. "Dead." He flipped him over, searched for identification.

Emma averted her face. "We have to call the police."

"And tell them what?"

"That a man is dead… that he tried to kill us."

"Again. Not us. You. This is who ordered the hit on you. I saw him at my father's."

The nausea was back. She swallowed. "This is him?"

"Yes. Ready to leave him now?"

"Absolutely not. We are calling nine-one-one."

He was back at her side now. "We are getting the hell out of here before someone sees and calls the cops."

"We can't just abandon him. I refuse to do that."

Max studied her, then gave a pained sigh. "How about a compromise? We get out of here and you call the police and report it on our way?"

"Deal."

"You sure you don't recognize him?"

She refused to look at the body again. "Positive. What's his name?"

Max flipped open the wallet he held in his hand, read over the driver's license. "Clarence Elrod. You know a Clarence Elrod?"

"No."

"If only this idiot had worn a seat belt while gunning us down, he'd be alive for questioning." Max jogged back to the pickup, dove inside. His voice was muffled. "Fuck. No cell. Car registered to some woman in Spring Valley. Probably stolen. I'll look into it later." After returning to her, he reached for her hand. "Let's go."

"Give me my phones back—or at least one of them. I have to call nine-one-one."

He fished the devices out of his pocket and handed them over.

She ignored the text notifications filling her screen, and dialed 911.

"Leave—"

"Yeah, yeah, yeah, leave you out of it."

Chapter 21

Though the Highlander was slightly banged up on Emma's side, it had stood up pretty well to the onslaught. Max preferred his cars, guns, and knives German, but the Toyota had impressed him. He pulled the rental out onto the road and headed toward Vegas.

He glanced at Emma. "How's your head?"

"Headache is fine, but I can't stop shaking. I know it's from the adrenaline leaving my body, but it's so surreal to not be in control of my own limbs. Look." She held up her trembling hand. "I can't control it."

Max rolled down the windows. The dry Nevada air chased any remnants of the air-conditioning from the car and made the insides sweltering. "This should help warm you up a little."

"I'm actually loving this dry heat." Emma extended her hand out the window. "I much prefer it to the New York humidity. Where are we going?"

"To a hotel. You need to rest, and I need to make a few calls."

Emma gave him a nod. "Sounds good. I don't even care which hotel. I just want a shower and some tea and to get under the covers and watch a rerun of *Friends*."

"In about an hour, you'll have your wish."

To his surprise, Emma didn't put up an argument. It was a testament to how tired she was. Expression wan, she rested her head against her seat and closed her eyes. The quiet lasted a moment. She turned toward him, studying him, prompting Max to glance her way as well.

"I need to know one thing. Why did you kill the ice cream shop owner?"

Max knew he was taking too long to answer. He didn't owe her an explanation. He didn't need to share his past, didn't want her to justify his actions. But she deserved an answer. She'd been through a lot today. His voice broke through the thick fog of silence that settled over the car. "He deserved it."

"Why?"

He shook his head. "Don't. Don't try to rationalize it. I killed the bastard. I took his life. Burned the whole place down to shit. The why doesn't matter."

"It matters to me."

He could tell that she wouldn't let it go.

"Why did you kill him, Max?"

"He was a child molester," Max spat out quietly, so quietly even he barely heard his own voice. "He abused my friend Matilda for years. She was too afraid to say anything. She was six when he started. She was twelve when I found out. There were other kids too. He deserved to die. I did it for Leslie's sister."

***

Emma couldn't breathe. He had punished a child predator, protecting his friend, freeing her from years of abuse. She didn't hold the crime against Max. "I'm glad you killed him then."

"I'm not a savior, Emma. I killed a lot of people. Got paid to do it. Don't mistake me for some hero."

His eyes were cold. His expression shuttered. He truly was, at the moment, the Ghost. She couldn't look at the icy monster he had become.

"Do you ever want to stop?" she asked, unsure of what she expected to hear.

"My life now is very different from my life a decade ago."

"But you still kill people?"

Max didn't need to respond. She already knew the answer.

"Someone wants me dead. But you want me alive. Why?"

Max glanced at her then. "Someone used my brother's name to put out a ten-million-dollar hit on my adoptive dad. I won't let anything happen to that man. I followed a lead, and stumbled on the hit being put on you... this one, in person, to my birth father. My brother wants you dead too."

"I don't know your brother."

"He was adopted when I was a kid after my parents gave up custody. There's no paper trail, no names. It was done through attorneys, and we can't track the paperwork. Milo is the name I knew him by, but he could be anyone anywhere now. I don't have a photo. I have nothing."

"I'll do my best to remember... but right now, that's not much to go on."

Turning toward her, he drank in her profile. Adrenaline still thrummed in his veins, but it wasn't the adrenaline that surged the blood through his body. He pulled the car over on the empty stretch of road, the late afternoon air shimmering around them. When he shifted the car into park, Emma gave a cursory glance around them before settling her gaze on him.

He leaned forward slowly, giving her every opportunity to move away, to stop him, to put distance between them. But she didn't do any of that. She leaned closer too, and their lips met in the desert-heated car.

Her lips were warm and soft, and when he dove deeper, she responded eagerly to his tongue. He groaned, cupping her face, threading his fingers through her hair, careful to avoid her injury. She released a tiny sound, and that unleashed everything within him. Dragging her over the center console, he pulled her against him. Her arms wrapped around his neck as she settled on his lap, pressing against his hardness as their mouths mated on a level so base and instinctive it shook him to his very core. His fingers dug into her buttocks, kneading, rocking her against him. The sun, the heat, the very desert around them disappeared and it was just the two of them—the two of them alone in the entire universe—finding and anchoring each other among the wild beating of the blood in their ears.

Max lost track of time, of his past, of his future, of where he was or where he could be—his only reality was Emma. He greedily sank his teeth in the hollow of her shoulder. Her head fell back and she moved against him, mewling to get closer. He wanted to plunge into her right then and there, to rip the thin cloth of her underwear out of the way and sink in to the hilt. To brand her as his.

To keep her forever.

The thought was enough to jar him out of the moment, and he jerked back.

Emma, disoriented, fell against his chest before righting herself. She glanced at his face, hers confused. Whatever she saw reflected in his features spurred her to move quickly back to her seat.

"Holy crap," she whispered, dropping her face into her hands.

Desperately trying to resettle his breathing, Max pulled the car back out onto the road.

He needed to put an end to the threat against Trevor and Emma as soon as possible so he could walk away.

Being near Emma for too long opened her to even greater danger: him. He wanted her, but he couldn't touch her. Vicious blood he'd inherited surged through him. He couldn't—wouldn't—expose her to that.

Chapter 22

They'd been driving in silence for almost an hour. Lost in thought, Emma barely noticed their surroundings until Max exited the freeway into an opulent neighborhood. She absorbed the tall palm trees, thick grass lawns, and large homes. Coming out of the sparse, beige Rose Falls, the contrast was marked.

"This isn't Vegas."

He glanced at her. "I figured you'd want something quieter."

They passed a row of fashionable boutiques and restaurants and turned down a wide private driveway, flanked by tall, lush palms.

According to the sign, they had just reached Green Valley Ranch Resort Spa and Casino. Date palms, Mediterranean cypresses, and a variety of native trees Emma couldn't name surrounded the large hotel, which was painted to reflect the colors of the desert around them.

Max pulled into the shaded valet drop-off. The valet opened Emma's door, but Max came around to help her out of the vehicle. "Your head feeling okay?"

"Peachy."

Max grabbed Emma's small luggage and motioned for her to go in first.

She hesitated. "We look like a mess."

"I'm sure they're used to it."

They checked in at a private desk.

"Walter Scott." Max extended a driver's license with the fake name to the concierge. "My wife and I are here for just the night."

They were shown into one of the most opulent rooms Emma had ever seen. The massive double doors opened into a large living room, with couches and armchairs to the left and a dining table seated for eight on the right. Two carved wooden barstools flanked a wet bar. Emma glanced up at the vaulted ceiling. The suite was enormous. Her NYC apartment could fit inside three times over.

A door led off to the bedroom. The concierge motioned for Emma to follow him through it as he played tour guide. Her gaze skimmed over the large bed before he took her to a second bathroom, with his-and-hers counter spaces, a glassed-in shower, and a gigantic tub.

The concierge directed her back into the living room and opened the glass doors that led onto the patio. Emma stepped onto the stone pavement. The dry heat of the late afternoon surrounded her, an escape from the air-conditioned air inside. The large patio boasted a sizable outdoor fireplace and an outdoor dining table. The outside warmth contrasted with the refrigerated interior, and all Emma wanted was to sit out here and think.

"We have a sand-bottom pool through there, and we can reserve one of the cabanas for you, if you'd like, while you're here," offered the concierge, pointing in the direction of the pool.

Emma shook off the offer. She could only imagine how much a cabana at this place would cost. "Maybe later. I think we'd like to rest."

"Certainly. Enjoy your stay."

Once the concierge left, Emma turned to Max. "Walter Scott?"

"Comes in handy to carry a couple of IDs. You hungry?"

"Starving. But I want a shower and pajamas, not a restaurant."

"Go shower. I'll order room service. Anything in particular you want?"

"I'll eat anything," she said. "You pick."

***

It was nearly five here. Evening back in New York. Max hadn't realized how hungry he was until he reached for the menu and his stomach grumbled.

As Emma disappeared into the master suite, he picked up the phone to order room service. He was rattling off a list of food items when the shower turned on in the other room. Emma's naked body was just an arm's reach away. His vision blurred as he imagined her in the shower, steam rising around her.

"Sir? Can you hear me, sir?"

The order taker's question brought Max back to the task at hand.

It took a moment for him to refocus, and he had to rescan the in-room dining menu to refresh his memory. Order finally placed, he let his head fall against the back of the hotel sofa. How did he end up in this situation? The one woman he vowed to avoid was showering, naked, a few steps away.

He needed a vacation. A getaway to clear his mind. To somehow purge the craving for Emma from his body.

136

He could go to Europe for a few days, or hop to Aruba for the weekend. Sun, beach, beer.

As a kid, he used to dream of travel. He wanted to go to Egypt to see the pyramids. To Tokyo. To Rome.

Matilda used to talk about going to Paris. She had loved to play dress-up, to pretend like she was eating croissants in front of the Eiffel Tower, instead of stale bagels in front of the local movie theater that would replay the same film six months out of the year.

"We can't even afford a movie ticket," Max used to scoff. "What makes you think you'll ever get to go to France?"

When he turned thirty, he traveled abroad for the first time. Colombia. Business trip. His job was to eliminate a bad guy. He killed that motherfucker quickly, and then explored Cartagena and Medellín, soaking up a moment he never in his entire life thought he'd have the privilege to experience: being a tourist abroad.

At thirty-two, after finishing a job in Croatia, he explored Eastern Europe.

At thirty-three, he took four weeks off and spent them in Western Europe. France, for him, was the highlight. He saw the *Mona Lisa* at the Louvre, rode to the top of the Eiffel Tower, strolled down Champs-Élysées, even took the train to Versailles. Matilda would have loved being there, he thought every second of that trip. He wished she could have experienced France. She'd never get the chance. She had killed herself at age seventeen, before she ever ventured outside of Rose Falls.

He had enough money to retire and live a lifestyle of luxury several times over, but his work with Trevor and Cynthia was too important. It saved lives. Still, he could get away for a bit. Chase thoughts of Emma from his mind, his craving for her from his body.

For tonight, he'd give her the bedroom. She could lock the door. He'd stay out in the living room, and keep his dick in his pants.

Max's noble thoughts evaporated as she stepped into the room. She wore one of the hotel robes, which hung down to her ankles. She was so beautiful, freshly scrubbed, her cheeks pink from the steam of the shower, that he forgot to breathe. Her still-damp hair cascaded in waves down her back. He wanted to sweep the tresses aside and nuzzle her neck. To strip her of the robe and take her right there on the king-sized bed a few feet away. He felt like an imposter, an intruder who didn't belong near her.

He cleared his throat, finding it hard to speak. "The food should be here soon."

She hovered at the entrance to the room, safely out of his reach. "Thanks, I'm starving. How did you get to Rose Falls so fast?"

"I took a jet."

"A jet? A private jet? If you have so much money, why do you keep doing what you do?"

"Killing those who deserve it is my good deed for the world."

After an uncertain pause, she walked over to the couch and plopped down next to him. "You said you retired."

"As a hit man, yes."

She tucked the robe closer around herself. "Now you do it for free?"

"It's..." He tore his gaze away from the exposed skin of her chest. "It's more complicated than that."

"I got time. Tell me."

As he met her gray eyes, Max hesitated. He hadn't

shared his background with anyone. Sharing the details with Emma would be rash and irresponsible. Entrusting her would expose not only him but Trevor, Cynthia, and the intimate group of people who put their neck on the line every day working for them.

"Max?" she asked, when he hadn't spoken.

She'd been attacked twice in Manhattan, knocked out by Leslie, then almost vehicular slaughtered in Rose Falls. She hadn't revealed his name or the details of his childhood he'd shared with her to the FBI agent or to the police. If someone could be entrusted with the details of his covert business, it was Emma.

He didn't trust easily, but he chose to trust her. "A dozen or so years ago, I found myself inside someone's home. Someone had taken out a hit on Trevor Martin."

"That reclusive billionaire? His foundation made a seven-figure gift to the New York Stop Domestic Violence Project last year."

"That would be him. I had been told, at the time, that he was supposedly behind a human trafficking operation in the cobalt mines in Congo. He had a sprawling mansion in East Hampton. The size of two of these hotels. The main door was unlocked, so I walked in. All the blinds were shut."

Max remembered walking into the dark, cavernous home. He had almost gagged at the stench of rotting trash, uneaten food, and stale alcohol. Moving slowly, he tracked Trevor to one of the bedrooms, where the older man lay surrounded by empty vodka bottles, clutching a tiny baseball glove to his chest.

"Trevor's only son had killed himself. He was despondent, holding a baseball glove that must have belonged to his son as a kid."

Something about the scene—of the grown man's tear-streaked face as he clutched his dead son's childhood toy—affected Max's every iota, and he slid his knife back into its sheath.

"I couldn't do it. Without thinking, I rushed to revive the guy. Got him into a cold shower, called the ambulance. I disappeared as the paramedics arrived."

"You saved the life of the man you had been paid to kill."

"I returned the retainer, and made it a point to learn who had hired me to kill him in the first place. The culprit turned out to be a competitor of his. He was the one leading the human trafficking ring in the Congo mines. I found him alone in his penthouse and proved a point. No one hires me under false pretense."

"What happened then?" Emma tugged her robe tighter.

"A year after the incident, Trevor found me. No one had ever surprised me until that moment. But Trevor Martin did. No one—not the police, not the FBI—no one could trace or find me, but Trevor had. You and Trevor have that in common."

Max closed his eyes. The day was fresh in his memory.

He had been sitting at an outdoor table in Madison Square Park when a figure appeared across from him, and Max glanced up into Trevor Martin's lined face. The man was in his sixties, but he looked at least ten years older.

Trevor pulled out the heavy iron chair with a scrape and sat. "You're the one who saved my life."

"I was hired to kill you."

"Then why didn't you?"

Max couldn't respond.

"That was the anniversary of my son's birthday," Trevor explained. "I wanted to die. Then you walked into that room, and for a moment I thought you were Calvin."

"I wasn't."

"I know you weren't. It took me a year to find you. Impressive body of work."

"I do what I have to do." Max watched the man, uncertain why he was there and doubting his decision to let the billionaire live.

"I want you to come work for me."

"I don't work for anyone."

"I think you might be interested in this particular opportunity."

Max had given Trevor Martin a new lease on life, and Trevor intended to put it to good use. Trevor's wife had left him when Calvin had been a baby, and he had raised the boy alone, with the help of a handful of nannies. He hadn't been the same since Calvin's passing, until a killer for hire had saved his life.

Max blinked himself back to the present and saw Emma watching him with rapt attention. "Trevor and I partnered on a new venture, together with his former IT security expert, Cynthia. We have a handful of hackers who work with us to identify criminals that Homeland Security, FBI, or Interpol can't track, and we eliminate them. That's what I've been doing for the last ten years."

"These are your seven-figure hits?"

Max shook his head. "My days of multimillion-dollar contracts are over. On paper, Trevor hired me to run the special projects division of T. R. Martin, and that's where I get my salary nowadays. That, and my investments portfolio."

"How is your brother involved in all this?"

Max hesitated.

She laid her hand on top of his. "I found my sister stabbed nineteen times, Max. I went through hell as they hunted for Austin, sat through his trial… I can handle whatever it is you tell me."

The sincerity in her gaze undid him. He flipped his hand to be palm-to-palm with hers, let their fingers intertwine, and told her the rest of the story. "Over the last year, we've been trying to bring down Mercury Marketplace, a dark web marketplace for human, drug, and weapons trafficking."

"I've never heard of it."

"It's the biggest marketplace for illegal products and services on the dark web. It allows vendors to post photos of their product, and for buyers to not only rate the product and seller, but to leave reviews. All under the anonymity of the dark web."

"Whoa."

He offered a terse nod. "The administrators facilitate billions of dollars in transactions, and make millions in commissions."

"How are they still allowed to operate?"

"Authorities from several countries have been after them for years, but no one has had any luck. Using the site's forum for services requested, someone offered a ten-million-dollar hit out on Trevor."

"On Trevor?" Realization dawned in her gray eyes. "Wait, *Trevor Martin* is your adoptive father?"

"He adopted me when I was twenty-six. It was a smart financial decision for both of us, nothing more. The authorities scanning the site had seen the message and notified him as well, but Cynthia saw it first."

Emma scooted closer. "Do they know who could possibly want him dead?"

"The username said MiloAugustus. Milo is the name my mother gave my little brother when he was born. Augustus is also my middle name. It could be a fake name. It could be someone else completely. We are looking at every possibility."

"That has to be some sort of coincidence. There must be hundreds of Milo Augustuses out there."

"No one knows my real name, much less my middle name or that I have a brother named Milo. The fact that this hit is on Trevor, who is connected to me… and Elrod told my biological father that you've caused Milo enough damage… I know deep in my bones that it's my brother."

"I don't know any Milos, Max. I don't even know anyone who remotely resembles you. I'd have told you if I did. How old would he be right now?"

"Twenty-two."

The creases deepened between her brows as she thought through it. "The only people who could possibly be upset with me are the abusive husbands and boyfriends of the women I help through the place where I volunteer. But I don't work with a single woman whose significant other is in that age bracket… What kind of damage could I have possibly done to someone I don't even know?"

"I'll get my answers from him soon enough."

She tugged her hand away from his. "You're looking for him to kill him."

Devoid of her touch, he stood, shoving his fingers through his hair. "I don't have a choice. I won't let anything happen to Trevor."

"Even if it's your own brother?"

He hated seeing the dismay on her face, tried to

explain. "I come from a very long line of bad men, Emma. I had hoped nurture would outweigh nature with him—he was taken away from my parents when he was just a baby. But nature won. Evil runs in our veins. The things I've seen… they haunt me."

Her voice softened. "That's why you spend your life ridding the world of bad people."

"And now one of them wants my adoptive father dead. I won't let that happen. Not to him. Not to you. I need to find out why he wants Trevor dead—and then stop him."

Chapter 23

Tap, tap, tap.

The sound of the knock flung Emma to her feet.

"Room service," Max assured her, as grateful for a respite from the conversation as Emma probably was. Stalking to the door, he let in the attendant. "I got us salmon, steak, salad, and fries."

A young woman rolled in the room service cart, setting the covered items on the dining table.

"And tea," Emma noted, surprise clear in her tone as the attendant set out the stainless-steel teapot and porcelain cups.

"You had said you wanted tea and *Friends* tonight," he pointed out, suddenly uncomfortable.

"That was… very thoughtful. Thank you."

Feeling awkward, something he never felt, Max tipped the attendant and closed the door behind her as she left them to their food.

Emma uncovered the dishes. "You also got chocolate cake."

The tips of his ears burned. He did his best not to brush at them. "I figured it would go with the tea."

"It's my favorite dessert."

"I know."

The energy in the room shifted. Emma must have

felt it too, because she dragged her darkened gaze away from his, cleared her throat.

Regardless, when she spoke, her words came out croaky. "Should we eat or do you want a shower too?"

Pulling out a chair at the massive dining table, he motioned for her to sit. "Let's eat first."

When she sat, he slid into the seat next to her, and they dove into the food, family-style. It felt strangely homey, sitting together like this, with Emma wearing nothing but an oversized robe. Shoving images of getting her naked from his mind, he tried to focus on chewing.

After they polished off the main dishes, she leaned over to pour the tea.

"How's your headache?" he asked when she resettled in her chair. "Has it gotten worse? The car incident couldn't have been good for you."

She took a sip of the steaming liquid. "If anything, that car assault took my mind off my headache and nausea. I think whatever your friend drugged me with has finally worn off."

Although she'd smiled, he couldn't let go of his unease. "Let me see the bump."

Placing her teacup on the table, she turned in her chair and tilted her head so he could access the head wound.

He circled the protrusion with a careful finger, hating that she'd been injured. "I still feel like you need to go get a scan."

"I feel fine. Much better after eating."

Max couldn't stop touching her now that he'd started. He skimmed down to her neck, to her shoulders, dug into the knots at the base of her neck. When Emma moaned on a breathy exhale, heat shot through his body.

"Oh, that feels good. I think that all the running around, trying not to get assassinated, made my tendons all tight. I haven't had a massage in years."

She was chattering again. He could read her relatively well by now, and knew that it meant she was nervous.

"Ooh, right there," she murmured, making his rock-hard dick strain against the zipper of his jeans.

Her skin was soft, fragranced with the hotel soap and lotion and that erotic Emma scent that was uniquely her.

She turned in her chair to face him, her eyes thoughtful.

His hands fell away.

"This is a problem still, huh?" When he nodded, she continued. "You want me."

His gaze strayed down to the deep V of her robe. He wanted to free her breasts and suck her nipples into his mouth.

A flush worked itself up from her chest to her face. Her cheeks were blazing red. "I want you too."

He stopped breathing. "I'll hurt you."

Emma tilted her head. "What do you mean?"

Max stood, stalked to the sofa. "I… um… I don't trust myself around you. Around anyone. The men in my family are all rapists, murderers, perverts… I'm no better. What if I can't stop when you need me to?"

Emma stood too. She approached him slowly, as one would a wild animal. Her pulse beat wildly in her neck, and her breathing was shallow, labored.

Fear? Desire? He couldn't tell.

"Have you ever… not stopped?"

"I don't trust myself to even try."

"Max… what are you saying?"

When she cupped his cheek in her soft hand, he jolted from surprise. Fighting the urge to nestle into her palm, he pulled it away from his face, pressed a kiss into its center before letting go. "I've… never been with anyone. I don't trust myself not to hurt you."

She ran her fingers along the spot he had just kissed even as her brow knitted. "You've never… had sex?"

"I can't chance it. What if I lose all control?"

Her breathing increased, became even shallower. He was afraid she was going to start hyperventilating.

She appeared to think about his statement for a long time; he could almost see the gears turning in her brain.

"I don't think you'd hurt me." Her throat worked as she swallowed. "You've stopped before. You've been around me when I was tied up. You didn't do anything then."

"I keep myself under firm control at all times."

Because he couldn't stop himself from touching her, he skimmed his thumb along her jaw. Her skin was velvety soft, warm… a temptation like none he'd ever faced. He wanted to pull her closer and kiss her. He wanted to push her away and run.

Emma leaned a fraction closer. "Kiss me."

"Don't," he warned.

"I trust you."

"How? Why?" Searching her eyes, he got lost in their depths, had to focus on her words when she finally answered.

"I've been scared of men ever since Austin stabbed my sister. Scared of my inability to tell the bad ones apart from the good after Austin. I thought he was such a good guy. He wasn't. I couldn't protect Riley because I couldn't see him for what he was."

"Emma—"

"I've locked myself away for years. You think you're evil and dangerous, but all you've done is protect me from the moment you met me."

"Because I need something from you," he pointed out.

"Is that all?" Emma asked, studying him. "That's the only reason you're here?"

Yes, he wanted to tell her. *No*, his heart screamed. He was here because she was opium to him. Letting go of her, he stepped out of reach. "You have information I need."

"So, this… this is how you interrogate people?" Her voice indicated she didn't believe him.

The last wall of his control began to crumble. "I want to fuck you."

"I haven't been with anyone in over seven years, Max. I don't take this lightly."

Before he could process her confession, she kissed him.

Her lips were warm and dry as they brushed against his. He froze, unsure whether to push her away or to pull her closer.

Rising to her toes, she sprinkled small kisses to his cheek, his jaw. "Max, I trust you. I've never said that to anyone before."

The dam broke.

***

He kissed her with all the longing she herself had been trying to contain since their first meeting. When his fingers tangled in her damp hair, angling her head to grant him better access, she couldn't fight the whimper of pleasure at the taste of him.

The sound pulled him back, his dark eyes concerned as they searched hers. "Did I hurt you? Is it your head?"

His fretfulness sent a bright ray of sunshine straight to her heart, filling her body with balmy heat. His fingers were nowhere near her head wound.

"No, not even a bit." She brought his mouth back to hers.

Skimming his hands down her body, he pulled her closer against him with a possessive growl, but it wasn't enough.

The layers of clothing were in the way. She needed all. Clothes. Off.

They reached for the belt of her robe at the same time. Undoing the knot, he tugged off the robe. The terry cloth material slid down her sensitized skin to pool at her feet, leaving her standing before him naked, exposed.

His gaze seemed to drink in every inch of her body. "Fucking perfect."

He fitted his large hand over her breast, grazed the taut nipple before sliding down to her stomach, lower. Each stroke made her tremble. When his mouth claimed hers, she arched against him, needing more. Max seemed happy to oblige. Wrapping his arms around her like a vise, he lifted her against him.

Making quick work of the short distance to the sofa, he sank into the cushions with her. She twisted out of his hold to straddle his lap, anchoring herself on the hard ridge that strained against the denim. The material felt rough against her sensitive flesh, but she relished the sensation, relished him.

His eyes turned completely black as he watched her from beneath heavy lids. When he ground up, sharp shards of pleasure pricked her nerve endings. She needed him to seat himself deep, to join their bodies together. If she couldn't lower herself onto the column of his erection at that very moment, she felt like she'd die. Her fingers trembled as she reached for his zipper.

"Tell me to stop," he ground out. The request, at such odds with her desperate thoughts, froze her.

Confused, she looked at him. The clear, unmistakable need in his tense face contradicted his statement. He wanted her as much as she wanted him, she could clearly see that, and he was terrified of it. Shifting closer, she let her breasts rest against his cotton-clad chest and pressed her lips against the rough shadow of his cheek.

"Never," she whispered.

"You're sure." The words were raspy and low, somewhere between a question and a statement. Vulnerability flashed across his face as his heart beat a wild rhythm through her.

"I am. Are you?"

"God, yes."

His terse statement spurred her to move lower down his lap, returning to her task. She slid the zipper open and released his hard length with shaking fingers. Her whole body trembled. Not from fear… from want. She couldn't believe this was happening, that she was naked, straddling Max, and she was holding him in her hand. She tightened her fingers, and his hips rocked into her. He released a guttural groan.

His penis was thick and large, impossibly hard, the skin velvet against her hand. She wanted to take him into her mouth, explore him with her tongue. Her intentions were delayed as he pulled her up to his face and kissed her deeply, his hands hot against her cheeks.

"Oh!" she yelped as she suddenly found herself staring up at the vaulted ceiling of the hotel room, flat on her back on the wide sofa.

Max stripped quickly before joining her again. His body covered hers, heavy and hard, his skin a searing contrast to the chilly room. His scent surrounded her.

"Tell me you want me," he demanded, his face desperate.

She gasped out a yes. Her lips wouldn't form another sentence as he drew a nipple into the warm cavern of his mouth, rolled it against the edge of his teeth.

Emma arched off the couch. His increasingly rough sucking shot myriad sensations through her, leaving her dizzy, engulfed by him.

His fingers slid between her thighs. His groan vibrated against her skin as he parted her folds, stroked through her damp heat. The sensation was sharp, the pleasure instant. Her head rolled back and forth against the couch as sounds she barely recognized escaped her. He continued the rhythmic glide until Emma ground herself desperately against his hand, demanding more. Yet he continued to torment, to shift just out of reach as she pushed herself harder against him.

Lifting her heavy lids, her gaze met his hooded one. He didn't break eye contact as his fingers teased her. The desire on his face froze her. The edges of her vision blurred—she had forgotten to breathe. She gasped for a lungful of air.

He slid off the couch and settled himself on the ground, readjusting her to face him. Spreading her legs with his hands, he made room for himself between her thighs. She felt open and exposed and vulnerable as he focused on that private part of her. He didn't move, just looked, and she grew shy and nervous at his focus. She shifted to close her legs, but his body held her open.

Then he lowered his head.

His breath washed over her, moist and warm, before he settled his lips on her and tasted her with his tongue. Repeating the glide, this time deeper, he explored her with his mouth, a little uncertain at first and then increasingly confident.

As he slipped two fingers deep inside, Emma couldn't breathe, couldn't think. Every cell in her body was focused on the sensations Max wrung out of her, the feel of his fingers inside her, the pressure of his tongue on her clit. His fingers moved in steady counter-rhythm to his tongue. It was too much. She tried to close her legs again, but he prevented her movement.

The thick slide of his fingers… the hot, raspy press of his tongue—Emma was lost to the feeling. Her inner muscles started to spasm, but he continued the unrelenting rhythm and then curled his fingers as his tongue pressed hard. The combination was too much. She exploded, arching off the sofa as the waves broke over her, swell upon swell. She sank, boneless, into the cushions.

When he planted a kiss to the inside of her thigh, she pried open a heavy lid and stretched her arms out to him, wanting him deep inside her now, but he moved out of reach.

"Max?" She watched his back as he retreated toward the bar. Confused, she sat up. "What are you…"

He dug through the tray at the bar, then held up a condom.

Oh. She'd forgotten about all that in her haste.

"The hotel provides condoms?" she asked.

"Vegas." She barely recognized his voice as he returned.

"What are they, like twenty dollars each?"

He ignored her attempt at humor, his eyes dark and focused on her naked body.

"I need to be inside you. Now," he growled. "Tell me you want me to fuck you."

She nodded, unable to say the explicit phrase even after sharing such a personal experience with him.

"The words."

"I want you."

It seemed to satisfy him. He exhaled in relief, moving over her. "Spread your pretty legs for me."

Hot all over again, Emma complied, shifting her legs open, the most private part of her spread for him again. She felt even more vulnerable now, as his possessive gaze raked over her.

She was still wet from her earlier orgasm, but his intensity drew even more desire from her.

"So wet for me," he murmured in satisfaction, covering her body with his. His mouth found hers in a kiss that left her breathless and writhing under him.

"Please," she begged, moving her hips closer to him. She'd never begged a man in her life, but she'd perish if he didn't hurry.

He growled low in his throat as he entered her, fully seating himself in one motion. He felt huge and thick inside her, and she strained to adjust to the sudden intrusion. She pressed her nose into his skin to inhale his scent. Inch by inch, her muscles relaxed.

He started to move, setting a powerful rhythm that left no room for thoughts. Her fingers dug into his shoulders, clawed at his back. His teeth sunk into her skin, marked her as his. Emma was powerless to contain her rasping gasps as her body fluttered around him.

His control had fled now. Nature had taken over and

he bore into her with increasingly powerful thrusts, whispering crude sex words in her ear that she found herself loving. She knew he was beyond cogent thoughts as he moved inside and against her with animalistic ferocity.

Her climax built, and she ground herself against him, the pressure inside her tightening to an unbearable knot that burst free.

He convulsed deep inside her, and his body twitched and shook against hers. When he collapsed against her, smooshing her all the way into the cushions, she didn't care. Feeling a strong sense of protectiveness over this man she should fear, she wrapped her arms around his sweat-slicked frame, wanting him closer. But he rolled off her too soon and, avoiding eye contact, stepped away toward the bathroom.

Emma sat up, suddenly feeling naked and vulnerable. She padded over to her robe and pulled it on, needing a layer of clothing as armor before he returned.

He was gone for so long that she began to worry.

When he finally emerged, his mask of control was back in place, his face devoid of all emotion. He was no longer the passionate lover who had whispered dirty love words into her ear. He was as cold as the Ghost, a stranger staring at her.

"You okay?" she asked.

"You needed rest tonight, and I mauled you like an animal."

She puffed out a breath of frustrated air. "I thought we talked about this—I don't have a concussion. Besides, I'm pretty sure it was me who mauled you."

"I… lost control."

"But you didn't hurt me. I'm absolutely sure, Max,

that had I told you to stop, you would have. Besides, I lost control too."

He headed into the alcove of the bar, grabbed a bottle of wine off the dark wood counter. Then set it back. Then gripped it again.

"I'd like a glass too, if you're pouring."

He looked at the bottle of red, returned it to its spot on the counter, before reaching down into the fridge and producing a bottle of champagne. "How about this instead?"

"I like it. Celebratory."

He gave her a dark look.

"I don't know what you're thinking right now, but I had a great time." She stood from the couch and walked over to the bar, climbing onto one of the padded stools. As she looked at him across the bar-top, she felt herself flush. "May I ask? How did you… if this was your first time… how did you know… you made it feel so good."

Max uncorked the cold bottle of champagne, concentrated on pouring out the sparkling liquid into two glasses. "Been known to watch a porn video or two… But, mostly, I just… kind of listened to you."

"What do you mean?"

"Your body… you're an open book. If you like when I do something, you sort of freeze and stop breathing. If you especially like something, your toes curl. And if you don't care for something, you don't react in any way. I sort of was just… you know… watching you, paying attention."

He handed her a flute of champagne, the bubbles dancing. He looked so uncertain and unsure of himself, that Emma set aside the drink and hurried to join him in the bar nook. She wrapped her arms around his neck and stood on her tiptoes. "You were incredible, Max. I forgot my own name."

He looked immeasurably pleased with himself at her statement. His arms closed like forged steel around her waist, and he pulled her into his naked body.

That naked body hardened against her. "I can't get enough of you." His fingers deftly untied her belt once more.

When they were both naked, he caressed her, sending shivers of sensation straight to her brain.

"How many condoms did they leave us?" Emma peered behind him at the tray.

"We'll ring for more when we run low," Max assured her, and lifted her up against the wall.

Chapter 24

They showered together and fell into bed, climbing under the covers. Emma brought the cake with her.

She leaned against the fluffy pillows, her cake balanced on her knees. Taking a forkful of the rich dessert, she extended it to Max. His mouth closed around the tines, and he pulled the morsel into his mouth.

Emma savored the next bite herself. "Delicious."

"Doesn't taste as good as you do."

Smiling, she leaned over and kissed his lips. She felt exuberant. Energy thrummed through her veins like effervescent bubbles in the champagne they never got around to drinking. "I want to go out."

"You can't be serious. It's almost nine. You've had a hell of a day. What you need is an early bedtime."

"I've been drugged, conked over the head, and almost run off the road today. But I've also been thoroughly pleasured, and I want to go out on the town with you."

"You need rest and hydration."

"We'll hydrate in our Uber. The Las Vegas Strip is just a short ride away. Let's go explore a little."

"Is that such a good idea?"

"I've locked myself away too long, Max. We go back to New York tomorrow. I want one evening of not thinking about the possibility of being killed and to have *fun*."

"I won't let anyone hurt you," Max promised, his face set.

"Then aren't I lucky you can come with me and play bodyguard? Come on, let's get dressed." Emma ate another bite of cake. "Darn, I wish I had another outfit. I didn't pack anything for a night out."

"It's Vegas. I'm sure we can find an open store on the Strip."

They did, first stopping by the Miracle Mile Shops, a mile-long shopping promenade at Planet Hollywood Resort and Casino, so Emma could find a dress. She picked out a short, silver, sparkly number, the beads clinking together every time she moved.

She shimmied in place. "How do I look?"

His gaze was soft when he replied. "Like a dream."

Wagging her eyebrows, she grinned. "You want to pick something glittery to match me?"

He tucked a curl behind her ear. "I'll let you be the shining star tonight."

Emma found strappy heels to match, the four inches putting her more level with Max's tall frame.

Max tapped his Walter Scott credit card against the card reader and accepted the small bag with Emma's original dress and shoes from the store clerk.

They exited the store into the indoor shopping promenade.

"Drinks. You want fancy or you want delicious?" Max asked.

"Delicious."

"I know just the place. You can't get margaritas like these in Manhattan."

Max took her to Nacho Daddy on the Strip, where they shared beer-battered tacos and spicy margaritas.

Max was right. Nothing in Manhattan compared.

"I want to go gamble," she declared, a teensy bit tipsy from the tequila in her drink.

Max proved to be very accommodating that evening. He kept his hand low on her back as they navigated the throngs of tourists who flocked on the sidewalk like schools of fish in too small a tank.

They headed to the Bellagio, proceeding along the dancing fountain to the lobby. Air-conditioned hotel air, suffused with cigarette smoke, replaced the dry heat of the outdoors. Emma glanced up as they walked farther inside. An expansive chandelier dripped from the ceiling in one elaborate glass bouquet, spreading outward in colorful tendrils. Notes of jazz wafted toward them from the piano bar near registration.

"Craps? Blackjack? Roulette?" Max's hand clasped hers as they navigated the crowded lobby.

"Craps. I've never played that and I want to learn."

Max led her through the throngs of guests toward a nearby craps table.

Her gaze lingered on a couple just ahead and recognition pinged. "Holy crap."

Instantly alert, Max scanned the crowd. "What is it?"

"That's my uncle." She pointed to the casually dressed, portly man she knew too well standing next to a very attractive blonde woman in a tight white dress as she attempted to take a selfie.

"Oh fuck," Max cursed, spinning around so that his back was toward the couple.

Emma looked at him. "What's wrong?"

"The woman."

"That's his new girlfriend, Keva. He got divorced a little bit ago, and I think that's his flavor of the month."

"I can't meet them." Max pulled Emma back into the crowd from which they had emerged.

"Why not?"

"I sort of dated her."

Emma's jaw dropped. "You dated Keva?"

"Kind of."

"You *kind of* dated Keva?"

"I can tell you all about it later, but she knows me as Jason Smith."

"Why does she know you as Jason Smith? Oh God. Did you try to kill her?"

"No. But I did kill her boyfriend."

Emma stared. "You dated her to get to her boyfriend?"

"She said they had an open arrangement."

"You dated Keva to kill the other guy she was dating?"

"This was years ago. Fifteen years ago. Sixteen, maybe."

"Think she still remembers you after all this time?"

Max gave her a look.

"Yeah. You're quite memorable," she acquiesced. "What do we do?"

"Leave the hotel."

"How many identities do you have?" whispered Emma as he pulled her out of the resort and casino.

"A few. I don't want to get you wrapped up in all that."

"I'm already wrapped up in all that, if it hasn't occurred to you. What happens at my next family gathering? How would you interact with Keva? Would I have to introduce you as Jason to my parents?"

"That's a moot point because I won't be going to your family gatherings."

Reality crashed over Emma like a bucket of dry ice.

What in the world was she thinking?

Family gatherings… introductions to parents… Max was a former hit man. His job involved killing people. Granted, he killed bad people, but still. He was wanted by the FBI. He wasn't take-home-to-your-parents material. Riley had already brought one violent man into their family. Emma wouldn't bring in another.

She stopped walking, freezing mid-stride on the sidewalk. The group of tourists behind them jostled as they attempted to walk around Emma and Max with annoyed grunts.

"You know I can never meet your family, right?" he asked.

"I think I just realized that now."

Panic entered Max's face. "You know we can never—that this can never—that we can't—that we are not—"

"Don't worry," she assured him, interrupting his failed attempt to get his words out. The tourists milled around them. Emma shifted away from them to a quiet spot next to the valet. "I'm not asking you to marry me or anything. We'll go our separate ways after we find your brother."

"Correction. I will find my brother. You're not coming anywhere near this mess."

"I'm stuck quite literally in the middle of this mess, if you haven't noticed."

"I'll take you to Trevor's castle in Germany. You'll be safe there. I've hired an army to watch over him while he's there."

Emma laughed. "I'm not jetting off to Europe to hide in a castle. I have a job. I have a life. My parents are returning from Italy soon, and I've missed them and my sister. I'm going to go see them in Cold Spring as soon as they're back."

"I'll take you to them in Italy."

"And put them in danger? Absolutely not. I can't take the chance that whoever wants me dead won't take a trip to Europe. No, I'm in it now. Soon as it's over, we'll go our separate ways."

"Just like that?"

"Yes, just like that."

His eyes flashed. "So you screw me and then just walk away?"

Emma studied his angry face. "Why are you mad? You just said that there's no us. You can't meet my family. I refuse to date someone in secret. What's the alternative, Max?"

He didn't have one, but he seemed primed for a fight.

"Listen…" She laid her hand against his jaw. "You and I have insane chemistry. We can leave it at that. I always thought I was happy in my little closed-off world, but I realize now that I was just scared. Scared of men, scared of lov—liking someone and not realizing their true nature, scared of making the wrong choice, scared of trusting someone. So I secluded myself, and I thought I was happy, but I'm not happy. Ever since I met you, I've had three—no, four, because I do count your friend too—attempts on my life, but this is the most living I've done in seven years. You helped me tackle my fears, Max. I trust you. You're a good person, despite whatever it is you think about yourself. I've learned to trust my own instincts again because of you. For that, I'll always be grateful."

He leaned his forehead against hers. "I can only hurt you, Emma. You shouldn't trust me. I can't be trusted, don't you see?" His arms wrapped around her and pulled her close. "My birth father went to prison when I was a baby—battery, assault—I will spare you the details. My uncles are all in prison. Two are on death row. My cousins? All bad seed. They've done horrible things. I thought my brother—my little brother who got to go to a good family as a baby—would be different. But he is just as messed up as me. There are no good men in my family, Emma. Violent blood runs in my veins." His eyes turned cold. The bars of his control snapped back in place, and he let her go.

Her body instantly missed the comforting warmth of his embrace.

"Cut the good person shit. You're saying that to make yourself feel better because today you fucked a murderer."

The statement was worse than a slap.

Emma turned around and ran.

***

Max watched her pry open the door of a cab from the nearby taxi line and slide inside, but didn't follow her. They both needed some space.

The cab pulled away from the curb and weaved into the traffic down Las Vegas Boulevard, and Max felt as though he had just kicked a newborn puppy. He made himself sick, but that was nothing new.

He came from bad blood, had done nothing saintly in his life. He didn't deserve someone as pure and innocent as Emma.

The guilt for not being able to protect Matilda still choked him. He tried working it away by killing pedophiles and murderers and predators, but that didn't

164

make him good. There wasn't a good bone in his body. Only evil all the way through. There was no happily ever after in his future, no love or family. Nothing awaited him but the loneliness of his own company and the darkness of days looming ahead. He didn't deserve anything more.

Emma was a beacon of light in his black world, so happy with her shining eyes and constantly smiling mouth. She had been through hell with her sister, and she still found the good in people. What a little fool. She was right. Her gut couldn't be trusted.

He wanted her more than his next breath. Now that she moved out of his immediate orbit, his body physically ached to be near her again. She had brought joy and light into his world. He had felt, for the first time in his life, happy—happy even as he himself got caught in the cross fire. How crazy was that? He'd gladly let himself be stabbed again just to have her near and around him once more. His body itched to follow her, to race back to Green Valley Ranch and apologize for his outburst.

She had opened herself up to him after years of seclusion, had let him make love to her, was vulnerable with him, and he tossed it back in her face.

Because he was a vile person.

Emma deserved better.

He wanted to go to the nearest bar and get blackout drunk.

Instead, he took a cab back to their hotel.

He couldn't leave Emma alone, and he needed his senses about him. Her life was still in danger, and he wouldn't let anything happen to her.

When he walked into the hotel room, he expected to find her curled up in bed. But the suite was empty. Emma was gone.

Chapter 25

Emma had run straight from the Bellagio to Harry Reid International Airport with just her wallet and her two cell phones. The work laptop and the few other items she'd left behind in the Green Valley Ranch hotel would have to be replaced, because she couldn't bear to see Max.

She got lucky; the last flight to New York was leaving within the hour. With only enough time to go through security and buy an extra-large sweatshirt at an airport boutique, she pulled on the sweatshirt over her sparkly dress and boarded the plane.

Unable to sleep during the red-eye, she landed in New York groggy and dejected on Wednesday morning. *Nothing that a cup of coffee can't fix*, she told herself as she stopped for a cappuccino right there at an airport cafe. Finally caffeinated, she caught a cab, looking ridiculous in her high heels and the gray sweatshirt, with Las Vegas embroidered across the front, over her jangling dress. The cab driver didn't bat an eye.

When she entered her apartment building, she half expected Max to be waiting in her lobby. She shook off the disappointment when she didn't see him. It was for the best. His outburst yesterday had stung, and she wasn't ready to face him again quite yet.

Dusty was at her neighbor's, but he must have

recognized her scent because he started meowing—she heard him all the way down in the lobby. Her neighbor would be at work until six, but she had given Emma a copy of her key so that Emma could retrieve the cat, which Emma had left in her kitchen cabinet for safekeeping. She'd get the key, grab Dusty, and then take a nap. Work emails were piling up, but she didn't have the energy to drag herself to the office today. She'd work from her apartment on her personal laptop after she had a few hours of sleep.

As she went to insert her key, she found her apartment door unlocked.

Great. I could have sworn I locked it, and of course I didn't.

She pushed the door open.

Something was off. Something was different. Something was wrong.

The drawers of her corner tables had been yanked wide open. Papers and random odds and ends now littered the floor. *Did someone rob me?*

A noise from her bedroom made her leap into the hallway. Pulling out her cell phone, she dialed 911.

"Nine-one-one, what's your emergency?"

"I think there's someone in my apartment. I just—"

Her door swung open and Emma almost screamed when she met the hollow face of Special Agent Russo.

"Ma'am, your address?" came the calm voice of the 911 operator.

"What are you doing here?" Emma emphasized, not hanging up.

"I didn't expect you back so soon," said Russo.

"Ma'am? Is everything okay?" asked the operator.

"Hang up the phone, Emma."

Emma gave the 911 operator her address, speaking clearly and urgently into the phone before Russo grabbed it from her and pulled her inside.

"Stop. What are you doing?" she yelled, as he shoved her onto her couch.

"*I know you know who he is*," screamed Russo. "*Tell me who he is!*"

"Who are you talking about?" Emma demanded, getting up. He rushed at her. In her hurry to escape, she tripped in her Vegas heels, falling cheek-first into the edge of her coffee table.

The sting was immediate. She tasted blood in her mouth.

"He killed my little brother! I need to know who he is!" Russo yelled down at her as she struggled to sit up.

"I don't know. I don't know anything."

"Why did you fly to Nevada?"

Emma prayed that one of her neighbors was home, that they heard the commotion.

"This is the first time he's ever messed up. We had someone who had interrupted him at the Crescent. They may not have seen much, but they were still present. Now the witness is dead. He's a fucking ghost. Why did you go to Nevada?"

The witness was dead? Max had been in Vegas with her this entire time, and he wouldn't have killed someone without just cause. She knew that now. *Who had killed the neighbor?*

Russo sank down to be eye level with her.

"Okay." She put up her hands. "I'll tell you what I know." *Dammit.* Emma needed to stall. *Where the hell was the police?* "But, Lincoln, my head hurts. Can I just have some water first?"

"I'm sorry you fell." He looked instantly contrite. "I didn't mean for you to get hurt. Emma, I'm so close to catching him. It… it's like a madness that's come over me. I need to know what my little brother ever did to him. I need to know who hired him. Why he killed him."

"I understand. I'd be doing exactly what you're doing if the situation were reversed. I get it. I'd feel the same exact way. I just need some water. Can I go get it?"

"Yes. Yes, of course."

Using the couch for leverage, Emma got to her feet, sorting through solutions. She had several things in her kitchen that she could use to stall the agent. One was a little pink Taser her mother had gifted her when Emma started running in the evenings around the Jacqueline Kennedy Onassis Reservoir. It was in one of her drawers. *But which one? How did a Taser even work?* Emma hadn't even charged it since she had gotten it.

The other was her pepper spray. It was in her wooden bowl by the fridge, along with the spare key that she used when she ran around Central Park. *That* she could use.

She also had knives. A beautiful Wusthof set she had bought at Crate & Barrel during a holiday sale. Twelve pieces. Sharp.

How to distract him long enough for her to grab her makeshift weapons? She'd left her work laptop in Nevada, but her personal one was still in the apartment. It was the perfect inducement to draw his attention.

"So," she said as she made her way into the kitchen. "Did you look in my laptop yet?"

Russo shook his head. "You interrupted as I was opening it."

"Bring it. I'll show you why I went to Nevada."

As he moved into the bedroom, she took one of the knives, tucking it into the pocket of her oversized sweatshirt. Then she reached for the pepper spray. Pepper spray wouldn't hurt him too badly—that was Plan A. All she wanted to do was to escape. Not to stab a federal agent.

He came out of the bedroom.

As soon as he approached, she jumped from the kitchenette and sprayed him with the pepper spray.

The cloud of bitter, caustic spray hit Emma just as much as it hit Russo in the tiny space. It sucked the breath from her lungs and burned through her eyes and nose and throat.

She stumbled back into the kitchenette.

Russo lunged for her through the cloud of toxin.

Emma tried to scramble away, leaping on her island to get to the door, but she didn't get far.

Grabbing her hair, he rammed her stomach-first into the countertop. The sharp edge dug painfully deep into her belly.

The knife in her pocket cut into her, and she screamed.

Did she just stab *herself*?

Still fisting her hair, he yanked her back from the counter. Emma reached for another knife from the knife block. Unable to see through the burning mist, she stabbed it into his thigh. Russo howled and let go.

She used the opportunity to scramble over the counter and rush for the door. As she darted into the hallway, she collided with a heavy body. Her eyes watered so badly she couldn't see, couldn't breathe. Coughing, she realized that she'd just plowed into one of two police officers.

She almost climbed up his heavy protective armor. "H-h-he's inside. He—"

"Go outside." The officer set her aside and strode forward. The two cops drew their weapons.

"No," Emma gasped. "Don't hurt him. He's upset about his brother. I'm okay."

They ignored her, coughing as they entered the apartment, the pepper spray heavy in the air.

More officers rushed up the stairs, grabbing Emma and pulling her downstairs and out of the building.

It was like a scene from a movie. Surreal. Why were there so many cops around? Were they all here for her?

Outside, an officer placed a thermal blanket around her shoulders. "Don't rub your face or eyes. That'll make it worse. You may want to take off your outer layer. It'll help. Are you hurt?"

"I think I stabbed myself with a knife while trying to escape."

The ambulance had arrived by then, and the policeman ushered her toward the vehicle. Once inside, the medics rinsed her eyes with a solution that stopped them from watering and offered oxygen to help clear the toxin from her passageways.

They treated her knife wound on the spot but urged her to go to a medical facility, nevertheless.

"No, I'm fine. I don't want to go anywhere. It's a surface wound."

As Russo, in handcuffs, was ushered into the waiting cop car, his eyes collided with hers.

"Ma'am, are you feeling okay?" asked a police officer, refocusing her attention. "We need you to answer some questions."

Chapter 26

Max drove straight from the airport to Emma's apartment. He had lost time getting to Green Valley Ranch, and then Trevor's plane needed refueling, which delayed him even further.

He had called Ezra to watch over Emma, but Ezra was on assignment in Thailand. Cynthia was en route back from Austria, so she couldn't step in either—her plane was farther out than his. Max was only a few hours behind Emma, and he didn't trust anyone else to watch her last minute. He hoped she'd be safe for the few hours until he could catch up to her.

Emma had messed with his mind in Vegas. He couldn't get the feel of her skin, the smell of her hair out of his head. He remembered the horror in her gray eyes as he accused her of fucking a murderer. He recalled how her skin had paled as she rushed for the cab. He'd made her sick. He'd made himself sick. He had broken the only person who had ever made him feel cared for, human. For that, he would never forgive himself.

Her face was branded into every cell of his worthless body. He knew that he should never come near her again, that he should disappear into the anonymous darkness where he was most comfortable. But his brother was trying to kill her, and he'd die a thousand times over before he let anyone harm a hair on her beautiful head.

As he turned down her street, Max froze at the sight of police and ambulance vehicles, their lights flashing.

It took him a second before he recognized Emma. She sat in the back of an ambulance, covered in a shiny blanket. Her legs dangled off the edge. Two police officers were asking her questions, writing things down as she spoke.

He shifted the car into park in the middle of the street and leaped out.

She looked up as he approached, and her eyes widened in recognition. Jumping from the ambulance, she ran the short distance to him. Her body crashed into his, her arms clinging.

Relief flooded him, and he pressed her close. Immediately, his nostrils started to burn and his eyes water.

"Have you been pepper sprayed?" He pulled her away to look at her. Her eyes were red and swollen; her whole face looked bruised. "What happened? Who do I kill?"

She hushed him. "The officers and I are almost done."

Max reached out his hand to shake theirs. "Xander Martin, Officers."

"This is my… um, friend," Emma added, still clinging to him.

"What happened here?" Max asked.

"A break-in that Miss Neely interrupted. Detective Warren will have some more questions for you, Miss Neely, but I think we are done here for now. Would you like for us to come up to your apartment with you? Make sure everything is safe?"

"No, my friend can help," Emma assured them. "Thank you both. And tell Detective Warren hello. He's a family friend." She thanked the medics as well, leaving her weather blanket with them.

"I interrupted Russo ransacking my apartment," Emma explained as she let Max into the building.

"I'll kill him."

Emma tensed. "Oh my God… *Dusty*. He must be freaking out. He's at the neighbor's but he heard me coming in." Rushing upstairs and into her apartment, she ran to the cabinet, retrieved a key.

Max stopped her by wrapping his hands around her waist. "You'll suffocate him with the spray on you."

"Ugh, you're right. Help me air this place out. I didn't think pepper spray would sting so much."

He gave her a gentle push toward her bedroom. "Go shower. It's in your hair and on your skin. And your clothes are soaked with it too."

"Don't tell me what to do," snapped Emma. "I'm still mad at you. I handled the situation myself. I know that I need to shower." She gave him a dismissive look. "You can go on your merry way."

"I'm not going anywhere."

***

Emma decided to let him stay for now.

In the shower, she turned the water to scalding hot, scrubbing her body with an oil-based salt scrub and rinsing her hair multiple times with shampoo and conditioner. The bandages on her hip got soaked, but she didn't care. It felt good to be clean.

Although she was shaky and nauseated, she also felt strong. Determined. She could take care of herself. She fought off a federal agent who was almost a foot taller than her and countless pounds heavier and she survived.

Max sneezed in the other room.

Good. He deserved it, that jerk.

Wrapping herself in a towel, she found him in the kitchenette, stirring something in her Garfield mug.

He handed her the cup. "Tea, with honey for your throat."

Taking it from him, Emma sipped the sweet liquid. "I think we should leave the apartment. Let it air out. But first, I need to reapply a bandage to *my* stab wound."

His gaze sharpened as he scanned up and down her towel-clad body. "He stabbed you?"

"I stabbed myself," Emma clarified ruefully. "I managed to cut myself with a knife in my pocket. Who does that?"

"Why did you have a knife in your pocket?"

"To fight off Russo."

"Through your pocket?" His gaze skimmed downward. "Show me."

Holding the mug in one hand, Emma dropped the towel with the other.

He studied the cut. Taking the tea away from her, he set it on the counter and pulled her into the bedroom, toward the bed.

"Here, sit. Let me take care of it."

She refused to sit. "I can do it myself."

"I know you can, but I need to. It's my fault you were here alone."

"Yes, it was, you butthole. I'm still angry at you."

"I know. I deserve it. Wait here. I'll go get the bandages. We should disinfect it again just in case."

Giving in, she sat. "There're a few bandages and iodine in the cabinet in the bathroom. Funny, I remember the situation being reversed not too long ago."

Finding what he needed, he rejoined her in the

bedroom and sank to his knees in front of her, all focus on her wound. When he poured the brown liquid onto a cotton ball and gently swabbed the shallow cut, Emma winced.

"Ouch."

"Sorry." He blew across her skin, then deftly applied the bandage. Wrapping his large hand around her thigh, he pressed a kiss on top of the dressing.

Emma's fingers curled into his hair, sifting through the silky locks.

Still crouched at her feet, Max glanced up at her. "I'm sorry about what I said to you in Vegas. I was angry at myself, and I lashed out at you."

"Thank you for the apology. I'm sorry that I abandoned you in Vegas."

"I'm glad you're safe."

"Me too." She brushed his hair off his forehead. "I'm so tired, Max. I haven't slept in what seems like days. I really can't think about what happened any more today."

Max stood. "Well, you're going to have to. Detective Warren called while you were showering. He needs you to come in to the station."

"He's a friend of my dad's," groaned Emma. "He probably already told my parents. They're going to flip. I better call them. What time is it in Italy?"

"It's the middle of the day there. Call them on our way to the station."

"Wouldn't it be weird for you to show up at a police precinct?"

"We'll make it work."

Emma left Dusty at her neighbor's for a bit longer, not wanting the poor animal breathing in the caustic toxin still lingering in her apartment.

The police station was located twenty blocks away. Emma wanted to walk, but Max insisted on driving her.

As she settled in the passenger seat, she glanced at her phone. Ten missed calls from her parents. While Max navigated through the Manhattan traffic, she spent the drive assuring them that she was fine and promising them that she didn't need them to return home or to hire her an attorney.

"I went to law school, Dad. If I need one, I'll know."

They parked the car several blocks from the precinct. Her phone rang again. Tim this time.

"Emma, are you all right?" Her sister in-law, Reese, spoke into the phone first.

Tim jumped in. "Uncle Jeremy called. I'm coming to get you right now. Stay with us a few days."

"The kids will be so excited to see you," Reese cajoled. "I can't imagine staying alone in that apartment after being attacked like that."

It took Emma five minutes to assure them that she was fine and decline their insistent offers to whisk her away to Cold Spring. By the time she hung up, she and Max had reached the police station.

Max settled his hand low on her back, leading her through the main entrance. Emma enjoyed the possessive heat of his touch, even though she knew she shouldn't.

She expected Max to stay in the waiting area, but when she was shown into what appeared to be a conference room, he followed close behind. Detective Warren and two men in dark suits greeted them.

She addressed her father's friend. "Uncle Jeremy… or should I call you Detective Warren? This is so surreal."

"Uncle Jeremy is fine," he said before glancing curiously at Max.

"This is… um…"

"Xander Martin." Max shook Detective Warren's hand.

"Can I get you two anything? A soda? Coffee?"

They both declined the offer. Emma looked anxiously at the two suited men.

The taller one extended his hand. "I'm Special Agent Ricardo Esteban. This is my colleague, Special Agent Ian Mitchell. First, I want to apologize for what happened to you. I assure you, we will be treating this matter with utmost gravity."

"Thank you. Do I have to go through what happened again?"

Jeremy pulled out a chair for her. "I'm afraid so."

"Is Lincoln okay?" she asked.

"Physically? Yes," Mitchell responded. "But he's undergoing a psychiatric evaluation."

"He's been after someone he called the Ghost, and he thought I knew who the Ghost was," Emma told them.

"Off the record," said Esteban. "Russo's half-brother was murdered awhile back. Russo hasn't been the same since. He thought he was onto something, despite us all telling him that he was grasping at straws. Attacking you crossed the line. We will make sure the proper disciplinary action is taken."

Emma offered a nod. "I hope he gets the help he needs."

"Yes, ma'am. Now, are you ready to answer a couple of questions?"

Clinging to the last reserves of energy, Emma settled in to regurgitate the events of the day one more time.

Chapter 27

What felt like hours later, she and Max exited the station and drove back to her apartment. Emma rested her head against the leather seat, exhausted.

Slowly, as though scared that she would move away, Max placed his warm hand on top of hers in her lap. As his fingers interlocked with hers, Emma's heart hammered. She savored the sensation as her nerve endings sought the solid connection to his.

Dammit. I like him. This is definitely going to be a problem.

When Max double-parked outside her brick walk-up, Emma glanced up at her windows, reluctant to go up. "I don't want to be in my apartment tonight. I'm going to pack a few things and find a hotel. I don't want to stay with friends and inadvertently endanger them."

"What if," offered Max, his hand tightening on hers, "you stay with me?"

"With you where?" asked Emma, confused.

"At my apartment. It's on the west side of the park."

"Your actual apartment?"

Max nodded.

Emma considered the offer. "One condition. Dusty comes with me."

After throwing a few items into her overnight bag,

Emma retrieved her cat and all his supplies, and followed Max out the door. He drove down the Eighty-Sixth Street transverse to a sprawling red brick building on Central Park West she had jogged past a million times before.

Max pulled into the discreet parking garage.

As they walked out of the elevator onto the ninth floor and he unlocked his apartment, Emma couldn't control her curiosity. *What was Max's place like?* She had imagined a shadowy unit, far away from prying eyes. Yet, when she stepped inside, she encountered the opposite.

She stood in the bright, wide hall from which various rooms branched out like spokes. A vast all-white kitchen with a mammoth island opened to her immediate right. An expansive living room lay to her left.

She set Dusty's carrier on the gleaming wood floor.

"You can let him out so he can explore," Max told her.

Emma unzipped the carrier, and Dusty emerged to cautiously sniff his new surroundings.

"The master suite is back this way." Max pointed to a spoke just behind her.

Emma stepped inside, her eyes falling on the king-sized bed, tightly made with nary a wrinkle in the bedding. Max set down her bags, the new one she packed as well as the luggage she had left behind in Nevada, in the corner of his room. She followed him through the master bedroom into another room. "Holy crap. Your bedroom has a living room."

"The real estate agent called it a sitting room." Max grinned.

He had a slightly crooked grin, Emma realized, charmed.

It appeared that Max had converted the sitting space

into a de facto library, the built-in shelves heavy with books. A comfortable-looking, worn leather armchair stood by one of the windows, which overlooked Central Park, the bright blue of the reservoir peeking from beyond thick green foliage.

"Bathroom is through here," Max said.

Emma gave the enormous tub a longing glance before she followed him back into the hall.

He gave her a tour of the apartment: the living room, the once-formal dining room that now served as his theater room, the office, then down another hallway to the guest bedroom, the other two bathrooms, the gym, and the informal dining room that connected back to his kitchen.

The entire place was decorated in shades of white and cream. It looked sleek, serene, almost minimalistic. Bold, colorful paintings in thick, matte frames covered the paneled walls, warming up the space with splashes of blues, purples, pinks, reds, yellows, and greens. They radiated vibrancy. Life. Hope. Calm. For the first time that day, Emma's muscles relaxed.

"This is one of the most beautiful apartments I've ever seen."

"When you grow up with nothing, you end up wanting everything."

Max set up Dusty's litter box in one of the guest bathrooms while she set out the water and food bowls in the kitchen. Dusty pranced over to her to make sure the location was up to his standards.

As she scratched her cat's ears, Max's footsteps approached.

He stopped at the threshold to the kitchen. Seeming tense and uncomfortable, he shifted from foot to foot.

"Make yourself at home," he said when she stood up. "Help yourself to anything in the fridge. I need to step away for a bit. But the alarm is on, and I'll be back soon."

"Step away? Where are you—" She suddenly understood. "Oh my God, no. No, no, no. You're going to kill Russo."

"Yes." Max didn't hesitate. "He hurt you. I feel bad he had to lose his little brother, but he crossed a line."

Emma closed the distance between them. "Max. Stop. You can't do that."

"I have to," he insisted, looking down at her angry face.

"No. No, you don't. You can't kill Lincoln. He's a good guy."

"He almost killed you."

"No, he didn't. The whole thing just spiraled out of control. You can't kill a federal agent. You can't kill Lincoln."

"He'll keep coming after you. He knows you know too much."

"I've told him nothing. I'll never tell him anything."

"He can really hurt you next time."

"I'd rather live with that than with knowing I let you kill him. Max. *Please*."

"Let's compromise. I won't make him suffer. How about that? Quick and painless. He won't even know it's coming."

Emma stared at him, dumbfounded. "That's your solution? A painless death?"

"Yes."

She paled. "Will you kill me too when you're done with me? Make it painless so it assuages your guilt?"

A muscle ticced in his jaw. "Don't be ridiculous."

"I refuse to let you do this. I won't have Lincoln's death on my conscience."

"It'll be on *mine*."

"No, Max. Let him be."

"He broke into your apartment. He attacked you. Look at your face. I won't let him get away with this."

"I won't let you kill him," Emma all but shouted, frustrated. "This is becoming a ridiculous conversation. I can't believe I'm arguing with you over this. This isn't how we handle adversaries."

"He hurt you, Emma."

"I'm fine. I'm alive. I'm here." Before she thought better of it, Emma wrapped her arms around Max's neck and looked up at his frozen, angry face. "I'm where I want to be. Please, Max. I beg you. Don't kill Lincoln."

Max stared straight ahead. Then, as if unable to restrain himself, he brought his face down toward hers, his gaze searching. His body relaxed. His arms clasped warm and tight around her. Their foreheads touched. "If he ever dares to come near you again, he's dead."

"Hmmm," Emma pondered. "Well, let's give him a warning first. It would only be fair."

"Am I operating on a three-strike kind of policy now?"

"Just for Lincoln. Deep down, you know you shouldn't do this."

"Fine," he allowed, his hungry gaze skimming down her body. "But I'm going to need some sort of reward."

Emma was more than happy to oblige. She tugged his face to hers. Their lips met, heat against heat, and Emma felt that familiar sensation again... of him, of safety.

He glanced at her hip. "Your cut feel okay?"

Emma touched the injury. "Stings a bit, but it's fine." She pulled his mouth back to hers.

His tongue probed inside, teasing at first, playful. Then the energy changed, and he dove deep, urgently making love to her mouth. She opened to him, her fingers raking through his hair, wanting him to feel as hot as he was making her. He broke away from her lips to trail hot kisses along her neck, nipped at her sensitive earlobe. Needing to feel his skin against hers, Emma pulled at his shirt, yelped as he scooped her up.

He carried her to his bedroom, to his bed. It pleased Emma to know that no other woman had ever been in his bed before. When he tugged the thin straps of her dress off her shoulders, the silky fabric fell at her ankles, leaving her in nothing but a strapless bra and panties. He discarded those next.

"Fuck." He froze. "No condom."

Emma collapsed against his mattress. "Where's my phone? I'm having them delivered."

"It'll be faster if I run down to the bodega. I'll be back in five minutes."

Like a flash, he disappeared.

Emma was left alone in his pristine bedroom, on the massive bed. The bedroom was done in the same white tones as the rest of the apartment, with similar bright paintings throughout. Curious, she hopped off the bed to explore his living space, starting with the reading room.

The books were clearly well-read, arranged without a particular order. Travel books, classics, biographies, and historical nonfiction all mixed together in a configuration only familiar to Max. She found a few Stephen King and John Grisham novels in the assortment.

Little knickknacks lined one shelf. Emma moved

closer to study the figurines and noticed that they were all little Garfields. Garfield holding a baguette. Garfield pouring tea. Garfield playing soccer. Garfield in a warm hat next to a Christmas tree.

"This is what I like to see. A naked woman in my bedroom."

Emma spun around at Max's voice, thoughts of his funny little collection forgotten.

She suddenly felt shy and awkward, naked in his room. "I like your bedroom."

"It's the first real bedroom I've ever had," he confessed quietly.

Emma, who'd had a room to herself her whole life, didn't know what to say.

Max lightened the mood, extending a paper bag out to show her. "I got the goodies."

She followed him to his island of a bed.

He flipped the open bag upside down, scattering dozens of condom three-packs like rose petals across the smooth bedspread.

Emma laughed. "What is this?"

"These are all they had. I bought every pack."

"Then we better make good use of them."

Max didn't have to be told twice.

***

Hours later, Emma stirred awake, her body pressed against a sizzling heat source. In an instant, she recalled where she was, whose body lay so close to hers. She shifted to look up at Max, who was fully awake and watching her with a shuttered gaze.

"Hey," she whispered, attempted a smile.

Max shifted as she sat up, his palm tracing down her spine. Hesitation radiated from him. "We have to find my birth father. He will know why my brother wants you dead."

"What a way to wake up," Emma said, sardonic.

"We have to get to the bottom of this."

"Do you think Austin's sister might be behind all this?"

"I was on my way to see her when I heard you were at JFK. Shower with me?"

Reluctant to leave the comfort of his bed, she shook her head. "You go on."

His lips nuzzled her cheek. "Come on, I need someone to scrub my back," he coaxed.

Emma grinned despite herself. "It is hard to reach some places."

"Mmhmm." As he nipped at her shoulder, his stubble left goose bumps on her sensitized flesh. "Help me out." He smiled against her skin. "I'll return the favor."

Emma allowed Max to pull her up and padded after him into the bathroom. She marveled at the shift of muscle under his skin as he moved. He reminded her of a panther. His toned ass flexed as he leaned into the shower stall to turn on the water.

"It needs a second to warm—" He turned away from the stall, his gaze darkening as he focused on her naked form. "Fuck," he groaned.

Before Emma realized his intent, he pounced. Suddenly in front of her, he wrapped large hands around her waist and set her on the white marble vanity just behind her. The smooth surface was cold against her skin and palms. Her nipples puckered. Anticipating what he'd do next, she leaned back on her extended arms. The move brought her breasts forward, and he pressed a wet kiss to each nipple before moving back to look at her.

"Put your feet on the counter," he instructed.

Emma complied, lifting her feet up to her butt.

"Spread your legs."

Her heart raced. Doing so would leave her scandalously open. Using the edge of the marble surface for balance, Emma complied, sliding her legs apart and opening herself to his gaze.

Max stepped between her thighs. He glided his hands down her shoulders to her breasts, skimmed over her sensitive nipples. Her head fell back when he leaned forward to pull a tight peak into his mouth. His fingers explored from her stomach to her thighs, rubbed along the delicate inner flesh. He used his thumbs to spread open her folds, already dewy with need, and massaged the slick slit. "So soft. So ready."

Her toes curled.

Max grinned, pleased. He fisted his cock roughly— once, twice—and Emma's eyes hungrily watched the movement. She inched closer, wanting him deep inside her.

Shaking his head, he produced a condom seemingly out of thin air and tore it open with his teeth. He slid his sheathed cock against her opening, spreading her liquid heat over himself. The movement sent sparks up her body.

He grasped her hips and pulled her into him in one slow swipe, impaling her fully.

She wrapped her legs around him as he started to move. When her eyes lifted to his, she found him watching her with a reverent tenderness that fully fractured Emma's heart.

"Kiss me," she begged, needing to feel the emotions reflected in his gaze.

Lowering his head, he kissed her with a worshipful softness that brought unexpected tears to her eyes.

His gaze bored into hers, even as her eyes brimmed. He used his mouth to catch the tears that rolled down her cheeks, so very careful of the swelling on one side of her face.

She clasped her arms around his shoulders, hiding her face in the crook of his neck as she sobbed. Max wrapped one muscular arm around her, bringing her tightly against him. His movements took an exacting rhythm as his hand slipped down to where they joined, finding the tender, throbbing peak. The added pressure sent Emma over the edge, and she collapsed against him even as he plundered into her again and again until he, too, found release.

Sobs racked her body. She couldn't control them.

Max pried her gently from his shoulder, his thumb carefully wiping the tear streaks on her cheeks. "Emma? Did I hurt you?"

She shook his head, but the tears came stronger.

"Sweetheart, what's wrong?"

Emma tried to speak. "I think… I think…" *I'm falling in love with you. I will miss you when you leave.* But she couldn't say those words to him. He'd flip out. He wasn't ready. Never would be. "The events of the day caught up to me," she offered instead.

He readjusted the angle of her head so he could study her face. "You sure?"

She gave him a wobbly nod. "It's been quite the few days."

Max didn't look like he believed her, but to her

immense relief, he seemed to let his doubts go, at least for that moment.

The steam from the shower filled the room. They'd forgotten about the running water in their haste. Max plucked Emma off the counter and took her hand, pulling her into the steamy, glass-paned stall.

As the water hit their bodies, Max hauled her close to him, blocking out the spray with his shoulders. She wound her arms about his waist and held tight, reveling in his heart beating so near hers.

He reached for the bodywash.

Lathering up the soap suds, Max settled his hands on Emma's shoulders, kneaded the knotted muscles. Pleasure slicked her as he worked across her breasts and then dipped lower, careful to avoid the recent wound on her hip.

Emma soaped him up in turn, gliding her hands over the hard breadth of his biceps. She trailed her fingers and her lips over the older scars on his chest and stomach, pressed kisses to the healing marks from his recent attack, one by one.

Max froze.

Afraid that she'd hurt him, Emma glanced at his face. A shuttered look had descended on his features. Her gesture to offer comfort was too much for him, and he was struggling to regain control, to constrain his feelings.

She wanted—no, needed—that carefully blank look gone from his eyes. She moved her hand south, over his taut belly to wrap her fingers around his cock.

"We'll drown in here if you keep doing that." His own hands caressed her body.

"Rinse us off," she murmured against his lips, giving him an open-mouthed kiss.

Max crowded her against the tile. As her back collided with the slick surface, she yelped. He caught the sound with his mouth, kissing her ravenously, frenziedly. Emma whimpered, needing him now.

When their gazes met, the need and vulnerability in his mirrored hers. Shaken, stunned, she wrapped her arms tighter around him, needing him to know that, with her, he was safe.

Chapter 28

As they climbed back into his bed, Max pulled Emma close. She settled against him, fitting perfectly into his body, her nose pressing into the crook of his neck.

Fuck. What had happened? He felt raw. Disoriented. As though a powerful wave had pulled him under and tumbled him against rock and sand, leaving him battered and drowning. The sex had been hot in Nevada, but today surpassed the wildest reaches of his imagination. She'd branded herself on him.

He had known from the very moment he met Emma that he should stay far away. She was dangerous. Addictive. The most potent of drugs—the kind that turned your brain to mush at the first sampling, the sort that made you do anything to get another taste.

When she relaxed completely against him, he knew she had fallen asleep. Limbs heavy, body sated, Max could have slept for days himself. Yet as he watched Emma snoozing quietly at his side, her arm curled across his chest, her head on his shoulder, he couldn't bring himself to close his eyes.

The moment was too rare. Too precious. Too unlikely. He was half-afraid that it might be a dream. If he let himself sleep, her vibrant presence next to him might evaporate, disappear. And he'd wake up alone. Again.

He stayed awake, wishing to remember this moment, when Emma so completely and utterly belonged to him. A dream he never even dared imagine.

Eventually he'd have to let her go, but for now he let himself bask in her presence. In the gentle swell of her body as she breathed, the velvet of her skin pressed against his, that unique scent of her floral perfume.

The princess and the monster. He was darkness, and Emma was light. What could he possibly offer her? A decent guy would walk away. Disappear, never return. Let her meet someone deserving of her.

She lay asleep, so trusting, so vulnerable. What a fool. She should be scared of him. She should be calling the authorities, not opening up herself to him so sweetly.

Unable to resist, he trailed his hand along her soft skin, stroked until she shifted restlessly under his fingers. He knew the moment she stirred awake, felt her satiated smile as she stretched over him.

Flipping her to her back, he settled between her thighs. "Yes?"

She pulled his head down to hers and let her ravenous kiss serve as reply.

Chapter 29

The next morning, Emma woke up to the smell of freshly brewed coffee. She had slept surprisingly well, on sheets so soft they felt like butter against her skin. Although she had fallen asleep with Max's arm heavy and possessive around her, his side of the bed was empty when she turned toward it, seeking him.

She brushed her teeth and splashed her face, careful of the heavy swelling and bruises on her cheek. Staring at herself in the framed mirror, she groaned. It looked worse today than it did yesterday. She'd definitely be working from home today.

Thursday promised to be another hot day in New York City. She reached for a dress, buttoning the daisy buttons down the front as she followed the sound of sizzling butter to the kitchen, her feet bare on the warm hardwood floor.

Max's back was to her when she found him at the stove, sprinkling cheese over the steaming contents in his cast-iron skillet. His muscles rippled under the white T-shirt as he bent low, sliding the skillet into the oven. Emma's gaze slipped quickly to his very nice ass, covered in gray sweatpants.

"Morning."

He turned at her voice. His eyes reflected that same raw emotion she had glimpsed in them last evening. It surprised her that he didn't attempt to veil them when he spoke. "I'm leaving you with Cynthia and a guard today. I'm heading to Long Island to speak to Leila."

The very name set her teeth on edge. "You think she might be responsible for any of this?"

"Highly doubtful, but I want to be certain."

The short distance between them seemed like an impediment. She crossed to him so he knew she meant business. "I'm going with you."

Settling his hands on her hips, he lowered his head to hers until they were eye level. "No, you're not. Her letters have terrorized you."

How could she make him understand? "You're not confronting Leila by yourself. It's something I have to do."

He tucked a strand of hair behind her ear. "I want you safe."

"Well, so do I. But you can't fight my battles for me."

"What if I conference call you in?"

"Don't be ridiculous." Emma wrapped her arms around his neck. The move pressed her breasts to his chest.

Heat flared in his eyes as he swooped down and captured her mouth with his, lifting her to the kitchen island.

Someone cleared their throat. "It's too early for a porno show."

Emma broke away from Max and hopped down as a gorgeous woman glided in from the hall, Dusty in tow. Her face, free of makeup, glowed. Were her eyelashes really that thick and long without mascara? She had piled her black hair in a haphazard knot atop her head, and a few tendrils escaped to frame her face. Her strappy linen dress displayed very long, very toned legs. Jealousy hit Emma like an unexpected right hook.

This must be Cynthia. Max never once mentioned how gorgeous his coworker was. He had shared that Cynthia had worked as chief information security officer at T. R. Martin International, a Big Five tech company that Trevor Martin had founded, until Trevor and Max recruited her for their new project. Her hacking skills kept proving invaluable to their endeavor. Emma had imagined an older woman with glasses and a short haircut. She had been very wrong.

"Hi, Emma." Cynthia shuffled the laptop she carried into her other hand before extending her right one to her. "I feel like I know you extremely well by now. I'm Cynthia Romer. I'm starving, and your boyfriend has been taking forever making breakfast."

Emma appreciated that Cynthia didn't comment on her swollen face and beat-up appearance.

Cynthia plopped her laptop on the gargantuan island and went to pour herself a cup of coffee from the tea and coffee station set against the dining room wall. Dusty jumped to the credenza, watching Cynthia with captivation. Cynthia picked up the cat, kissing the top of his head before setting him back down. Dusty looked smitten. "Emma, want tea or coffee?"

Emma joined her at the coffee station. "Coffee, please."

Cynthia bypassed the fancy espresso machine for the hot coffee in the drip coffeemaker. She poured the dark liquid into a mug for Emma as well. "I have some updates on the man who almost got you guys killed in Nevada—Clarence Elrod. Clarence is an adoption attorney. Max, he used to work for the Dudley Legal Group. He quit a year before the practice shut down."

When Max stared at Cynthia from across the room,

Emma's head swiveled between them. "What's the Dudley Legal Group?"

"That's who facilitated my brother's adoption," he explained. "They closed shop years ago, but he wasn't the attorney on that case. What's he been doing since?"

Cynthia took a sip of coffee. "Personal life? He's got a wife and two kids in Park Slope."

Emma's heart lurched. "Oh God! How old are his kids?"

"Best to not think about that." Cynthia waved off her comment. "Clarence wasn't too creative. I looked up his public Facebook. He had a pet bunny named Logan. Logantherabbit is an email linked to a crypto wallet for one of the vendors on Mercury Marketplace."

"What did he sell?" asked Max.

"He sold babies."

Emma gasped. "*To whom*?"

"Couples who want kids but can't adopt through the legal route for whatever reason went through him to get a child on Mercury Marketplace. He has—had—an almost all-five-star rating."

"Fuck," said Max. "How many ratings?"

"Too disturbing to mention. He was costly, but his clients say he's worth it. I've asked my team to find who else was working with him. And then we can figure out where they're getting these babies."

Emma sank into a chair at the dining table. "What kind of disgusting place—"

"That's just a tip of an iceberg in comparison to some of the other things vendors are selling," said Cynthia. "Just to be sure, I looked for any connection to Austin or Leila through the marketplace. I didn't find any. But Max wants to verify in person. While I'm working on the virtual trail, you two are heading to Long Island."

Dusty, perceptive to his owner's unease, jumped on her lap, offering comfort.

Max brought over plates and utensils, setting the table. "We're having breakfast first."

"About time," grumbled Cynthia.

Emma didn't think she could eat. *How could they be so blasé about someone selling babies through the dark web?*

Max went back to the oven to pull out the egg dish. Returning, he set the sizzling cast iron on a cork trivet in the middle of the table. Fragrant steam rose from the cheese-topped frittata.

Cynthia didn't hesitate. She scooped a large helping onto her plate before Max had the chance to even slide his oven mitt off. Scooting in closer to the table, she dug in.

Emma placed a slice onto her plate too. Although the dish looked and smelled delicious, she had lost her appetite. "A father of two is dead, and he was running an underground child trafficking ring."

"We won't tell you what monstrous things Derek Harbor was doing," answered Cynthia. "These people need to be stopped."

"How do we stop them?"

Max helped himself to the food also. "By shutting down Mercury Marketplace and figuring out who the key people are. We stopped a dark web child abuse site last year—this one is giving us more trouble with access, but we'll get there. I need to figure out how my brother is involved."

Emma pushed the food around her plate.

She felt Max's gaze on her as he spoke. "You don't have to go to Long Island with me. I'll handle it and report back."

Facing the sister of the man who tried to kill Riley didn't make it to her list of top ten things to do today, but she was going. No question about it. She took a sip of the scalding coffee, needing the familiar jolt of caffeine to calm her nerves. "I'm going."

"I'll work from here until you guys are back," said Cynthia.

Chapter 30

After breakfast, Cynthia retreated to Max's office on the opposite side of his apartment, taking her laptop with her. Dusty pranced behind his new friend, tail happy.

"Ready?" Max raised a brow at Emma.

"Just need my purse."

When she walked into his bedroom, he followed. She glanced up when he closed the door.

"What are you doing?" she asked as he crossed to her.

In response, he turned her, nuzzled her neck.

Leaning against him, she angled her head to give him better access. "Max… Cynthia is next door."

"She's rooms and halls and walls away… but you'll have to be very, very quiet just in case." He pulled up her dress, slipped his fingers under the thin fabric of her underwear. "Fucking so ready for me."

Her head fell back against his shoulder. "We can't do this right now."

"We can do whatever the fuck we want." Flipping her to face him, he reached for the buttons of her dress, a desperate edge to his movements.

Brushing his hands away, she undid the buttons before he could rip them and pulled off her dress and bra. When he palmed her breasts, lifted them to his mouth, she bit her lip on a whimper.

"Shh," he whispered against her skin as he sat her on the bed, tugged off her panties. "You don't want anyone to hear, do you?"

His skillful fingers found her, slipped inside, teased her with lazy strokes. Blood roared in her ears.

And then he sank to his knees, wedged himself between her thighs, and settled his mouth on her.

"Oh God." She fought to draw in air.

Wrapping his arm around one thigh, he held her in place as he laved at her center. She undulated against him, breathless with need. When he closed his lips around her clit and sucked, the intense pressure threw her over the edge and she came in a kaleidoscope of sensation, biting her lip hard to not make a sound.

"You want this," he murmured against her. "You want me."

"Yes." Her breathing was ragged as she sank, boneless, into the mattress.

Shedding his clothes, he shifted her higher up the bed. He sheathed himself before joining her, filling her completely in one powerful stroke.

He never stopped kissing her, his assault on her mouth frantic, rough. Lost to sensation, burned by the intensity in his gaze, she let him pillage. The sounds of their lovemaking echoed in the room as he plunged into her in a desperate, barely leashed frenzy, until they found release together. He buried his groan against her neck, his sweat mixing with hers.

When he kissed her cheek, the words almost spilled out.

I love you.

I'll miss you when this is over.

But she kept quiet, refusing to frighten him with the

powerful feelings that coursed through her body. As he resettled next to her, she pressed her ear to his heart, let its solid beat soothe her aching one.

Max mistook her silence for concern about their upcoming meeting. "You don't need to go with me to Leila's."

She'd almost forgotten about their unpleasant errand. "I absolutely do. Leila is my problem, and I will handle her."

"Then we should go. We gotta drive halfway across Long Island."

Chapter 31

Leila Skylar lived a stone's throw away from Stony Brook University, where she worked as an assistant professor. A perfectly trimmed lawn bordered by a medley of blooms in heavy clay pots led up to her single-story home. If the very thought of Leila didn't set Emma's teeth on edge, she'd have admitted it was a cute place.

Emma had handled pressing job matters from her work phone during the drive and felt caught up by the time they arrived at Leila's charming neighborhood. They parked across the street and crossed the tree-lined road to the house.

As Max rapped against her lacquered door, Emma's heart beat in her eardrums while they waited.

A dog barked inside.

Footsteps.

The door swung open.

Leila froze when she saw Emma. "What the hell are you doing here? And what's wrong with your face?"

Before Emma could say anything, Max stepped forward. He held up Leila's latest missive and flashed it in front of her face. "I read the charming little message. We're here to talk about it."

Leila's eyes narrowed. "I have nothing to say."

Emma cut in front of Max to confront Leila. This

202

was her battle to fight. "You seem to have a lot to say. I'm getting tired of recycling your mail. Say it to my face."

"You are the reason my brother killed himself," spat out Leila.

"How?" demanded Emma, confused.

"He was sorry—so sorry for what he did to your sister. So repentant. Riley forgave him. Your parents forgave him. He wrote such kind letters to them, from his soul. You refused to read his letters. Refused to even accept them. Filed a complaint about them. He was drowning in guilt. He sought forgiveness. He never received it. It's my goal in life to make sure you never forget what you did—that you rejected his apology."

"I'd do it again in an instant. I will never forgive him for what he did. My family said forgiving him helped them heal. Well, not forgiving him helped *me* heal. We're here to tell you to stop the letters." She glanced at Max, who looked quite impressed. "We're also here to find out if you're paying someone to kill me."

"What?" Leila's face contorted in bewilderment.

"Did you hire… what's that man's name?" Emma looked at Max.

"Clarence Elrod," he supplied.

"Did you hire Clarence Elrod to take out a hit on me?"

Leila blinked. "Who?"

"If you're lying," Emma warned, "you know we'll get to the bottom of this."

"I don't know any Clarence Elrod," said Leila, clearly dazed at their accusation. "I'd never pay anyone to kill anyone. I'm mad at you, but I don't wish you dead."

Emma studied her for a long moment. "Okay. I believe you. But stop sending the stupid letters. If you have to, email me—save a tree, and I can send them straight to spam." She turned to Max. "May I have a moment?" Because Max looked hesitant, she laid her hand on his arm. "Please?"

He didn't appear happy about it, but he jerked his chin toward the driveway. "I'll be right there."

When he stepped away, Emma turned back to Leila. "Listen… I'm sorry your brother is dead. I don't forgive him. I won't forget. You said you don't wish me dead. Know that I never, ever wished your brother dead—once he was convicted. Riley survived, justice was served, and that was enough for me."

Leila gave a brief nod. "Is someone really trying to kill you?"

"It seems so."

"It's not me. I don't think it's anyone in my family."

"That's good enough for me. If you ever want to talk, you have my number—and please stop with the letters."

Turning away from Leila, Emma reached Max just as his phone rang.

"It's Trevor." He brought the cell phone to his ear to answer. Glancing back to make sure she followed him back to their vehicle, he stepped into the street.

She heard the car before she saw it.

The red sedan squealed as it sped out from the corner, gunning for Max. On sheer instinct, Emma leaped from the sidewalk. She collided with his solid frame, shoving him out of the vehicle's path, and sending them both tumbling to the hard ground. Focused on getting to Max, she hadn't even heard the gunshot.

Max rolled over her, releasing his gun from its holster and taking a shot in one seamless move. The bullet shattered the back window, but it didn't stop the getaway. The car zoomed away as quickly as it had approached.

Leila ran up to them. "You weren't kidding! That man shot at you!"

Crouching over Emma, Max ran his hands feverishly over her body. "Were you hit? What the hell were you doing, running up to an aimed gun like that?"

"Me? He was trying to run you over. I reacted to save your life. Let me up."

He released her. "Are you hurt?"

"I'm fine. Are you hurt? I tackled you pretty hard." Leila's and Max's words finally sank in. "Wait… he had a gun?"

***

The drive back to Manhattan was silent. The air in the car sparked with electricity from the tension emanating from Max.

The three had decided to not involve law enforcement in the drive-by since Leila hated cops as much as Max did. Max had dragged Emma back to his car, slammed her door shut, and took off. He still hadn't looked at her.

"Why are you mad?" Emma asked, deciding to prod the electrified force field around him.

"Don't. Speak." The words were squeezed through clenched teeth.

"What's wrong?"

"*You fucking dove in front of a bullet!*"

"*I didn't see the bullet.* I only saw a car charging at *you.*"

"And running toward it was your solution?"

"Yes. He would have hit you."

"Screw me. My job is to keep you safe. I got distracted for a minute… God, Emma, do you realize what could have happened?"

He was puffing out air like an angry bull.

"You were on the phone—I panicked. If something happened to you, I couldn't handle it—"

"Don't," he ground out.

"Don't what?"

"Don't continue. I don't need to hear it. I keep telling you over and over again there's no us, and you keep forgetting. You and me? We are a business transaction. I keep you safe. You help me find my brother. In the meantime, we have great sex. Nothing more."

Emma stared at his tense form. His fingers held on to the steering wheel tight enough to snap it. His chest rose and fell in angry huffs, like he'd sprinted a marathon, the color high on his cheekbones.

He had called Trevor's adoption of him a business transaction too, but she doubted that encompassed the full extent of their relationship.

"You're right. I misspoke."

His head snapped to look at her. "You understand why—"

She put up her hand. "No need to beat a dead horse. Focus on the road."

Chapter 32

When they arrived back in Manhattan and parked at his building, Emma jumped out of the car, eager to no longer be sharing a small space with him. She wasn't mad at him or particularly hurt by his outburst. The situation clearly scared him—even though he didn't want to admit it, he was worried about her. He wouldn't have searched her so hysterically for bullet wounds otherwise. Comprehending what drove his outburst didn't make it any less annoying, though, and she needed some space.

They rode up to Max's apartment in silence. Cynthia had made herself comfortable on one of the sofas in the living room. A bag of potato chips leaned against her hip, and she munched between her wild typing. Dusty snoozed, curled at her other side. He barely reacted to Emma and Max's return, content to be next to his new friend.

Cynthia looked up when they entered. One glance at their faces had her rising. "I should go."

"I have to call Trevor back." Max stalked to his office. The door slammed.

Cynthia gave Emma a look. "Wine?"

"God, yes."

They headed into Max's kitchen, and Cynthia pulled out a Lambrusco from Max's wine fridge. "I like sweet and sparkling. Will this do?" When Emma nodded, Cynthia poured the red liquid into two crystal glasses, then clinked hers to Emma's. "I've known him for a long time and he can be grouchy. But I've yet to see him all befuddled like he has been since he met you. I think you discombobulate him."

Emma took a sip of the chilled, effervescent wine. "He discombobulates me too."

"You're his first-ever girlfriend. There's a learning curve."

"That's a good reminder, but as he told me today, we're a business transaction."

Cynthia rolled her eyes. "Trevor and Xander always say that about their relationship too, but it's a crock of bull. It's clear how much they adore each other. Give him time."

Emma took a longer sip, noticing Cynthia had used the name that Max took after Trevor adopted him. "It's just… it's complicated. For instance, when we were in Vegas, we ran into my uncle and his new girlfriend. Max used to, as he said, sort of date her to get to her boyfriend."

Cynthia's eyes rounded. "No."

"How do you move past that?" Finally seeing the humor in the situation, Emma laughed.

"Want me to dig up some dirt on her so your uncle breaks it off?" Cynthia offered.

"Not yet. He swaps them out every few months, so it's only a matter of time. But that's a handy skill to have."

"My dirt-digging services are at your disposal." Cynthia grinned. "I won't even charge you."

Max walked into the room, stopped when he saw her and Cynthia giggling. "What's so funny?"

"Why'd Trevor call?" Cynthia countered.

"Our call got disconnected at Leila's. He wanted to make sure I was okay."

Cynthia turned her back to Max as she mouthed "Business transaction" to Emma and rolled her eyes.

Emma smiled, feeling a tendril of hope blossom for the first time in hours.

Her phone rang. Her parents.

"It's my family," she explained to Max and Cynthia as she answered the call.

"How are you feeling, dear?" asked her mother.

"Tim said you declined his offer to stay at their house. Was that a good idea?" demanded her father.

"Did you at least stay in a hotel?" Riley added.

"I'm fine, guys. I feel great. I stayed with a friend."

"Who's the guy who came to the station with you?" her dad asked.

"That's… um… that would be Xander Martin, a friend. I'll tell you anything you want to know when you're back stateside, but for now please put it out of your minds."

"We're already stateside," said her father.

"We switched our flight as soon as Jeremy called about the FBI agent. We just exited customs," her mom chimed in. "We're going to be at your apartment soon. We are taking you to Cold Spring with us."

"You're back in New York early?"

"Of course," her mother said. "We almost lost one daughter—we aren't about to risk losing two. We'll see you in your apartment in a bit."

When Emma hung up the phone, two expectant pairs of eyes watched her.

"My family decided to return home early from

Europe because of what happened with Russo," she explained. "They're at JFK. They left their car at their friends' house in Brooklyn, which means they'll be at my apartment in under an hour. I have to go."

"Whoa," Max jumped in. "You are not going anywhere."

"Don't tell me what to do. I'll be back in a few hours."

As she turned for the door, Max released a resigned groan behind her. "Hold on. I'm coming with you."

"Dusty and I will hold down the fort," Cynthia called after them.

Chapter 33

The mess that Russo had left in Emma's apartment served as a stark reminder of what had so recently transpired there.

An ache split Max's jaw at seeing the disarray. He forced himself to unclench his teeth. Slightly better, but anger still gripped him. Russo had managed to break in and attack Emma in her own home while he had lagged behind.

"I need to clean this up before my family arrives." Emma knelt to gather the items scattered across her floor.

Together, they made good time setting the place to rights.

Emma glanced around her apartment, looking pleased. "Good as new."

Max pulled the filled trash bag from the bin in the kitchen. "I'll take the trash out—"

The sharp screech of the apartment buzzer cut through his offer.

"I think that's them." Emma rushed to the buzzer, letting in her family.

Max left the trash where it was.

Emma's family burst into her apartment like a whirlwind. Her father, a robust gentleman with pronounced folds between his brows, held the door open for his wife and daughter.

Her mother, thick, dark hair bouncing about her shoulders, rushed to Emma as soon as she crossed the threshold. A cloud of perfume trailed behind her as she enveloped Emma in a tight hug. "We were so worried. I couldn't sit still the entire flight."

Riley entered next. Blonde and slim, her posture faultless, she reminded Max of a ballerina. She made a droll face at Emma. "The flight attendant had to tell her to sit twice."

"Look at your poor face!" Emma's mother gasped, laying her palm gently against Emma's unbruised side.

"I'll kill him," growled Emma's father. "No one lays a hand on my child."

"I tripped. It looks worse than it feels," Emma assured them.

Not a single person noticed Max's presence until her father suddenly turned toward him. "Who the hell are you?"

"Dad!" Emma chided. "This is Xander Martin."

"The guy from the station?"

"Yes. Please be nice."

"I'm always nice," he muttered, extending his hand to shake Max's. "Roger Neely. My daughter's been hurt. I'm jet-lagged and sleep deprived. We're double-parked, and our luggage is in the car. We are here to scoop up Emma and be on our way."

"I'm not going to Cold Spring with you. I'm staying here. I have things to tie up."

"What things?" her father scoffed. "We are not leaving you in an apartment someone broke into—you fought him off with pepper spray." He turned to Max. "Where were you when all this was happening?"

"He was out of town. Now, I really appreciate you all being here, and I know I made you worry, but everything is under control. Er… Xander will stick around. I'm perfectly safe."

Emma's mother approached Max. "Hi, Xander. I'm Deanna. I'm a hugger," she warned him a second before her arms closed about him.

He awkwardly hugged her back, not used to such shows of affection.

"I'm sorry we barged in like this. It's very unsettling to hear that one's daughter has been attacked in her very own apartment, so we are all still processing and on edge."

"I'm Riley," added her sister, giving him a small wave from across the room. "It's nice to meet you."

"Tell us about yourself, Xander." Her father sank into the couch cushions and eyed him expectantly.

"Umm…" Max thought about it. He'd never been in this situation before, and he didn't know what to say or do. Should he sit down on the couch because Emma's father was sitting? Or should he stand because her mother and sister hadn't sat? What was the polite thing to do?

In a round of panic, he realized that he was nervous… he wanted them to like him. He, who'd never cared whether anyone liked him or not in his entire life, wanted to make a good impression on Emma's family but had no way of knowing how to go about it. He hovered in place, unsure what the courteous thing to do would be.

He glanced at Emma.

She must have seen the panic in his eyes. "Let's everyone sit," she announced brightly. "I'll make tea."

"We're double-parked," Roger repeated.

"If you're blocking anyone, they'll honk," Emma assured him.

Everyone settled quickly, and Max found three pairs of curious eyes all focused on him.

"What do you do, Xander? Emma here has a law degree she doesn't use."

"Dad likes to bring that up any time he's feeling cranky," Emma pointed out from the kitchenette with an amused smile. She hovered by the kettle as she waited for the water to boil.

"I don't have a law degree," Max said. He didn't know what spurred him to add, "I run the special projects division at T. R. Martin International."

"You related to Trevor Martin?" asked Roger.

"Trevor is my… um, father."

"Trevor Martin the *billionaire* is your father?" Riley asked, eyes huge.

Max gave her a nod, feeling awkward. He shouldn't have revealed his connection to Trevor's company, or to Trevor, but he bafflingly wanted to impress Emma's family, wanted to anchor himself in something respectable, and the words had just come out.

"How did you and Emma meet?" Deanna glanced between Max and Emma, who still remained in the kitchen.

Would that water never boil?

"Xander came to my rescue," answered Emma, finally leaving the confines of the kitchenette. She set out cups in front of everyone.

"Need help?" Max stood, desperate for an escape or an activity to do.

"Nope." She smiled. "Sit. Here, the Garfield cup is for you. Since you're a fan."

Max had seen the television series as a kid, but he barely remembered it. He had never read the comic strip. He accepted the cup.

Max spent the next hour surrounded by Emma's

family. The Neelys got along well, their closeness obvious. They laughed, they teased, they argued, they joked. Every interaction made it clear how much they loved one another. Max found himself enjoying his time with them, even with Emma's father. Although the man came off gruff and bristly at first, his tenderness for his family was clear. Max could get used to this easy family time, if he let himself. He refused to let himself. Once Emma was safe, he'd walk away and let her move on with her life.

***

Watching Max interact with her family made Emma feel… mopey. They were getting along swimmingly well. Even her father came around. He was always a porcupine with newcomers, but Max had won him over too. Her mother, who'd been desperately begging Emma to start dating again, was almost giddy. Even Riley, who tended to be reserved around strangers, openly laughed and joked with Max.

But Max would leave.

He wasn't the settle-down, be-with-family type.

He had a dark job and a dark past, and Emma knew he'd walk away as soon as they found whoever it was trying to kill her and his adoptive dad. He continued to remind her of that over and over again.

When Riley yawned, her family decided it was time to head home. They tried to cajole Emma to join them in Cold Spring one more time, but she refused once more.

"This weekend then, you both have to come to Cold Spring," Emma's mother announced. "Xander, you can meet Tim and Reese and the kids. I'll make apple pie. I won't take no for an answer."

Emma almost laughed, watching Max control his reaction to her mother's invitation. He appeared to be completely calm on the outside, but the muscle in his jaw said otherwise.

She provided a noncommittal response on behalf of them both, and her family exited in the same flurry of activity with which they entered her place.

As soon as she closed the door behind them, she turned to face him. "I'm hoping we'll find your brother by Sunday and then I can go and see my family. I wouldn't jeopardize them until he is found. Don't worry, I won't drag you along."

His body tensed.

Oh boy, here we go again.

"You know that once he's found, you and I can't…" Max began. "What are you doing?"

Maintaining eye contact, Emma undid the buttons down the front of her dress. "Taking off my dress," she explained innocently, shimmying out of it.

His eyes fastened on her breasts.

She unclasped her bra next, struggling to make the move appear sexy. *How does one bend their elbow that way and still look suggestive?*

"What game are you playing?"

"No game. I just can't have this argument again." She dropped her panties.

With a groan, he lunged for her.

Chapter 34

"I like your family," Max said as he lay next to Emma in her bed. He wished they could be back in his apartment, rolling across his king-sized mattress, but her sun-speckled bedroom was warm and charming, and she seemed much more relaxed in her own space. He was glad the pepper spray had aired out.

"They're great, aren't they?"

When she curled closer into his body, Max felt a strong sense of contentment. She belonged there, cuddled up next to him. He didn't know how he was going to let her go.

"Tell me about your parents," she said.

His limbs tensed. He had just met Emma's parents; it made sense that she'd be curious about his. Yet he never discussed his upbringing with anyone. He fought through the lead that settled low in his stomach.

Emma glanced at him. "You don't have to," she hurried to add, her eyes soft and understanding.

He hesitated. She had given him an out. He could shift the conversation, and she wouldn't press further. But looking into her upturned face, he couldn't refuse her. She deserved to know where he came from, the past that had forged him.

"They had me young. Barely knew my birth father.

I've had more interactions with him the last two weeks than I had in my entire childhood. He spent most of it in prison. I doubt he realizes we are related. Stepdad One hated me. Never accepted that he now had a son. Stepdad Two broke a few bones several times before child services stepped in. Mom loved him and the drugs they did together. Had a couple of foster families. Some were okay. Others not. Had too many court appearances to count as a kid. At the last one that I ever bothered to attend, my foster parents said my mom would be there, that she was on track to fight for me, to take me home. I was so stupidly excited. I even packed what little stuff I had. So eager to come home. So dumb. She never showed up. She chose Husband Three over me. And I stayed in the system. One of the stepdads is in prison. It doesn't matter anymore. They don't mean anything to me. They aren't family. For a few years, I was thankful my brother made it out, got a good family, had a chance to be good. But now I know differently."

"You share your biological father with Milo?"

"Yep. He and my mother linked back up at some point when I was around fourteen. She got pregnant again. I was living in Rose Falls at the time, and Mom lived back in North Las Vegas. As hard as they try to find foster placements that are near the bio parents, the reality is that most available foster homes can be as far as two hours away. I saw the baby once before he was put up for adoption."

"Where's your mom now?"

"Anyone's guess. After I supposedly died in the caves, I couldn't really look for her. Tried to find her when my brother's full name popped up on the dark web, but no luck. She'd been homeless a bit. Maybe she finally succumbed to the drugs she loved so much. A shame, really. She was one of the smartest women… so vibrant, full of life. The times she wasn't using… she was a force."

He glanced down at Emma. She looked so deeply sad, and Max realized he knew so much about Emma and her life, while she knew very little about him, only heard about the hard life he'd led. He wanted to share something personal about himself with her, something happy. "She was a good mom, despite it all. Some of the happiest memories of my childhood are because of her. The best Christmas I had as a kid was when I got a bike. I was seven or eight. One of the stepdads was MIA for months at that point, and Mom was sober again. It was just the two of us that Christmas. We splurged on takeout. The heat was out, so we snuggled under layers and layers of blankets and watched *Home Alone* on VHS.

"No matter how hard times got, she always got me a gift for Christmas and for my birthday, even if the gifts were small. That year, I wanted a bike so bad. I knew we couldn't afford it, but a kid could dream. The next morning, I got a bike. I couldn't believe it. I don't know how much that bike cost her, but it was the one thing I treasured most out of all my possessions. I'd probably still have it to this day, but I couldn't take it with me when CPS came later that year."

A tear leaked down Emma's cheek.

Fuck. He didn't want her pity. Didn't want her sorrow. Never wished to make her sad. He had never shared that Christmas memory with anyone before. All these years, he had kept it safe deep inside his cold, dead heart, a kindling crumb of his past that he couldn't bring himself to extinguish.

He had tucked that small part of himself away and safe as a reminder that he wasn't born the monster he had become, that he hadn't always been the hit man who dowsed life in exchange for cash, the vigilante who hunted and killed people he himself convicted. Once, he had been a child who had a wonderful Christmas, and he wanted Emma to know that part of him. Instead, he made her feel sorry for him. He realized his mistake too late, when her big, gray eyes brimmed with tears.

"Don't cry," he said, his tone chiding, wiping at another tear that streaked down her cheek. "I can afford a million bicycles now."

Emma ran her fingers under her eyes, quickly recovering. Face sober—but no longer sad—she studied him from beneath dark, wet lashes. "You and I had very different childhoods. My happiest Christmas was getting a puppy. I never had to worry about not having heat or food or whether or not my mom would start using again." She skimmed her hand down his stomach, wrapping it around his penis.

"What are you doing?"

"Getting you hot."

"You trying to fuck me because you feel sorry for me?"

"Don't be silly. Your story made me *very* sad. I want to make you happy."

Max grabbed hold of her wrist. "You do make me happy," he said quietly, needing her to know that he meant it.

Emma slid down his body. "Let's see if I can make you happier."

Chapter 35

Emma's heart thumped in her eardrums as she stood at the sink and watched Max load the dishwasher, cleaning up after tea with her family. She wasn't supposed to have fallen in love with him, had tried so hard to fight it. Long ago, she had encased her heart in steel and barbed wire because she had never wanted to be vulnerable again.

It hadn't worked.

Where did she go from here?

He didn't want a future with her—he didn't want a future with anyone. As soon as the threat against Trevor, and by extension her, was over, he'd skedaddle right out of her life.

Would telling him she loved him change his intent to leave? Absolutely not. If anything, it would speed up his departure. Their connection, whatever it might be for him, terrified him. Making it into anything more serious would be too much for him to handle.

She couldn't force him to stay with her. He'd be encaged. He'd feel trapped. He'd rue the chains. He'd resent her. His childhood had made him terrified of being close to anyone ever again.

She had always known that her upbringing had been wildly different from Max's, but she hadn't understood the full extent until she heard the memory he had shared. If that memory had been his best one, a holiday with takeout and no heat, what had his other holidays been like?

Growing up, she knew that her parents would always keep her and her siblings safe. They were exceedingly close even now. They had especially come together after Riley had been stabbed. They handled her attack and long path to recovery as a cohesive unit, providing one another with a support system they desperately needed.

Max never had her safety net. His parents hurt him. Abandoned him. Destroyed his childhood hope and innocence. Max had to adjust to the dark, unfair world in which he grew up. He had to survive and he did, coming out of it with a targeted purpose to protect those who couldn't protect themselves.

He lived a lifestyle of decadent luxury now, in his spacious apartment on Central Park West. What he had to go through, what he had to overcome, to be the man that he was today… Russo had called him the Ghost, but that was just a silly moniker. Max was no ghost. He had a soul and a heart, and she loved him.

On that vanity in his apartment, after he had made love to her so gently, the thought had hit Emma like a tetherball to the face, and she was infinitely sure of it today. She loved the illusive Max Clark, and she had never been more terrified.

She tried to steer her thoughts to safer ground, but tension tightened her throat. Coughing to clear it, she grasped for a tone of normalcy. "Wait, that one is hand-wash only."

Max handed her the Garfield mug. "Why do you think I'm a Garfield fan?"

"Because of the figurines in your bedroom. They're adorable, and it's adorable knowing you collect them."

Max shook his head. "I don't really follow Garfield.

My mother collected those when I lived with her as a kid—she gave me some when I went to my first foster home. I kept them all this time. It's silly, but it sort of reminds me of being a kid."

Emma kept her tone neutral. "Your mother is a Garfield fan?"

"Was. Don't really know much about her now. Finding out what happened to her has been like pedaling in sauerkraut."

Her blood, which had begun to chill, froze now. "Until Rose Falls and Dr. Ross, I've only heard one other person use that phrase."

Max cocked his head. "My mother used to say it all the time. I guess I grew up with it."

"What's her name?"

"Ramona Clark. Why?"

"The woman who used that phrase gifted me the Garfield mug."

He stiffened next to her. "You think that could be my mother?"

"I'm not sure… she wasn't from Nevada. She had a kid." Emma thought back. "I started volunteering at the Stop Domestic Violence Project about a year after Riley's attack, working with domestic abuse victims, helping them access the resources they need—counseling, housing, pro bono attorneys. I worked with a woman, Carmela Griffith, who'd left her abusive husband because he hit her kid. The kid was sixteen and starting to adopt some of her husband's violent tendencies. She left to protect her son from following in his footsteps."

Max took out his phone and typed Ramona Clark into the internet search bar. A couple of photos popped up. "Is this her?"

Emma studied the image. "It could be. Carmela has long, straight hair and her face… I don't know. Maybe. The eyes look similar."

"What's her son's name?"

"Adrian. I really felt for the kid. He was whip-smart, but sheltered. Homeschooled, a little anxious about the world. Quiet, polite. Always on his phone or laptop. I suggested he get out there, start volunteering, see what he might like to do before he applies to college. College wasn't something he'd considered, but he seemed interested… I sent him links to a few paid internships for high school-aged students and a couple of college scholarships he could apply for. I think… I *think* one was from the Calvin Martin Foundation, but it was so long ago. I work with so many people, send around so many links." She reached for her phone. "Let me see if I can find it in my inbox. Do you think that's your younger brother? I thought you said he was adopted by someone else?"

"That's what I remember, but there are no papers or any documents. And this Adrian would be the same age as Milo. It could be him."

"The one who wants Trevor and me dead?" Opening up her email, she ran a search. "Here… yep. I had shared a few links with him years ago. One to a paid internship at T. R. Martin I'd found online. And one to a college scholarship through the Calvin Martin Foundation I also found online. Thought they could be helpful to him."

Using his own phone, Max searched for Carmela and Adrian Griffith online. Several people popped up, but none matched his mother or brother in age.

"I'll have Cynthia find recent photos of them." His eyes lifted to hers. "But this is how you are connected, Emma."

Chapter 36

His mother and brother were in New York. He hadn't heard from the woman in two decades. Hadn't even imagined she'd be on the East Coast. Or have his little brother with her.

"You've met them. My mother and Milo."

"If it really is them, yes, six years ago, they were in New York." She frowned. "Carmela and I stayed in touch for a while, but I haven't talked to her in years."

"What was she like?" He kept all expression carefully out of his voice. Emma had met his mother. Had talked to her and Milo. Had known them.

"Carmela was really nice. She was in a hard spot, but she wouldn't let it get her down. Very solutions-oriented. Funny. The best, most boisterous laugh. I had a really great time working with her."

That sounded like his mother. In the episodes when she was sober, she had been an unstoppable force.

"You have an email address for Milo?"

"I do. Wait, I helped them find an apartment unit. I probably still have Carmela's number saved in my phone."

The muscle in his jaw twitched. Emma had his mother's phone number.

"Call it." His voice sounded strangled to his own ears.

Emma scrolled through her list of contacts. When she found the right one—Carmela Griffith—she dialed it, setting her phone to speaker mode.

Max waited for the ring.

"We're sorry. You have reached a number that has been disconnected—"

As Emma hung up the call, disappointment doused him. "Fuck."

Emma looked at him with a hopeful expression, so at odds with the darkness crashing through him like a midnight ocean storm.

"I can take us to her apartment. I don't remember the exact address, but it's at the corner of Tenth Avenue and I think Forty-Eighth Street. I can find it once I'm back in that area."

"Let's go."

As they made their way to his car, his pulse pounded louder with each step to his vehicle. He hadn't expected his mother to be alive, much less in Manhattan. He had lived in the city for years. Had they ever crossed paths? Walked by each other without even realizing it?

He held open the passenger-side door for Emma.

How would she react to seeing him again? Otis hadn't recognized him during their encounters, though he had barely been around. His mother would remember him—wouldn't she?

He merged into the traffic.

"Her apartment is above a small grocery store," said Emma. "Once I see it, I'll know her building."

Miraculously, the grocer was still in business.

"There. That's her apartment building." Emma pointed to a five-story brick structure on the corner as soon as they reached Forty-Eighth.

A green awning hung above the ground-level shop, displaying *Corner Market* in thick, white lettering. Four stories of apartment units stacked above the shop. Max glanced at the small park across the street from the building. Not a bad place to live with a kid. He parked the car illegally in front of a fire hydrant.

"I don't know her unit number because we used to meet right out here. But maybe a neighbor remembers her." Emma unbuckled her seat belt.

He wanted to do the same, but his muscles refused to cooperate.

She glanced at him, her brows fusing in puzzlement. "Max?"

His mother and brother lived in Hell's Kitchen. Less than forty fucking blocks from him. So fucking close, and he had never known.

Now that he was here, he didn't think he was ready for a reintroduction.

But he had no choice.

Emma's and Trevor's life depended on him figuring out who hid behind the username MiloAugustus. If it was his brother, why did he want Trevor dead? Where did he find ten million dollars for the contract?

He released his seat belt and reached for the door, following Emma to the entrance to the units upstairs.

After studying the apartment intercom system and the faded names next to each unit number, she rang the super. No response.

"I'm going to go down the list," she told Max and buzzed the first apartment in the row of call buttons. No answer. She tried the second.

"Who is it?" an irritated male voice questioned.

"We are looking for Carmela Griffith."

"Fuck off."

Emma rolled her eyes at Max. The sun, diffused by gathering clouds, made her skin glow like alabaster. Unable to help himself, he leaned down and pressed a kiss to her cheek. He felt her smile, and she leaned into him as she rang the third unit. He liked having her so near him.

"Yes?" another male voice answered.

Max pulled Emma in even closer as he spoke. "We are looking for Carmela Griffith. She used to live in this building."

"Carmela moved out years ago."

"Do you know where she might be now?"

"Nope."

"What about her son?" asked Emma.

"Didn't know she had a kid."

Emma gave Max a dejected look before leaning closer to the intercom. "The phone number I had for her is disconnected. Do you have another number?"

"Never had her number to begin with."

"Do you know how long ago they moved out?" asked Max.

"A few years, at least."

Chapter 37

When they stepped away from the building, Emma assumed he'd want to return to his car, but he didn't. Instead, his warm hand engulfed hers, and he pulled her across the street to the park.

The small playground was bordered by overhanging trees. Storm clouds gathered and thickened overhead. A breeze, heavy with the scent of impending rain, ruffled the foliage above them. Max paused at the sign on the gate—Hell's Kitchen Park—and turned to face the building where his mother once lived.

"You met my mother out here."

"I did. Right at this corner. But I haven't been here in years." Emma glanced at him. "How come?"

His eyes never strayed from the building. "All this time, I thought she was dead. But she lived within a few miles of me. Milo lived within a few miles of me."

She threaded her arm through his and leaned into his body heat. "We will find them. I promise you, Max."

"Do you think she'll be happy to see me?" Before she could respond, he shook his head. "Don't answer that. Guess we'll find out one way or another."

"I think she'll be very happy to see you," Emma said, though deep down, doubts spiraled.

"We never lived next to a playground like this, when

I was little. If we did, I don't remember ever visiting one. I know Milo would be too old for the monkey bars and the slides, but I'm glad to know he had access to this space. Even if he had outgrown it." With one final glance at the park, Max led her back to his car.

Once back inside the vehicle, Max dialed Cynthia. "Find out what you can about a Carmela Griffith. We think that's my mother's new name. Either Milo now goes by Adrian—or she has another kid. Emma shared links to an internship at T. R. Martin and to a scholarship from the Calvin Martin Foundation with Adrian. She has an email for him and an old number for her."

Emma rattled off the email address and phone number, and Cynthia promised to call back soon.

The atmosphere inside the car felt as silent as a monastery as Max maneuvered them back to the Upper West Side. He pretended to focus on the road, but she knew he battled a contingent of demons inside. His own mother had lived so close to him, yet he had thought her gone this whole time. His own brother had been just a brisk jog away.

Max's phone rang less than a handful of minutes later. When he tapped the car display to answer, Cynthia's voice projected through the car speaker. "Four years ago, the Calvin Martin Foundation had given Adrian a full tuition scholarship to pursue his bachelor's degree when he was ready to apply to colleges. He declined."

"Does Trevor know them?" Emma asked.

"Just called him. He's never met them before. Adrian's email is no longer active, and I can't find a trace of him or Carmela after they moved out of their Hell's Kitchen apartment three years ago. I can't find a single visual for them. It's weird. Like any document or picture of them got wiped."

Emma glanced at Max. His knuckles had turned white from gripping the steering wheel. "What about her ex-husband? The abusive one?" she asked Cynthia.

Through the phone, she could hear Cynthia's fingers flying over the keys. "He died. Drug overdose. No suspected foul play."

"That's odd," said Emma. "She never once told me he did drugs."

"I do have a possible lead on Otis," offered Cynthia. "He has a property registered to him in Brooklyn."

Chapter 38

"I'm dropping you off at my apartment," said Max.

Emma twisted in her seat to look at him, lifted her chin. "Heck no. I'm coming with you."

"I'm not taking you into his lair," he snarled. "He was hired to kill you."

"I am in this now, Max. I'm going."

His thunderous gaze pinned her. "What do you think I'm going in there to do?"

The question silenced her, made her turn away from him to stare out the window. Naively, she'd assumed they would confront him, but that's not what Max intended to do. Max's job involved killing people—granted, bad people, but killing people nevertheless. That was why he aimed to go to Brooklyn to find his biological dad.

"We need to call the police," she said. "We need to call the FBI. All the authorities."

"We aren't part of law enforcement, Emma. What we are doing is not exactly legal, is it? Trust me, this will be best for all. I'll go, find out what he knows and why he keeps coming after you, and end it. It's what I do."

"No." Emma shook her head. "You can't keep losing a part of your soul like this. There has to be a better way. We'll call—"

"Who? Who will you call?"

She faced him again. "Uncle Jeremy. NYPD can start their own investigation. Or those two agents who came to tell us about Russo. The FBI can get involved. You need to leave it to the authorities."

"They're going to fuck it up. Law enforcement agencies have been trying to crack into Mercury Marketplace for years—they've accomplished nothing. Authorities have never done anything to help me—they didn't help Matilda. They never intervene until it's too late. I'm taking care of this on my own. Starting with Otis."

"I won't let you do that, Max."

"*He's been trying to kill you!*"

"Don't raise your voice at me. I know what he's been doing. I still won't let you go in and murder him. Max, you know that's not right."

"What would you have me do?"

"Call the fucking authorities." Emma, who rarely swore, had enough.

"In this case, I am the authorities. I left my piece at my place, rushing out after you. I need to grab it, and I'll drop you off."

"I'm going with you."

"You're not coming within a mile of that man."

"I'm not letting you go alone—I won't let you execute him."

The first raindrops fell as Max pulled into the loading zone in front of his apartment building. "I'm done with this conversation. You'll wait for me upstairs. Let's go."

"Absolutely not." She crossed her arms. "You're not going alone."

"You want to argue about it right here in front of my neighbors?"

Emma considered it. "Fine. We can take it upstairs. But you're not leaving me behind."

Max tossed the keys to the doorman. "Watch it for me for a minute. I'll be right back."

"We'll be right back," Emma corrected, and flounced in front of Max into the lobby.

They didn't speak until they exited the elevator and walked into Max's apartment. He strode down the hall toward his office.

"Don't touch anything in there," Emma commanded, right behind him. "We're calling the authorities. They need to take over."

Max spun around. "Don't you see? I have to end this. I won't let anything happen to either you or Trevor. It needs to stop. I'm the one who has to do it."

"You're going to kill your own father?"

"Easy."

"I don't believe that. You can't kill your own dad in cold blood and not feel an ounce of regret. That's not you."

His voice crackled like ice. "You don't know me."

"I know you're not a monster. I know you can't just go in there and kill your own flesh and blood. It's not you."

"*It is me!*" Max yelled, the sound bouncing off the walls of his cavernous apartment.

She wanted to challenge him, to tell him to prove it. Deep inside, though, she wasn't so sure he wouldn't, if only to demonstrate to himself that he really was the monster he thought himself to be. But if he really did kill his parent, she knew with absolute certainty that it would destroy him—it would haunt him for the rest of his life.

Max turned away from her and resumed his path to his office.

Rooted in place, unsure of what to say or do next, Emma didn't follow him. She didn't hear the door they'd left unlocked open. Didn't see Lincoln Russo enter the apartment.

When Emma glanced up and saw him raise his weapon, she screamed.

***

Max, almost to his office, sprinted back toward Emma. He came up short, watching Russo aim a Glock at her.

His own weapon was still in the safe in his office. Too far.

Emma raised her hands. "Lincoln. Put down the gun. What are you doing?"

"I've been watching you, Emma. Watching you with him." Russo encompassed Max with the muzzle. "Xander Martin. The billionaire's son. You didn't even exist until the adoption papers were signed ten years ago. Your jet was in Nevada too. You went there. Why? What do you know?"

Max had lived through a lot in his life, but he had never known fear like this, watching the disgraced FBI agent aim his firearm at Emma. She looked terrified. Max would do anything to protect her.

"I killed your brother."

At the statement, Russo swung the Glock away from Emma.

Good. Focus on me, asshole.

"You killed Phillip?" Russo's hands shook so much, Max doubted he was aware that he still held the gun. "Why would you kill a kid?"

"Your brother is Phillip Russo-Wellesley. He died

while having beer on his still-docked sailboat. I'll tell you everything. Just let her go."

Russo's weapon cut back to Emma.

"Hey," Max called out, needing his attention back on him. "She's done nothing here. You want me. Let Emma go, and you can do whatever you want to me."

"Lincoln, can you please put down the gun? You don't want to hurt anyone. You took an oath to defend. Lincoln, please."

Russo motioned toward Max. "She stays. You tell me. What did he ever do to you?"

"I was hired to kill him. It was a long time ago. I took contract killings then, but only to eliminate people who deserved it. Your brother raped someone's daughter. He was found not guilty on a technicality. I was paid to bring him to justice."

"My brother wouldn't hurt a fly."

Russo's denial ran deep. "You know that's not true. You sat at that trial. You heard the evidence. You heard Allie testify."

"You executed him!" Droplets of spit flew out of his mouth, hung in the air.

"Yes. I did. But Emma didn't. Let her go. I'll go anywhere with you."

"Tell him the rest," Emma said to Max.

Max shrugged. "There's nothing more to tell."

"Xander hunts bad people, Lincoln," said Emma, using the name the agent knew. "He finds child abusers and human traffickers and arms dealers online and stops them. He's not the cold-blooded Ghost killer you think he is."

"He killed my brother!"

"It sounds like your brother deserved it."

"Emma," Max cautioned sharply.

"Look, I get it, Lincoln. I know you want justice. Someone else wanted justice for their daughter—for what your brother did to her. Aren't you tired of this endless circle of violence? You have your answer, but it won't bring him back, will it? You're a good person. You're excellent at your job and your job makes a difference. Don't screw that up."

"I am excellent," scowled Russo, keeping the gun aimed at Max. "I do my job and I do it well. I always follow the rules. Well, guess what? That hasn't helped. Following rules and staying within the bounds of my role didn't get me to the Ghost. No, breaking those rules did. And here we are."

Max took a step forward. "I'll leave here with you right now. Just let Emma go."

"I should take both of you out right here. Taking you into custody will lead nowhere—between your daddy's attorneys and her sob story with her sister, you'll both walk."

Max eyed the weapon. If he rushed Russo, tackled him, the gun would go off while he had it aimed at him, and Emma would be able to escape. Emma would be safe. He estimated the distance to the agent, ready to leap.

Russo sighed, swinging the gun back to Emma. "But you know what? I like rules. I believe in the bounds of the law. That's why you're both coming with me."

"Where?" Emma asked.

"I'm turning you both in. The authorities can deal with whatever outlaw business of justice you're in. I wash my hands of you both. Hurry up. Let's go." He motioned toward the door with a jerk of his head. "Now."

Russo directed his gun at Max, then held Emma in

its frame. "Move." He led them out into the hall. "Hands where I can see them, or I shoot Emma first."

The elevator door dinged at the end of the hall, catching them all by surprise.

None of them expected the weapon trained on them across the stretch of hallway.

Max's father didn't hesitate.

He aimed his small pistol at Emma and discharged.

Max had never moved so quickly in his life. Russo forgotten, he dove for Emma, covering her body with his. Blood sprayed at him as a stray bullet hit Russo. The man fell to the ground with a grunt.

His father's handgun jammed. Max and Russo saw it at the same time.

Leave it to his father to carry the cheapest possible micro pistol.

Russo raised his weapon and fired. Max's father collapsed to the ground, but didn't pause, crawling into the elevator like a crab.

"You okay?" Max ran his hands over Emma's body.

"I am. Are you?"

"Yes."

"Oh my God, Lincoln!" Emma extricated herself from beneath Max and rushed for Russo. A bullet had hit him square in the chest, and blood was everywhere. "Call nine-one-one."

Max was already dialing.

"Who," gasped the agent, "the fuck was that?"

Emma put Russo's head in her lap as Max stripped his shirt and applied pressure to his bullet hole.

"That's the man trying to kill me," explained Emma. "Xander's been protecting me from him."

"We can't," wheezed Lincoln, "let him escape."

"Don't talk," cut in Max. "I think the bullet punctured your lung. The medics should be here soon. Here, turn this way. I know it hurts like a motherfucker, but this angle will keep your lung from collapsing."

"Why…" Russo continued, straining, "why are you… helping me? Shouldn't… shouldn't you… want me dead?"

"I did yesterday, when you attacked Emma. But she's right. You're a good guy. The world needs more people like you."

The paramedics, police, and fire department descended on the building in minutes. Max's father had disappeared, though the cops were searching the perimeter.

Russo was moved to a gurney and rushed away to the nearest hospital. Emma and Max, stained with Russo's blood, answered innumerable questions. Max held Emma closely to his side, afraid to ever let her go again, his sweatshirt covering her blood-splattered body. Even the sweatshirt and body heat weren't stopping her shivering. As she drooped more heavily against him, he knew she was starting to wane. Her body begged to feel safe, and he needed to get her out of her bloodied clothes and warmed up.

He'd never pulled out the big guns before—his adoptive father's name and connections. But if there was ever a time, it was now. "My father is Trevor Martin. Here's our family attorney's business card. All future questions can be directed through her. My girlfriend and I need to get cleaned up—it's been a hell of a day."

Chapter 39

He called me his girlfriend.

His girlfriend.

Emma had almost been killed thrice today—by two different men—and still had Russo's blood on her, but the most shocking part of the day was Max calling her his *girlfriend.*

Had he meant anything by it or was he trying to get the questioning wrapped up?

His familiar hand wrapped around hers as he led her into the master bath, stripping them both.

Emma glanced at his face. He looked aloof, distant. Methodically, he turned the various knobs in the shower until hot water fell in a steady stream from the rain showerhead. He hustled her inside and followed her into the steamy heat.

He was clinical about washing the blood from her, his fingers impersonal as they lathered soap over her skin. Even his detached touch set off sparklers in her nerve endings, her nipples pebbling as he traced her skin with his soapy hands. Moisture pooled between her legs.

When she skimmed her hand toward his penis, he stayed her attempt, encircling her wrist with his fingers and tugging her away before she could get closer. He turned off the water.

She didn't like this Max, this withdrawn stranger in the gigantic shower stall with her.

"I'll get fresh towels." Stepping out first, he padded across the room to the linen closet against the opposite wall.

Before Emma could stop herself, she launched at him. As if anticipating her movements, he turned and caught her, hauled her to his chest.

"I was so scared for you," she whispered against his skin.

"Scared for me? Emma, he had a gun trained on you. I was terrified for you."

"You told him everything about killing his brother. He'll tell someone and they'll take you away."

"I'll gladly spend the rest of my life in prison, would take the electric chair, if it means that you're safe."

Emma tangled her fingers in his hair. "Don't say that. I can't even think it."

"I need you." He strode with her to his bed. "Now."

He made love to her frantically, as though his very next breath depended on it, while the summer storm battered at the windows.

"Mine," he growled against her skin as he pounded into her. "All mine."

Emma knew without a shadow of a doubt that she never wanted anyone else but him.

She must have dozed off, because she woke to sensation. He was all around her, inside her, moving with deliberate slowness. Her eyes opened, and he kissed her, not quickening his luxuriantly unhurried pace even as her legs tightened around him, urging him to move faster.

"Nuh-uh, I'm in charge right now," he whispered into her ear. "And you're going to be a very good girl and do everything I say."

"I don't follow orders," she protested weakly.

"You're so wet for me. I love that. Can't get enough of you."

His words turned deliciously dirty, and Emma found herself getting wetter, wilder, clawing at the sheets. He teased her leisurely—wickedly—slowing whenever she was close, causing her to beg and plead and moan.

"I want to be in charge now. I want it faster. Please."

Despite her pleas, he made love to her slowly, almost despairingly. Her inner muscles clenched tight as she trembled and convulsed under him again and again, sinking her nails into his back.

He came on a growl against her neck, spilling himself deep inside her.

Chapter 40

"Fuck," Max muttered when he got enough breath in his lungs to speak again. "I was so hot to be inside you—"

His tongue couldn't formulate the words. White spots danced across his vision as he thought of what he had just done. His rashness and stupidity could have gotten Emma pregnant. Growing up the way he had, he had long ago decided that he would never have children. He wouldn't let his vile bloodline continue. It would end with him.

He could almost see Emma's mind working, as she did calculations in her head. "I think we should be fine." She sounded composed. Sensible. Her unflappability at a moment like this, when sheer panic coursed through his bloodstream, rankled. Maybe she didn't understand the repercussions.

"Emma, what if you're pregnant?"

"We should be okay," she repeated in that same unconcerned tone, though a hint of wariness entered her expression.

His teeth ground together as his head pounded. "I need to go."

Emma looked around them, as though to remind herself of where they were—his apartment. "Go where?"

"I need air. This was a bad idea." His lungs burned every time he attempted to breathe.

"You need to elaborate."

Why was she not having a proportional reaction to this momentous fuck-up? What part of the equation did she misunderstand? He could have gotten her pregnant with his evil DNA. There was no future for them. His line ended with him.

Emma attempted to move closer to him, but he couldn't handle the nearness. His body reacted on its own, leaping out of bed. Away from her. He moved so quickly that his heel caught on the rug, and he landed on the hard floor with a jarring thud.

Her eyes widened as she leaned over the edge of the bed. "Are you—"

"I'm fine." He leaped to his feet. She looked so beautiful, naked and flushed in his bed. A part of him wanted to lunge for her, to sink into her welcoming heat, and make love to her again and again. A larger part—the part that restricted his breathing, gripped his neck like a noose—wished to run. "I don't want a kid with you."

The sentence hung in the air for a tense moment.

Emma's eyes filled with tears.

"I don't want to have kids with anyone," he rushed to clarify. *If I did, I'd only want them with you.*

It was too late. Her lip quivered.

He almost fell to his knees at her feet. He wanted to pull her into his arms and kiss away the salty droplets that gathered on her lashes. To press his ear to her beautiful heart and feel its steady beat. He forced himself to stand stock-still. To not move closer even when a tear spilled down her cheek, tearing at his insides.

"You don't understand—" he began, needing to explain himself. Maybe if she understood, she wouldn't look at him with her huge tear-rimmed eyes, as though he had just slapped her.

"No, you don't understand!" She wiped at her tears with the knuckles of one hand. The other fisted the sheet she had pulled tightly to her chest. "I tried so hard to fight it. Knowing that you don't want anything beyond this. I told myself to remain distant. To let sex be sex. To not fall in love with you."

The floor gave out beneath his feet. "Don't—"

"No, *you don't*. I've fallen in love with you. Stupid as it was. As much as you continue to remind me that this means nothing to you, it means something to me. I love you, Max. I couldn't fight it. I tried. I really did."

He tried to reason with her despite the ballooning panic. "You don't love me."

The tears came stronger. She kept clearing her throat to get the words out. When she spoke, the anguish in her voice ripped his insides apart. "You want to be a wild animal out there all alone? *Go*. I don't think I'm pregnant, but I'll have this baby alone if I am. You keep saying you don't want anything beyond sex. Have it your way. But I can't keep making love to you as though it means nothing to me."

Although he could tell that she had more to say, her gasping sobs restricted the words. She shook her head in frustration, sending tears to fall around her like shooting stars.

"I…" Yet he didn't know what to say.

She took a deep lungful of air, exhaling it slowly in a struggle to control her ragged breathing. "Just leave me alone," she finally whispered, turning away.

Chapter 41

Max had shattered her heart.

Deep down, she'd known it would happen all along.

He'd never led her to believe otherwise.

She had accidentally freed the foolish romantic in her, the one she had locked away seven years ago. Now she had to deal with the consequences—of loving someone who did not want her love, who did not love her back. She'd get over it. Eventually. Tonight, she'd let herself weep.

She had a strange sense of catharsis when she had said the words. As much as his rejection hurt, she had spoken the truth, had told him how she felt. She hadn't let fear drive her to hide her true feelings. She had admitted that she loved him, and she was proud of herself for saying so. When it would all be over, at least she'd have no regrets.

The rain had stopped a long time ago. Dusk bled into nightfall outside the windows before her tears finally dried. Her face was hot, her lids swollen. Dragging herself to the shower, she stood under the cold stream until she recovered a modicum of her normal self again. After tugging on a pair of pajamas, she headed to the kitchen. She'd dehydrated herself with her tears and needed a glass of ice water. Maybe two glasses of wine.

The lights had been left on throughout the

apartment, but Max was nowhere in sight. Dusty snoozed on one of the sofas in the living room. She filled her glass with water from the fridge and followed the hallway until she stopped in front of the open door to Max's office.

He sat behind his desk, his computer screen bathing his face in an icy-blue light. His fingers pressed to the furrow between his brows, and it didn't seem like he was paying much attention to whatever the display showed.

When she entered, he glanced up. His eyes focused on her, widened.

He jumped to his feet so fast, the chair shot out from behind him and crashed against the wall with a thump.

Gaze glued to hers, he swallowed. "Emma—"

Seeing his face shattered her broken heart into even smaller pieces, their sharp edges shredding her. She held up her hand to interrupt. "Please, let me say this. You've never led me to believe you felt anything for me other than lust. I fell in love with you all on my own, and I'll deal with it on my own. I'll be okay. I promise. I just can't stay in your bedroom anymore."

"Take my room. I'll take the guest room."

"No. I want the guest room. I can't sleep in your bed."

It looked like he wanted to speak—to argue—but after a beat, his shoulders drooped. He nodded.

"I'll see you in the morning," she offered.

Another nod.

There was nothing more to say.

Chapter 42

"I just got back from the hospital," announced Cynthia, walking into Max's kitchen the next morning.

Emma had just turned on the Breville to make herself a cappuccino. It was a sugar-milk-and-caffeine kind of day. The machine whirled and whizzed as it expressed a double shot of espresso into Emma's cup. Emma turned on the milk frother, glancing up as Max strode into the kitchen.

He looked as terrible as she felt, she noted with an ounce of petty satisfaction. His hair stood every which way, and dark shadows gathered under his eyes. When his gaze collided with hers, a muscle ticced in his unshaven jaw.

Cynthia, oblivious to the tension, scooped up Dusty, who came to greet her, and joined Emma at the coffee station. "Russo came out of surgery splendidly. He'll make a full recovery."

"Thank God," Emma breathed. "He saved our lives, he acted so fast."

"He told the authorities that the suspect came out of nowhere and started shooting, and he had to discharge his weapon. Weapon was registered in his name, legal, and your stories matched up well enough. The attorneys assure me you all will be fine. When I spoke to him, he asked me to tell you that he won't share what he'd learned." Cynthia's lips pursed as she looked between Max and Emma. "You trust him?"

"I do, yes," said Emma. "He's a man of his word. He had sought answers, and now he's found them. I'd like to go visit him."

Max gave Emma a dark look. "Over my dead body. Your bruising isn't even healed yet."

"We'll discuss it later." Emma, cognizant of Cynthia in the room, waved off his comment.

"There's nothing to discuss. You're not going anywhere near him."

Emma tensed. "Don't tell me what to do. I want to go see him, and I will." She looked at Cynthia. "Coffee?"

Cynthia threw a sideways glance at Max, shifting Dusty higher in her arms. "I can make it."

Needing to keep busy, Emma turned back to the espresso machine. "I got it."

Max's voice reached her over her shoulder. "Stay with Emma. I'm going to go to Brooklyn. Talk to my father."

Emma spun around. "Over my dead body," she said, echoing Max's earlier phrase.

"That's not an image I need in my brain right now," Max ground out.

Cynthia, watching the two with acute insight, stepped back. "On second thought, I think I'll get a cup of coffee at the cafe on the corner."

She set Dusty on the kitchen island and retraced her steps to the exit.

The front door snicked behind her.

Max's hands dug into the marble edge of his kitchen island. "You're not setting foot out of this apartment until I find Otis."

"I won't let you kill your own father."

"What I do is not up to you."

The words stung like a whip. She picked up her cup of espresso, the milk and sugar forgotten. Refusing to cry in front of him again, she let the scalding caffeine soothe the tears clogging her throat.

When the heavy silence settled in the room and pricked at her nerve endings, Emma glanced up to find Max staring at her with an inscrutable expression.

"Fine. I won't go to Brooklyn," he said. "I'll send my colleague Ezra. I'll ask him to find out why Otis has been so adamant about coming after you. There has to be more at stake than five grand. Does that work for you?"

Emma's heart sped up at the alternative proposal. He had taken her adamant reaction into account. She tried to keep her voice even. "Thank you. That works for me."

"You and I can go back to my mother's old apartment. We'll find the super. See if he remembers anything."

How can he be so attractive even looking this exhausted?

So unfair.

I shouldn't be in his company for this long. He has some potent pheromones wafting my way as we speak.

"I'll go change." Emma set her cup in the sink.

She moved to exit the kitchen, to flee to the safety of her room at least for a little while. As she hurried past him, he snagged her hand.

His fingers twined through hers, sending a tremor to zing through her. Or maybe it zinged through him. He clasped her hand so tightly that it was impossible to tell. His thumb traced slow circles against her skin, shooting restless need through her veins.

She wanted to close the distance between them and nip at his jaw, to stand on her tiptoes and kiss his mouth. To feel his arms wrap around her, lift her. To have him—

When she tugged away her hand, he tightened his hold for a beat before releasing her. Sinking her teeth into her lower lip, she braved one quick glance at his hard features before she fled his presence.

This attempt on her life had to be stopped so that she and Max didn't have to continue to orbit each other. Seeing Max crushed her heart every time, and she could only handle so much pain without imploding. She hoped Ezra would get some answers, or she'd figure out a way to track down Otis herself.

They drove back to Carmela's old address in silence. Max kept glancing at her as he navigated through the heavy morning traffic, but he didn't speak.

He pulled over at the fire hydrant again. She forced her eyes not to linger on his fingers as he shifted the gear into park.

Tap, tap, tap.

An insistent knock on Emma's window startled her. She looked up to find an older man in a white wifebeater frowning at her through the glass. "You can't park here."

"We're here for just a moment," offered Emma, opening the door and joining him on the sidewalk. The warm humidity of the air contrasted with the car's air-conditioned interior and sent goose bumps up her arms. "We're looking for the building super."

"Which building?"

"This one." Emma indicated it with a nod.

He gave her a guarded look. "You're looking for me."

Emma's muscles sagged with relief. She tensed a

moment later when Max came around the car and laid his hand at the small of her back. His touch jolted through her, heating her blood. Despite everything, she wanted him.

"We're looking for a former tenant of the building. Carmela Griffith and her son, Adrian."

The super's body relaxed as his eyes lit with recognition. "Carmela was a great resident. Never any problems. Didn't complain. Kept to herself. Shame she moved away."

"And the kid?" Max probed.

"Great kid. Never saw him, never gave me any trouble."

Emma didn't want this to be another dead end. "Do you know where they might live now?"

He shook his head. "She didn't leave a forwarding address."

"What about their things? Did they take everything with them?"

"Apartment was spotless. Cleaner than when they even moved in. Great tenants, like I said."

Max pulled out his phone, diving into his images folder for a picture of Otis. "Have you ever seen this man visiting?"

The super shook his head. "I don't think so, and I always remember a face."

Emma took the phone from Max, searching for a photo of Clarence Elrod online. "What about this man?" She extended the phone to the super.

The super snapped his fingers. "Yes. I remember him. He helped them move out."

Clarence Elrod knew Max's mom and brother. Nausea clawed up Emma's throat. The man who died trying to kill her in the Nevada desert somehow knew Max's family.

How had they met? What was the extent of their relationship? She followed Max back to the car, lost in thought. She didn't realize they had pulled away from the curb and into the gathering traffic until a loud honk from one cab driver to another brought her out of her racing thoughts.

Max had set the direction south.

"Where are we going?" His apartment building was located the other way.

"To see Mrs. Clarence Elrod."

The last person Emma ever wanted to face. Her palms began to sweat. "I'm nervous to see her," she confessed. "Her husband died chasing us. She has two kids. What do we even say to her?"

Max gave her a considering look. "Want me to drop you off at my apartment? I can have Ezra meet us there and stay with you until I'm back."

She wasn't going anywhere. "No, I'm sticking this out to the end. I just wish it were all over by now."

Max anchored her hand with his on her lap. His heat burned through her as their fingers interlaced. She should shake him off, move farther away from him, but she couldn't make herself do so. Tightening her hold, she brought her other hand to rest on top of his, pretending that the simple touch didn't send her heart skipping and nerves buzzing. Pretending that the weight of their joined hands resting on her thigh didn't tear at her broken heart.

"I hope it's over soon too," he said in a jagged voice.

That would be the end of them, though. Emma tried to breathe through the pain. They'd figure out why his brother wanted Trevor and her dead and stop him, stop his father, and then Max would disappear back into the darkness from which he'd emerged. She'd be free to resume her old life, as monotonous as it now seemed to her.

She hurried to change the subject, to chase the dejecting thoughts from her mind. "What do we even ask her?"

"I want to know the extent of her husband's connection to my mother and brother. She has to know something."

Brooklyn seemed even hotter than Manhattan that day. The sky burned bright blue, the sun baking them to the pavement. As Max and Emma made their way to the Elrods' brownstone on Fifth, she looked longingly at the coffee shop next door. An iced coffee would hit the spot. Not that she needed the caffeine—her anxiety was already sky-high in anticipation of seeing the wife of the man she saw die.

When they buzzed her apartment, Nancy Elrod refused to let them up.

"I'll be right down," she told them through the intercom.

A tall woman with straight blonde hair, dressed in a white tennis dress, emerged from the building a few minutes later. Her every limb was a collection of taut muscle.

She must lift a lot of weights and often, thought Emma, impressed.

She gave them a once-over as she stopped a few feet away. "I'm Nancy. How do you two know my husband?"

Nancy looks so normal. So run-of-the-mill. Does she know of her husband's dark web activities? Is she involved in his baby selling business? If she were, Emma wouldn't hesitate. She'd report her to every law enforcement agency on either side of the Mississippi.

Max's voice brought Emma out of her racing deliberations. "We don't know him. But I'm looking for my mother, and we were told he knew her."

Nancy crossed her arms. "Who's your mother?" Her gaze drifted to Emma. "My God, are you okay?"

Emma had almost forgotten about the bruising still swelling her cheek. "Fell off the bed," she offered, recalling her explanation to Dr. Ross. People didn't ask follow-up questions when a bed was brought into conversation.

Max redirected Nancy to the question at hand. "My mother is Carmela Griffith. Clarence helped her and her son, Adrian, move about three years ago."

Nancy frowned. "Carmela and Clarence go way back, but they haven't interacted in years. I'm not even sure she's still in New York. I can't help you, sorry. She and my husband lost touch a long time ago."

Was she lying?

She seemed truthful, but if she had a hand in her husband's business, she had something significant to hide. Emma expected Max to press further, but he didn't.

He pulled out a business card. "If you remember anything, however trivial, please call me."

Nancy took it from him. "Hope you find your mother," she offered, and turned back for her building.

Chapter 43

They were halfway to Max's apartment when the sound of Emma's phone ringing broke through the heavy silence in the car.

The picture of Tim's face appeared on the screen. Emma slid her thumb over the phone to answer, setting it to speaker.

Her brother's voice rushed out on one breath, panic saturating every word. "Emma, Janie's been hurt. Some asshole ran the stop sign on Mom and Dad's street. She's barely conscious. The doctor suspects an intracranial hemorrhage." Tim's voice broke. "She's just a little child."

Tears burned her eyes as she fought back a sob. "I'll be right there. Which hospital?"

"I'll text you the address."

"I'm on my way now. Did they catch the driver?"

"Hit-and-run."

The tears made it hard to see the phone screen. Blindly ending the call, she swiveled to Max. "I need to go to Cold Spring. You don't have to come with me."

Max didn't hesitate. "I'm driving you."

"Do you think it's Otis? Is he coming after my family?"

Max's jaw clenched.

Oh God. He did *think so.*

"Take my phone and call Cynthia. If there are cameras near the incident, she may be able to click in and see what happened and who drove."

"Good idea." Emma's hand shook as she reached for Max's phone.

***

The small town of Cold Spring, just fifty miles north of Manhattan in the Hudson Highlands, was refreshingly cool compared to the steamy heat of Manhattan. The town's location—flanked by Hudson River on one side and steep mountains on the other—had kept it small and contained since its founding in 1818.

Max managed to get them to the hospital from Brooklyn in just over an hour. Emma had chattered anxiously as he drove, sharing a brief history of the town with him. He knew that talking soothed her anxiety and managed to pick up a fact or two about Cold Spring.

The three-story, red brick medical building stood at the edge of town, surrounded by a small green lawn and sparsely planted pines. He pulled into the half-full parking lot.

Just an hour earlier, he had anticipated learning more about his mother—Carmela Griffith, as she'd become known. But Nancy had known nothing. Was Nancy lying about being unaware of any recent interactions between her husband and Carmela?

Although Cynthia hadn't found a link between Nancy and her husband's business, Max had his doubts. She seemed relatively calm for someone whose husband had just died. Clarence had obviously taken things into his own hands after Otis failed to terminate Emma. Did he do it at Milo's orders? Or Carmela's? Was the hit-and-run that injured Emma's niece related?

Thoughts of Clarence and Carmela and Milo dashed from his mind when he saw Emma's tense face. Now that they had arrived, she looked like she never wanted to leave the safety of his car.

***

Painful memories crashed through Emma as she stared at the glass-and-brick structure. She had shed so many tears in this hospital as Riley fought for her life in the OR, the idea of now returning to see injured Janie threatened to break her. She got out of the car anyway.

"They're on the second floor," she told Max as she hurried toward the glass entrance.

He kept pace, a silent and solid presence next to her.

The smell of antiseptic hit her nostrils as they entered the building. Heading for the elevator, Emma shook off the memories that the scent unearthed. It broke her to realize how familiar she was with the hospital, and how little had changed inside in seven years.

They found her family in the waiting room—her mom and dad, Riley, and baby Finn. Her parents sat next to each other in the square-back chairs, her dad's arm draped protectively around her mom as she rested her head on his shoulder. Her parents had always found solace and joy in each other. It was a powerful example Emma longed to emulate. Riley sat cross-legged on the floor and entertained Finn with colorful toy cars.

Her mom jumped up when she saw them. "Tim and Reese are with Janie," she explained, enveloping Emma in a hug.

The familiar scent of her soothed Emma's frayed nerves, and she held on tighter for an extra few moments. After Emma let go, her mom hugged Max as well.

"How is she?" Emma scanned the faces of the adults in the room. "What happened? Did they find who did it?"

Her mom rushed to provide some answers. "She's doing better. It could have been so much worse. They thought she had a brain bleed, but now they're saying a grade 4 concussion. And a dislocated elbow."

"She was on her bicycle just at the edge of our driveway. I glanced away for a second," said her father, looking alone and dejected in his seat.

Emma saw the guilt etched in his features. She was thoroughly familiar with the feeling. Sinking into the chair next to her dad, she took his hand. "It's not your fault, Dad. All the kids are biking up and down that block all the time. That driver should have stopped. You're not at fault here."

She knew her words would make little difference in the guilt coursing through him, but she hoped he would see the truth in them eventually.

"Can't believe someone would drive away after running over a child." Riley shuddered. "What a monster."

Baby Finn wiggled from Riley's lap and tottered toward Emma with a happy smile, arms extended. Scooping up the baby, she tossed him in the air as he giggled and squealed, then settled him on her lap and pressed a kiss to the top of his auburn head.

She felt Max's gaze on her and glanced up. He flicked his away and found a seat a few chairs away from her, reaching for his phone. His fingers raced as he typed.

"The cops are checking with the neighbors for footage from their doorbell cameras," said her mom.

Her father restlessly ran his fingers through his hair. "I should have had one installed years ago. I will as soon as I get back home. This is all my fault."

"What were you doing right before the car hit her, sir?" asked Max.

Instantly, Emma felt defensive. "What are you asking?"

Emma's dad considered the question. "I was watching Janie as she started doing loops on her bike in front of the garage. Her tire looked a bit flat, so I turned away to get the pump. Told her to wait. I should have made her come with me."

"Would she have listened?"

"No. I should have dragged her."

"If Deanna were with her instead of you, would you blame her?" Max asked.

"Of course not! I'd blame the idiot going fifty in a residential neighborhood."

"You don't really know me, sir, but I've lived with guilt a long time. I can see it in you. An asshole sped through a stop sign. There was nothing you could have done at that moment. Don't let the guilt eat at you when you would have not blamed anyone else for your exact actions. Guilt can be gluttonous."

Her dad offered a noncommittal huff and sank deeper into his chair.

"That's beautifully said, Xander," said Emma's mom. "I wholeheartedly agree, Roger. It wasn't your fault."

Emma glanced between her two parents. "Did you see what the driver looked like? What kind of car were they driving?"

"A white sedan," said her dad. "Didn't get a look at the driver."

Emma exchanged a look with Max. Otis had been driving a red vehicle previously, but he could have acquired another car since then. Russo had injured him in the shootout—what if he had outsourced to someone else?

If the goal were to terminate her, attempting to run over her niece made little sense. Emma prayed it was just a coincidence.

The incident had caused her to do the one thing she had sworn to avoid—see her family before the hit on her had been stopped. She would ensure that Janie was fine, and then she and Max would return to Manhattan and end this threat once and for all.

Finn wiggled out of her grasp. She lowered him to the floor, expecting him to toddle to Riley or her parents, but the baby set a sure-footed path for Max.

"He wants to say hello to you, Xander," cooed her mom. "He loves new people."

Emma watched as Max eyed her baby nephew with mistrustful uncertainty. He clearly hadn't spent much time around children before, but Finn had never met a stranger he didn't love.

He stopped right in front of Max and stared at him with wide eyes. Then he smiled and reached out his plump arms, asking to be picked up. Max didn't look like he was going to do it. He stared at the toddler, immobile. The baby's smile faltered. Suddenly spurred into action, Max leaned down and scooped up Finn, setting him on his knee.

Emma's heart lurched at the interaction.

The baby, now settled on his new friend's lap, leaned against Max's bicep and glanced up at his face. He offered another smile.

Max stared at Finn as though he were a creature he had never encountered before. The corners of his mouth tentatively tilted up as the baby kept grinning at him. Delighted at the reaction, Finn giggled. The sound of pure joy. No one was immune. At the laugh, Max responded with a wide, warm smile and pulled the baby in closer. Finn rested his head heavier on Max and settled in with a content sigh.

"Aww," her mom observed. "Finn made a new friend."

"I've never held a baby before," confessed Max, looking at the child resting on his lap.

"Well, you're a natural."

Max missed Riley wiggling her eyebrows at Emma. When Emma's lips pressed together, Riley immediately understood to lay off the teasing. "Emma, would you go with me to get a cup of coffee?"

Emma nodded. "Of course."

Max shifted. "I'll go with you."

"We can go by ourselves," Riley assured him. "Stay here with Finn."

Emma suspected that Riley had a boatful of questions, and she wouldn't be able to ask them if Max tagged along.

Max had already stood, adjusting the baby higher up his body. "I insist."

Emma knew he wouldn't let her out of his sight, not with the contract still out on her life.

Finn laid his hand on Max's mouth, giggling as Max puckered his lips against his palm.

Charmed by the interaction, Emma froze, watching the two of them.

When she didn't move toward the door, Riley

prodded her with a light poke to her ribs. "Emma? Coffee?"

"Yes." Emma blinked back to reality. "We'll be right back," she told her mom and dad. She ignored the delighted grin that Deanna shot her husband and exited into the hallway.

***

Max balanced the baby's slight weight on his hip as he followed Emma and her sister to the coffee machine at the end of the hall.

"Dad is going to drive himself up the wall with guilt. Do you remember how he was after my incident?" Riley turned to Max as she explained. "He hovered for a good two years. Emma hovered too, but Dad went beyond. He and Mom would have slept in my room if I'd let them. That's how paranoid they were afterward."

"Well… you did flatline twice," Emma pointed out.

Riley rolled her eyes, waving off her sister's comment. "I had to get them a puppy just to give them something else to do."

The baby chose the moment to place his little hands on either side of Max's head and turn his face toward his. He giggled happily at Max as their eyes collided. Though the child had auburn hair, his wide gray eyes looked remarkably like Emma's. Holding the little human sent sheer panic through Max. Emma could be carrying his child. She said the possibility was slight, but he knew that it wasn't zero. He didn't want to curse the world with his offspring—he couldn't even begin to guess what kind of monsters they'd grow up to be. Yet while staring into the large, innocent eyes of Emma's nephew, Max couldn't possibly imagine how anyone related to Emma could be anything but good.

"He loves to be tossed up in the air," offered Riley, smiling at her nephew.

Max considered the child. His bones looked so fragile. That couldn't possibly be safe. "I'll leave that for the experts. I'm still learning the ropes."

He let his gaze sweep over Emma. She kept her focus on the coffee machine, appearing hyper-focused on the small menu of options.

Footsteps at the other end of the corridor alerted him. He faced the approaching figure with hesitancy. Maybe he should have warned him.

"Hey, Tim," Riley said as the newcomer caught up to them with quick strides.

Tim Neely blinked at Max, as though he, too, needed a moment to process. "What the fuck are you doing here? And why are you holding my kid?"

Chapter 44

Emma's head whipped between her brother and Max. The two men squared off in the hospital hallway, glaring at each other. The tension and animosity radiating from them scalded her. "Do you two know each other?"

A long pause.

Then Tim shook his head. "No. We don't."

Riley's blue eyes studied the two men. She gave Emma an unconvinced look. "That was a strong reaction to a stranger," she noted reasonably to Tim.

"This is Xander Martin," Emma added, though she had a feeling Tim already knew that.

Her brother strode forward and extricated Finn from Max.

Knowing this wasn't the time to investigate the connection between the two men, Emma moved on to the more pressing question. "How's Janie?"

Tim gave Finn a kiss on his plump cheek. "She's doing better. Reese is with her. They want to keep her overnight just in case."

"Can we see her?" asked Riley.

"I don't want to overwhelm her with too many people. Maybe if you guys go in pairs?"

"We can do that," Emma readily agreed.

Tim looked like he'd fought his way through hell. "I'm going to go give Mom and Dad an update. Can't believe someone would plow that way through a child and take off."

"They still haven't found the driver?" asked Emma.

He shook his head. With a hostile look at Max, Tim led the way back to the waiting room.

***

Max never thought he'd have to face Tim Neely again. He hadn't thought of the guy in ages. Even though Cynthia had flagged the connection, Max didn't think they'd have a chance to interact. His relationship with Emma was finite, after all. Yet here they were.

Tim led the way to the waiting room to give an update to his family. Riley followed close behind. Emma's deliberately slower pace put her at the back of the procession.

When Max hung back in the hallway, she stopped and glanced at him. He indicated with a nod that she should go on; he'd watch from here. The Neelys didn't need him intruding on their family huddle.

Emma hesitated, eyes searching his. When she understood that he wouldn't follow, she trailed her siblings into the waiting room.

He positioned himself in the hallway where he could see Emma. Emotions—relief, concern—flitted across her face as Tim updated his family on his daughter's status. As though feeling the weight of his gaze, Emma looked straight at him.

Max had to physically restrain himself from striding forward.

Emma, seeming to feel the same force, took a step toward him.

Tim, sensing her intent, caught her elbow to stall her progress. He whispered something in her ear. Emma gave her brother a perplexed look, but didn't attempt to make her way toward Max again.

***

Emma fought hard to keep her eyes from straying to Max. He leaned against the wall in the hall that led to the waiting room, a lone figure just out of reach. Her every limb pulled at her to go to him, to take his hand and bring him into her family's close-knit circle. Yet when she had made the attempt a few minutes earlier, Tim had insisted they needed to talk. Now wasn't the place or time, but questions ticker-taped through her brain.

Her gaze drifted to Max again. Nope. She couldn't do it. She couldn't leave him standing there alone, just outside the orbit of her family. Her heart sped up with every step that took her closer to him. He seemed surprised at her approach. Silently, she threaded her hand through his arm and tugged him toward the waiting room.

He hesitated. "I don't think that's such a good idea."

She dropped her voice to the lowest decibel. "How do you know my brother?" The question had been burning through her for minutes now.

Max's expression didn't change. "I'll tell you everything on our way home. Now is not the time."

"Emma?" Tim appeared next to them. "Why don't you and Riley go see Janie first?" Clearly, he didn't want her anywhere near Max.

Emma studied the two men. She contemplated staying and questioning them, but the draw to see Janie pulled stronger. "Fine. But when I'm back, I need one or both of you to tell me how you two know each other."

***

As soon as Emma and Riley headed for Janie's room, Tim jerked his head toward the stairwell. "Talk outside."

Max prickled at the idea of letting Emma out of sight. The threat on her life still loomed, but he owed Tim an explanation for his unexpected relationship with his sister.

The two stomped out of the hospital and along the narrow path paved through the lawn.

When they were far enough away, Tim swiveled to face him. "What the fuck are you doing here?"

A valid question. No use beating around the bush.

"Someone wants your sister dead. There's a hit out on her life."

Tim's pale face whitened even further. Shock flashed across his features. "What the hell? Who? Why? What'd she ever do to anyone? Is that what happened on Wednesday?"

The headache throbbed in his temples again. "No, that was only tangentially related. She did have a few run-ins with cars this week. A few guns too."

Tim blanched. The man looked like he would pass out if he didn't sit down immediately. "You think someone did this to my daughter on purpose?"

Max spoke the truth. "That makes no sense to me, but Cynthia is looking into it."

"Fuck," Tim breathed out. "Keep me updated?"

"Of course. You'll hear as soon as I do."

Tim stared at the conifers in the distance. "She know what you do for a living?"

"Yep."

"She okay with it?"

"Doesn't matter. Soon as she's safe, we'll go our separate ways." A petite redhead approached them from the hospital, her auburn hair the exact color as baby Finn's. "Your wife?"

Tim followed Max's gaze. Warmth suffused his features. "Yep."

Reese stopped in front of the two men and frowned. "What are you two doing out here?"

Tim pulled her into his side. "Reese, this is Xander Martin."

She offered a polite smile from the safety of her husband's hold. "I put the two together when Deanna told me you're Emma's new boyfriend just now. Figured Tim would freak."

Clearly, Tim didn't keep secrets from his significant other.

"He's not her boyfriend," insisted Tim.

Max fumbled for words as possessiveness surged through him. He wanted to claim Emma as his, but the image of her tear-streaked face from earlier stabbed through his gut. He couldn't assert any hold on her—he had refused that right last night.

"You're not her fucking boyfriend," repeated Tim, even more irritated. "She can do better."

Max wasn't one to argue with a solid point. "On that, you and I agree." He turned to Reese. "Know that your husband's former colleague is trying to find footage of what happened to your daughter."

"I appreciate that." At the mention of Janie, Reese glanced anxiously at the hospital. "We should head back."

***

When Emma and Riley walked into Janie's room, the little girl looked so small lying in the hospital bed, the scraped skin on her face red and raw.

Emma tried to dislodge the bone-deep strain that had settled on her like a weighted blanket. Her niece didn't need to see the worry in her aunt's features. She had been through enough as it was, and required calm and happiness.

"Look, Janie, you and I match." Emma framed her still-swollen cheek to show her niece.

Janie smiled drowsily. "Did you get run over too?"

"Actually… yeah. But this is from something else."

Reese, who had exited the room briefly, returned, trailed by Tim and, behind him, Max. Emma didn't even need to see Max to know that he had entered the room. She felt his presence in her nerve endings. "Janie, this is my friend Xander."

Janie managed a polite wave, but she looked exhausted.

"I think she's had enough visitors," said Tim, noting the same. "I'll have Mom and Dad swing by and see her next, then we're calling it a day."

Emma maneuvered back to Max, despite her attempt to stay far away. His familiar scent felt like home. Her overwrought muscles relaxed as soon as his heat surrounded her.

"Ready to go?" he asked.

At her fatigued nod, he leaned down and pressed a kiss to the top of her head.

Tim, watching the gesture, tensed.

How in the world did Max know her brother? And why didn't he tell her?

A few minutes later, after saying goodbye to her

family, she and Max headed for the exit. They were almost out the hospital door as Tim caught up to them.

"I need to speak to my sister."

Max crossed his arms, placing himself between her and Tim like a nightclub bouncer. "Can it wait?"

"Fuck no."

Max didn't budge.

Emma stepped in front of him, laying a hand on his bicep. "Give us two minutes?"

He glared down at her, but acquiesced. "I'll be outside."

Although he exited the glass doors, he didn't stray far, pacing just outside the entrance.

Tim didn't beat around the bush. "You need to stop seeing him."

The command tore her gaze away from Max. "What?"

Her brother had never dictated whom she saw in her life. The sudden mandate jarred her.

"Trust me on this."

Emma frowned, not sure where to begin. She lowered her voice, not wishing to draw the attention of the visitors in the lobby. "I don't think you understand… I'm not seeing him."

Tim scoffed. "Are you blind? You guys keep mooning at each other. You don't know this guy, Emma. I do. You don't want to be with him."

Emma kept her voice to a bare thread of a whisper. "How do you know him?"

Tim didn't elaborate. "Doesn't matter."

"It matters to me. Tell me."

His lips pursed. He scanned the lobby. When he appeared satisfied that milling visitors and darting medical staff weren't within earshot, he continued. "I used to work for him."

Maybe she'd misheard. "*Excuse me?*"

"Briefly. I quit."

"Like… actually work for him?"

Her brother had been an ethical hacking penetration tester for years. She hadn't suspected he'd ever venture into anything outside of cyber security.

Tim huffed out a breath through his nostrils. "He told me you know what he does for a living."

"I do," Emma offered quickly, eager to hear the details.

"He recruited me to join his hacking team. I quit when Xander shared how they deal with the perpetrators. He was upfront, which I respect. But it wasn't my style. Couldn't be a part of it. I quit before I started."

"You didn't tell anyone about their venture?"

"I told Reese, but that's it. I see why he does what he does. I just don't want to be a part of it. And I certainly don't want you anywhere near him."

Emma slid her gaze to Max, pacing just outside. "You don't have to worry. He doesn't want me anywhere near him either."

"If you think that, you're crazy. His eyes home in on you every time you breathe." Tim's phone rang. He answered it instantly. "Yes? Wow, okay… he's there now? Thanks for letting me know." He returned his attention back to Emma, his entire body reverberating. "They arrested the man who hurt Janie. Drugged out of his mind. Crashed his car a couple miles from here. He's at the station now."

Emma sagged in relief. Janie hadn't been hurt because of the contract out on her. She was hurt because of some irresponsible idiot who drove high. "I'm glad they found him."

"Me too… the alternative was unthinkable."

***

Janie's less serious prognosis and the fact that her attack didn't appear related to the attempt on Emma's life buoyed Emma. She looked like she could dance an Irish jig up and down the parking lot as she met him outside and updated him on the call Tim had received from the police.

"I'm so relieved. No threat to my family, and no internal bleeding for my niece. Some rest and relaxation, and she'll be back to her usual self."

"I'm glad to hear that," said Max. Though he had asked Cynthia by text to look for a link between the arrested addict and Otis, he refused to rain on Emma's parade. "Do you want to stay a bit longer?"

Emma considered it. "Nah. If we stay any longer, Mom will insist you and I spend the night, and I really do want to minimize family time until we find Otis. But before we head back, can we go get some ice pops?" Her eyes lit up with the words. "I feel like celebrating."

Max's lips curved up at her exuberance. "Ice pops it is."

He wasn't a fan of small towns, but even he had to admit that Cold Spring was charming. He navigated the car down Main Street as Emma pointed out her favorite boutique, her preferred brunch spot, and the pub she had yet to visit.

"I love how well-preserved the old buildings are here. It's like stepping back in time. The paletas shop is just ahead," she said, all but dancing in the seat next to him.

He allowed himself a brief peek at her glowing face. How had she become the very center of his world in such a short time? She anchored him to a life he desperately wanted—one he knew that he could never have. The idea of their impending goodbye churned through him, a chalky dread settling in the pit of his stomach like valley fog.

"Here we are. And look, perfect, parking right in front."

Max pulled into the open spot she'd indicated.

He knew that they'd go their separate ways soon, understood that he had no right to touch her. Yet every fiber of his being wanted to keep her close to him. Unsure of whether she'd welcome the gesture, he took her hand as they set foot on the sidewalk. Although she tensed, she didn't pull away. They walked the short distance to the paletas shop holding hands.

Glossy photos of fruits and berries decorated the bright-white walls. The displays showcased the fruit bars in neat, colorful rows, sorted vertically by flavor. Emma ordered a chocolate bar, and he settled for a tropical option. Ice pops in hand, they strolled down Main Street, and Emma pointed out her favorite bakery.

"They sell the best coffee. It's always a treat to get coffee and croissants there."

"It must have been nice growing up here," said Max, noting her excitement at being back in her hometown.

"Sometimes I found it boring," Emma admitted. "But it's a nice place to live." A pause. "One day, I'd like to move back here to raise a family. I'd have built-in baby-sitters. It's quiet and safe. Manhattan is only a drive away."

The idea of her leaving Manhattan caused unexpected panic to rise through him. He knew that her life after they found Otis and stopped Milo would cease to involve him, yet the reminder jolted him. All he had wanted when he had met her was to be rid of her and the uncomfortable emotions her presence stirred in him. Now the thought needled.

Suddenly in a bad mood, he bit into his ice pop, letting the stab of cold against his teeth chase away the thoughts thundering in his brain. He tossed the rest of the ice cream into the trash and redirected them back to his car. "We should head back. I doubt strolling out and about like this is a good idea right now."

She didn't argue.

As she walked alongside him, her arm brushed his. His heart raced at the small contact. Without thinking, he pulled her to a stop. Confusion flashed in her eyes. A tiny droplet of chocolate danced on her lip. He reached out and brushed it away with his thumb, stroked across her lower lip. The small touch wasn't enough. A pulse beat wildly in her neck, and he hoped she felt the same desperate need that he did. Taking a chance, he lowered his head and kissed her.

When she laughed against his mouth in surprise, the sound shimmered through him. "I don't think this is the time."

He forced himself to pull away.

As though unsure about what to do next, Emma let her forehead drop to his chest for a mere moment. His arms twitched to engulf her slight frame and hold her tight, to bring his mouth back to hers. The weight of her head lifted. She gave him a quick look from beneath her lashes, and then she stepped away, taking the warmth with her.

***

He'd kissed her. Right there on Main Street. Emma had to delve deeply into the last embers of her self-control to extricate herself from his hold and to move away. The distance she'd put between them had nearly killed her. Yet his continued closeness would have destroyed her even more.

Could she give herself fully to him knowing what they had was temporary? Knowing that he didn't want to love her back?

Emma barely noticed their drive back to Manhattan, her mind zipping from thought to thought. When the sound of an incoming call reverberated throughout the car, she realized that they had almost reached his building again.

Cynthia's voice rang out through Max's car speakers. "Ezra just called. No sign of Otis at the Brooklyn property, but he did find a car in the garage linked to the drive-by that killed the Crescent witness."

Max's confused face mirrored hers. "Otis killed the witness? Why?"

"Looking into it." Cynthia paused. "I'm glad Janie is okay, Emma. But the guy they arrested? Otis was his dealer."

Emma's head spun. It was too much of a coincidence. "You think Otis sent someone to hurt my niece? Why? What does she have to do with a hit on me?"

"I'm looking into that too," said Cynthia. "It doesn't make sense."

"Have Ezra—"

"Already done," Cynthia interrupted Max. "He's on his way to Cold Spring. Emma, he'll keep watch over your family."

Max caught her hand. "You want me to drive you back? Would you feel better being there?"

Emma considered his question. "You trust Ezra?"

"With my life." The sincerity in his expression was clear.

"Then I think it'll be safer for them if I stay in Manhattan."

"Agreed. Cyn, get the company protecting Trevor to send another team to Cold Spring. Emma's got a lot of family. Ezra will appreciate the extra hands."

"On it." Cynthia hung up.

Emma lowered the car window to let in fresh air. "I want to throw up."

He gave her hand a reassuring squeeze. "Ezra and the security team will watch over them. I swear, I won't let anything happen to your family. Or to you."

Looking into his earnest eyes, she believed him, yet anxiety gnawed.

Chapter 45

As they walked inside Max's apartment, a flashback of their fight last night sent fresh pain roiling in Emma's stomach. She didn't know how long it would take for them to stop the contracts on her and Trevor, and she couldn't imagine living this close to Max for days—or worse, weeks—on end.

Her love for him clawed at her, despite her best intentions to tamp it down. How could it not? He'd anticipated her need to return to Cold Spring, had readily offered to drive her. On top of Ezra, he'd hired an entire security team to watch over her family. He'd ensured their safety.

Gratitude. I feel gratitude, not hopeless love. Remember that.

Trying to distract herself, she headed to the kitchen, pulled open his French door refrigerator, kept her tone light. "You hungry? There's only so much an ice pop can do."

Max joined her by the fridge.

When Dusty ran out to greet them, twining between Max's legs, he knelt to pet him. Watching Max be so sweet to her cat made her want to jump his bones. She refocused her attention on the contents of the fridge.

"Want to order in?" Max asked, rising from his crouch next to the Himalayan.

"I'll find something to whip up." Closing the refrigerator door, she opened the pantry. "I need something to do or I'll fall apart."

"Come here," he murmured before pulling her against his steady heartbeat, rubbing reassuring circles on her back.

Despite knowing better, she burrowed closer.

"Your family is safe. Ezra and the security team protect world leaders. They're pros. There's no safer place for your family than with them right now."

She swallowed against encroaching tears and pulled away. "It's a lot to take in. I'm okay now. Thank you."

He released her, but remained close.

She stared blindly into the pantry. She and Max didn't have a future together. They came from different worlds; they wanted different things. Max refused to be confined to a relationship, to a family. He had seen a lot in his life, believed that he was genetically predisposed to despicable things. She would never be able to convince him otherwise, even if she knew better. The realization would, someday, have to come from him. She wouldn't wait around and waste her time, not when she had already squandered seven years hiding in her apartment, too terrified to live her life.

She'd always be grateful to him. He'd helped her escape her fear of trusting men because, despite it all, she trusted him. Even if he didn't see it himself, he was a good person.

Their time together was finite. She didn't want her memories to be tainted with this painful tension between them. They were both adults, and could revert to their easy camaraderie until the threat was over and they could separate for good.

Could I handle being intimate with him knowing that he could never love me? I think so. It's not like he can break my heart even more than he already has.

Might as well make lemonade out of the sour lemons dealt to them.

How do I broach this new proposition to him?

She didn't have much recent experience with men, and she definitely didn't have any experience with offering to be friends with benefits—with an expiration date. Yet she wanted this, wanted him. She couldn't imagine being near him and not touching him.

Decision made, she closed the pantry door. Counted to three, exhaled, and took a step toward him.

He froze, only a muscle in his jaw flexing.

Now or never.

Finding a boldness that surprised even herself, she leaned in. "I want to taste you," she whispered in his ear, feeling feverish and forward.

His eyes turned black, welded to her lips. "What?"

Emma assumed he was sure he'd misheard.

"You and I are not meant to be. I accept that. I still want you, and you want me too. Let's make the best of a crappy situation and just…" She wanted to say *fuck* but her lips wouldn't form the words.

"Just what?"

Emboldened, she found and stroked his hard length through the denim of his jeans.

"Fuck," Max breathed.

His hands closed around her breasts. He thumbed her nipples through her satin tank and the thin bralette beneath, sending molten heat to flow through her.

"I'm in charge now," she told him primly, reaching for the button of his jeans. "You have to listen to my directions."

When she slipped down his body, Max pulled her up. "Floor's too hard."

It warmed Emma to know he cared about her knees.

He dragged her toward a couch in his living room, plopping himself onto the leather. Emma sank between his legs on the plush rug.

I can do this. I can make love to him without crushing my heart. She didn't know whether she wanted to prove it to herself or to him.

Her fingers closed around the thick column of his erection. Not breaking eye contact, she ran her tongue along his sensitive underside, drawing a moan from deep within him. Encouraged, pleased, she licked around his head, reveled in his groan as her mouth closed over his hard length. She needed him to feel the same blinding pleasure he always drew from her, to bring him to the same precipice, to drive them both crazed with need while keeping her emotions strictly at bay.

He dug his hands into the edge of the couch as she worked him with her hand and mouth, taking him deeper each time. The sound of his erratic breathing echoed in her ears, mirrored the wild beating of her heart, spurred her on. She took him to the edge, felt him go feral, overcome; loved that he trusted himself around her to relinquish control.

When the last vestiges of his orgasm subsided, she let her head fall on his thigh. Unbidden, misery swirled. She'd sought to flip their relationship back to the physical, but she wasn't so certain she'd succeeded.

His fingers brushed through her hair. "Fuck. That was incredible. You're incredible. I'll never forget this."

The finality in his statement ripped at the shattered bits of her heart.

She told herself to suck it up. She could do this. She could get over her feelings and let them be physical until they said goodbye.

"What was that?" asked Max a few minutes later, rezipping his jeans.

Emma tried to keep the mood light. "I believe that was called a blow job."

He gave her a dark look.

She shrugged. "You said it best earlier. We have great sex. I agree. I want it to continue until I can go back to my life. No demands. No expectations."

Max looked as if he were trying to do abstract algebra in his head. "Are you sure you can handle that?"

Not really, no. "Yes. I'm an adult. We've got time to kill. Might as well make the most of it."

He studied her for a long moment. "I don't want to make this harder."

"You're not," she assured him, even though she wasn't feeling that confident herself. "Let's stick to the physical until we find Otis and your other psychotic family members. Then we never have to see each other again."

"Just sex until then?"

"Yes. Just sex."

***

Max felt like he had just won the lottery and discovered a secret stash of gold bullion all in the same day. A fathomless relief spread out from the pit of his stomach.

Being with Emma brought him infinite happiness. He had thought them to be irrevocably over last night, yet she had surprised him once again. To celebrate, he wanted to pop open a bottle of champagne and drink it from her belly button.

"You're sure?" he repeated. "No takebacks."

"Yes."

He scooped her up in his arms, but she swatted at him. "Food first."

Setting her back on her feet, he tossed together the fastest salad in history. Emma topped it with watermelon and feta, adding a summer-themed twist to the plates. He watched her eat three bites before he couldn't take it any longer. His lips took a playful nip at her neck.

"You're in a hurry," she observed, eyes dancing.

"You done yet?"

Emma set down her fork. "I can finish it later."

He swooped, carrying her back to his bedroom, where she belonged. He had missed her last night. Lying across his enormous, cold mattress all alone, his body had burned to be near her, yet he couldn't bring himself to violate her request, couldn't seek her out in the guest room to which she had escaped. Now she was open and willing in his arms once more.

Setting her on his bed, he kissed her cheeks, her mouth, her jaw. Her body belonged to him. *She* belonged to him. For however long they had left together. When she reached to strip her clothes, he pushed her hands away, impatient.

Once she lay naked across the bedspread, he kicked away his own clothes and joined her, crushing his mouth to hers, needing to taste her, reveling in her throaty hum of desire as she kissed him back. He trailed open-mouthed kisses down her stomach, lingered over the tremor of abdominal muscles underneath his tongue. His face ducked lower.

She pulled him up. "Need you inside me. Now."

He loved it when she wanted him closer. Once sheathed, he entered her. Her body began to convulse under him almost instantly, and she cried out, grasping at his biceps, her nails sinking into his skin. God, how he had missed her.

His own need thrummed through his blood, but he refused to rush it. He refused to rush *this*. By sheer miracle, she was back in his arms, back in his bed. He intended to enjoy every gasp, every sigh, every shudder. He drew out her crest, then took her up the next one. When she arched into him—nails scoring, body trembling—he couldn't hold off any longer. With a groan, he powered into her with all the intensity burning his body, needing. To. Show. Her. That. She. Was. His.

She fell apart under him, with him, her thunderous heartbeat matching his own. He collapsed next to her and pulled her close, twining his fingers through hers.

A shiver raced through her. Tugging the sheets over them, he wrapped his arm around her and pulled her tighter to him. Instead of relaxing, Emma tensed. She wriggled out of his grasp.

His brow furrowed as she edged herself all the way off his bed and set her feet on the ground.

"Where are you going?" he asked, confused. Irritated.

"To shower and check my email. I have some work to do still."

The aloof mask that descended on her features as she moved away chafed.

"What the hell was this?"

Now she looked confused. "What?"

"Were you horny and wanted a booty call?"

"Didn't we just talk about this?" She pointed in the

direction of his living room. "Just out there. A few minutes ago. Sex. No strings. Until we go our separate ways when the hit is stopped. Why are you mad?"

She had been mewling for him to be closer just minutes ago, and now she looked at him with detachment. He had thought they'd laze in bed, chatting and enjoying the afterglow. Maybe she'd even let him fondle her a bit more. She had been upfront with him about their new relationship—he had accepted her terms. It just hadn't occurred to him how different this would be.

"I have work I need to get to before the weekend. I'll see you a little later."

As she disappeared through the door, he felt like something precious had slipped through his fingers, and he had been too distracted to catch it in time.

He couldn't demand they go back to the way they were. After all, he couldn't give her the future that she deserved. His lineage ended with him—he wouldn't curse the world with his offspring. If he could, he'd sterilize his brother too. The Clark line needed to end.

As much as her sudden distance hurt, it was for the best. She deserved better than to be with someone like him. She deserved everything she had ever wanted in life, and he could never give that to her.

Chapter 46

Emma needed to rinse the scent of Max from her body.

Sex like that had been a terrible idea. She'd thought that she could do it, that she was strong enough to remain detached, but she wasn't. She loved him, and making love while knowing that he didn't feel anything for her had torn at her. Setting the shower water to scalding hot, she let the stream cleanse the memories.

Her broken heart wept, but she refused to do the same. What was done was done. She'd learned her lesson—she couldn't make love to Max as though she wasn't irrevocably in love with him. The experience had almost broken her, and she would never repeat it.

Trying to refocus her attention, she pulled on her loungewear and settled in on the guest room bed. When she opened her work laptop, three hundred emails greeted her.

She managed to make her way through a handful of them when she heard what sounded like the thump of dozens of footsteps. *Was it coming from the hall? From outside the apartment?*

She set her laptop aside and followed the sound down the hallway toward the main door. Definitely coming from outside Max's apartment.

Max was at her side in an instant, weapon drawn. It

looked like he had hastily pulled on his jeans, but hadn't gotten to his shirt.

"Stay here," he told her, and strode forward.

The doorbell rang.

She joined him at the door. "Assassins are now announcing their arrival?"

Max swung it open.

Trevor Martin stood at the doorstep. Behind him, wide-shouldered, square-jawed giants, each one armed to the teeth, lined the corridor.

The men nodded in acknowledgment to Max, clearly familiar with him.

Max's adoptive father, the elusive billionaire with a $10M contract out on his life, had returned to the States.

She'd read many articles about Trevor Martin, especially after he'd made the donation to the nonprofit where she volunteered. He was more petite in real life than she had imagined, with closely cropped silver hair and kind eyes.

"What the hell are you doing here?" demanded Max, lowering the gun. "Coming here is the stupidest thing you can do. I told you to stay in Germany."

"I'm not one to run and hide." As Trevor moved his gaze to Emma, he recoiled in surprised horror before schooling his features.

She knew how the bruising on her face looked, especially to someone not expecting it. Her fingers flew to the swelling.

Max's arm twined around her waist, pulling her into his side. She had barely handled the sex earlier; she couldn't manage his nearness now, especially when he was bare-chested and smelled this good. Trying to act casual, she took a heedful step out of his reach.

Trevor directed the next statement to Emma. "Xander hired an army of ex-special forces from every country imaginable to watch over me. I figured you and I together can figure out why his family wants us dead."

He strode into the apartment, but the army of giants stayed out in the hall. Emma could only imagine what Max's neighbors thought about the continuous commotion this week.

Max made a belated introduction. "Trevor, this is Emma."

"Nice to meet you, Mr. Martin."

He waved away her attempt at pleasantries. "Please, call me Trevor. I hear you've been having quite the few days."

"It's been eventful ever since I met… er…"

When her voice trailed off, Trevor helped her out. "Yes, Xander has been known to keep people on their toes."

"Why are you here?" demanded Max.

"An FBI agent attacked you. I refuse to hide out in Europe while your life is in peril."

"No one took out a ten-million-dollar hit on my life," grumbled Max. "You need to go back to Germany."

"Out of the question."

"I have my hands full with her." Max jerked his head toward Emma. "I can't handle both of you." He looked like he was ready to kick both Trevor and Emma out of his apartment.

Trevor gave Emma a perceptive look. "You'll have to forgive my son. He's not usually this rude."

Max jolted at the moniker. "You know what? It's a good thing you're here. Take her back with you so I can finally have some peace and quiet."

"Cynthia tells me you figured out Xander's real name." Trevor continued as though Max had never spoken.

"I did. So did you."

"Ah, but I had all the money in the world to do it, and it took a whole year. It took you just over a week."

Emma grinned. "Don't underestimate a girl and her laptop."

Trevor smiled widely, waving her toward the kitchen. "What do you say we have some tea and you can tell me all about that."

Emma instantly liked Max's adoptive father. Tea had always been the key to her heart. "That sounds like a great plan."

Trevor knew his way around Max's apartment. He headed straight for the tea station, turning on the electric kettle and setting out two cups.

"What kind of tea would you like, Emma?" He reached for a canister. "I'm partial to Irish breakfast myself."

Max cut in front of him and thrust the decaf alternative into his hands. "You're not supposed to be having caffeine. Here, this one is similar enough."

Trevor took the canister of decaffeinated tea from Max's hand, opened the lid, and dropped a bag into a cup. "Emma? Do you want real tea or the fake crap?"

Emma chuckled. "I'll have the decaf in solidarity."

Trevor added a bag to her cup as well.

The sound of Emma's phone ringing reached them from the counter. She had left both cells next to each other and glanced at the screen of the ringing one. "I have to take this. It's work. I'll be right back." Seeking the privacy of the guest room, she left the two men to catch up.

"Go put on a shirt. This isn't *Baywatch*," she heard Trevor tell Max as she answered her phone.

***

"I like her," Trevor announced as soon as Max returned fully dressed.

"Who doesn't?" Max grumbled. "You shouldn't be here. It's not safe."

"I'm not going to hide out in my castle while you put your life on the line. It was fine for a day or two while you were determined to get to the bottom of it. It's been two weeks. Enough is enough. Maybe brainstorming together will help us end this."

"Does Cynthia know you're here?"

"She's on her way, but stopped to get bagels. Said your house has no carbs, and she's even resorted to smuggling in chips. Now tell me what that was about." His head tilted in Emma's direction.

"There's nothing to tell."

"One minute, you're looking for Otis; the next, a girl is moving in with you."

"She hasn't moved in with me. Otis wants her dead too. I'm trying to keep both of your stubborn asses alive long enough for me to track down Milo."

***

By the time Cynthia entered with an extra-large paper bag from Ess-a-bagel, Emma had completed her work call. She sat across from Trevor at the dining table, answering his questions about her cat. Dusty had already made himself comfortable on Trevor's lap.

Cynthia laid out the bagels, spreads, and lox across the wooden surface before ripping into a sesame bagel with her hands. "Help yourselves, everyone."

Max walked over to the cupboard to grab plates. He handed one to Cynthia as she chewed.

"Ramona changed her and Milo's names," Emma said. "She would have to have gotten new IDs somewhere. Think she'd go through Mercury Marketplace? Maybe she was a buyer on there?"

"Mercury hasn't been around that long, but she could have changed their names again." Max looked at Cynthia. "Can you pull up customer reviews for any New York-based document forgers?"

Cynthia set aside her bagel and flipped open her laptop just as Max's cell rang.

Emma glanced at the screen. Unknown number.

Max set it to speaker. "This is Xander."

"Hi…" came a female voice. "This is Nancy… Nancy Elrod. We met earlier today." She hesitated. "I know you're looking for your mother. I kept something from you because I… well, I don't know. I've been feeling so guilty to not have told you. You should know, and I'm sorry I didn't tell you earlier. You see… my husband lost touch with your mother after she got married."

"Who'd she marry?" asked Max in a lethally quiet tone.

"She married a man named Larry Bief."

Chapter 47

"Who's Larry Bief?" asked Emma after Max hung up.

Max's jaw ticced as he sank into a chair at the dining table.

Emma wasn't sure that he realized he'd ended the call. Dusty, perceptive to the tension, moved to Max.

"We shut down a dark web child abuse site last year. Larry Bief ran it," explained Trevor.

Emma's pulse pounded against her eyeballs.

"Larry had a wife—Cara. Cara Bief is Carmela Griffith is Ramona Clark," said Cynthia. "Fuck. I hadn't seen the connection." She looked at Emma. "We terminated Larry and shut down his site, but nothing indicated his wife or kid were involved."

"His kid's name is Ryan," Max added. "I'm assuming that's Adrian Griffith, formerly Milo Clark."

Cynthia dove into her laptop. "Ryan Bief owns several properties across the tri-state area. Including a unit at the Crescent."

How could a kid afford that?

"Where is he right now?" asked Max.

"I'll track him down. Your mother too." Cynthia flipped her laptop around. "Here's her new face."

The plastic surgery had made Max's mother almost unrecognizable—not only to Max, who last saw her decades ago, but even to Emma. The woman looked years younger, pounds trimmer. Her hair went blonde, her boobs went double D. She had a new nose, a new chin, and, by the looks of it, new cheekbones. Even the shape of her eyes had changed—they were now wider, decidedly uptilted, and, most likely with the help of contacts, bright blue.

Emma considered Nancy's earlier statement. "Nancy said Elrod and your mother lost touch. Do you think she knows that's not true?"

Max shrugged. "It's probably what he told her."

"And here's a photo of Ryan Bief." Cynthia turned her laptop toward them again.

They stared at the kid's New York State ID card—Emma could see a vague resemblance to Max, with the dark hair, dark eyes, and set mouth.

Cynthia spun the computer back to face her, and her fingers raced over the keys. "That's the only photo I got. He doesn't have a social media footprint. *Fuck*."

Max studied his colleague. "What?"

Cynthia looked grim when she glanced up from the screen. "I checked the seeking services part of the marketplace again. Trevor's contract went up in price. Fifteen million to anyone who takes out both him and Emma Neely. Posted again by a MiloAugustus."

Chapter 48

Where did Milo get the money for the multi-million dollar hit and why was he focused on Trevor and Emma? Was he only a customer on Mercury Marketplace, or did his connection run deeper?

"See if you can find a link between Milo and the administrator for the marketplace," Max said to Cynthia. "I have a feeling there's a connection. And see if my mother is tied in any way."

Emma considered his statement. "Something isn't adding up. Before, he offered ten million for Trevor, but only five thousand dollars to off me. Why?"

"Maybe he's cheap. If you grow up in poverty as I did, you start to appreciate the value of a dollar. You don't toss it around, even if you suddenly have millions." He gave her a look. "You really can't get over that he only paid five grand to have someone take you out?"

"Well, it's an insultingly low amount."

Amused, Max reached for her hand that lay between them on the table. When she moved hers away, he felt the loss in every cell.

"Out of all the people in New York, he had Clarence Elrod hire your dad. Does he know Otis is his father too? And your mother…" Emma clutched her mug of tea.

His mother, who assumed him dead. Ironically, he had supposed the same of her until recently. She swapped around identities as often as he himself did. Guess it ran in the family. The thought of seeing her again inspired a surprising tendril of anticipation. Despite everything, he wanted to see her.

He remembered her animated facial expressions, her carefree laughter that people often thought too loud, the feel of her arms around him as she read him a bedtime story when he'd been a little kid. Time had dulled the feelings of anger and bitterness and disappointment, but had heightened the good memories of her.

Max pushed back from the table. Sitting close to Emma yet having her shut off from him hurt. "What about her?"

"I got to know her well," said Emma. "She left an abusive husband to protect her son. Granted, I didn't know about her prior three husbands, including Otis. But she left an abusive husband… only to marry someone running a child abuse site?"

"Maybe she just can't pick 'em," offered Cynthia.

***

Emma's heart ached for Max. What this must be like for him. His only blood relatives were really messed up. Murder. Contract killings. Dark web activities. They were linked to pedophiles and human traffickers. This was who shared Max's DNA. No wonder he never wanted children. She wouldn't either, if she were him.

She observed Trevor and Max. The strong bond between the two seemed obvious, even if neither acknowledged it. When Trevor had reached for the caffeinated tea earlier, Max had practically wrestled it from him. He cared about the man.

Trevor cared for him in turn. Why else would he have returned to the country where he was wanted dead upon hearing that his adoptive son had been attacked?

They both might think their relationship was a business decision, that the adoption was fiscally responsible for them both, but Emma agreed with Cynthia. The two loved each other.

Max hadn't experienced love in his childhood from anyone—except maybe from his mother, when she had been sober. Emma knew that he cherished those few-and-far-between memories.

"First thing, you both need to get the hell out of Dodge," Max told her and Trevor. "Go to Germany. Go to Bali. I'll get you more guards. You'll be behind a wall of weaponry."

Emma lifted her chin. "I'm not running away. I've already felt on the run this week just being across the park from my apartment. Besides, how long would we have to do it for? I want to see my family on Sunday."

"That isn't happening."

The comment was a bucket of ice water thrown at her face. He was right. They were safer without her around.

She asked the rhetorical question. "When will it all be over?"

Max laid his hands on her shoulders, sending energy zinging straight to her private parts. Her body remembered all the clever things his fingers had done to her, the pleasure he could draw. Her toes curled into Max's warm hardwood floor.

She wanted to lean into his strength, but she had to protect her sanity. He couldn't give her what she needed, refused to take what she offered.

Emma stood, removing herself from his hold, and went to the kitchen. She'd learn not to yearn for his closeness. She'd learn not to ache for him.

"I'll make sure it's over soon," Max promised as she set her cup in the dishwasher.

If she missed him when he was just a few feet away from her, how would she handle their final goodbye?

***

Max, who'd never sought contact or closeness with anyone, craved Emma's touch. She had offered it so easily to him before, so naturally. Now she avoided it. Eluded him. He didn't like it. She was holding a part of herself back, and he demanded it all, selfish as it was.

Max felt the weight of Trevor's attention on him. He cocked a brow. "What?"

Trevor lowered his voice. "You can't stop looking at her."

He returned to his chair at the table. "I don't know what you're talking about."

Cynthia glanced up from her screen. Her head swiveled from Trevor to Max before she stood and made her way to Max's office, leaving the two men at the table alone.

His father kept his voice muted. "You clearly like the girl. What's the problem?"

"There's no problem. I promised to keep her safe, and I will. Now that we're close to finding Milo, we can go our separate ways."

"Why would you let her go?" whispered Trevor, clearly puzzled. "You two obviously like each other. Explain it to me."

Max hesitated. Emma was setting the few plates from earlier into the dishwasher, out of earshot of their quiet conversation.

"I can't give her what she wants."

Trevor's perceptive gaze settled heavy on Max. "Can't or won't?"

Before Max could answer, Cynthia returned, looking distraught. She set her laptop on the island. "Max, Cara Bief is dead. An apparent self-inflicted gunshot wound only several months after we stopped Larry. I can't yet track Ryan."

Emma reached Max in quick strides. "Oh God, Max. I'm so sorry." She folded herself around him, trying to offer comfort even as her own eyes filled with tears.

He absorbed her nearness, locking his arm around her waist. Numb, cold, he tried to process Cynthia's words.

His mother had killed herself? Did she know of her husband's dark web activities? By terminating Larry, had he caused his mother's death? Where was his brother?

He pulled Emma closer, letting her anchor him as his thoughts raced.

Dusty bumped Trevor's calf. Trevor leaned down toward the cat.

The window exploded.

Chapter 49

The sniper missed.

A $15M contract killer missed his mark because Trevor had leaned down to pet Dusty.

Chaos erupted. The army of hired guards rushed inside, hustling Trevor and the group away from all windows, keeping them low to the ground. Someone activated the switch on the wall panel, and the blinds across the entire unit slid shut.

"You both need to go *now*." Max practically pushed Emma into the arms of one of the guards. "I'll double your pay—just keep them both safe."

"I'm not going anywhere." Emma looked outraged. "I told you before. I'm in this."

"Are you fucking nuts? You are not in this. I end this. Today. You're going with Trevor."

"I'm not leaving you here alone."

"Neither am I," said Trevor. "We all go together. Or we all stay."

His lungs burned as he tried to control his thunderous breathing. "You're both fucking nuts. I'm not taking no for an answer." He glanced at the guards. "Take them away."

Short of dragging their clients away kicking and screaming, there was nothing the paramilitary team could do.

Max tried a different tactic. "Go with them for now. I'll find you both later today."

Emma glared at him. "Absolutely not. I am staying."

"Do you know the media circus that's about to erupt?" demanded Max, grasping for anything that would get her to go to a secure location. "Do you want a repeat of what happened seven years ago? They'll hound you as soon as they recognize your name."

When she lowered her head, he knew he'd hit a nerve. Emma wouldn't want to relive that again. Yet when she lifted her eyes, her gaze looked resolute. "I don't care. I'll live through the madness again. I'm not leaving you alone to deal with this by yourself."

Trevor's hand settled on Max's shoulder. "We're handling this together."

Max didn't know whether to be grateful or angry.

Cynthia, who had been speaking into her cell the last few minutes, hung up the call. "We have backup en route. We can head down as soon as they arrive."

By the time they assembled in the building lobby, the team of attorneys and the T. R. Martin International PR team that Cynthia had called swooped in to deal with the fallout. They helped wrap up questioning swiftly, earning every penny of their astronomical salaries. They even sent a window replacement team, who appeared within the hour. Sometimes Max forgot how much money talked.

He could still hear helicopters—probably police and media—circling above the building. It wasn't every day that a sniper attempted to kill an elusive billionaire in his son's Central Park West home.

Cold sweat broke out on Max's skin even thinking about what could have been. The sniper had almost killed his dad. If Trevor hadn't bent down toward the cat at that exact moment, he would be dead. Max wasn't a religious man, but he said a grateful prayer. His father was alive and well. Emma was alive and well. He'd do everything in his power to ensure they continued to remain so.

Max kept Emma at his side the entire time, marveling at the feel of her so close to him. He never wanted to let her go again. This was what he wanted, Emma next to him.

When she had stepped away with that detached expression earlier that day, he had felt a numbing hollowness. The void had almost engulfed him. Yet she was back in his arms now, and he intended to keep her there always.

They had a lot to discuss. He had a lot to think about. Yet he knew without a shadow of a doubt that they could make it work. The alternative was unthinkable.

He told the police and the FBI everything he knew about his mother's and brother's identities, leaving out his own connection to them. As mistrustful as he was of authorities, if sharing their many prior lives helped stop the impending threat to Emma and Trevor, Max would cooperate.

Chapter 50

The heat radiating from Max soothed Emma's rattled nerves as the investigators concluded their questioning. Max had shared every detail about Ramona and Milo Clark, aka Carmela and Adrian Griffith, aka Cara and Ryan Bief. Emma understood that trusting authorities wasn't easy for him, and was glad that now the NYPD and the FBI could add their weight to the investigation into his mother and brother.

A familiar figure entered the building. Relieved to see Detective Warren, Emma took a step toward him, but Max pulled her back with a searching look.

"It's Uncle Jeremy," she explained as Max followed her gaze.

More familiar faces entered the lobby. Special Agents Esteban and Mitchell beelined for her and Max. Not quite ready to go through the exact same questions, she squeezed Max's arm. "Give me a minute to talk to Uncle Jeremy, and I'll be right back."

Trevor's security team had spread themselves around the lobby, keeping a watchful gaze on her and Trevor. Now that the NYPD had built a secure perimeter around the building, the reporters and gawkers had been removed from the already-crowded lobby and sent to loiter outside.

"After a citywide manhunt, we caught the sniper," Uncle Jeremy announced as soon as she reached him. "I wanted to tell you that personally. How are you feeling?"

"I'm good." She glanced around the lobby, still crawling with law enforcement. "This is a lot. Brings back bad memories."

"I can only imagine."

"Any updates on Ryan Bief?" asked Emma, hoping for at least something she could share with Max.

Jeremy lowered his voice. "Yes, but it's confidential. Can we go somewhere quiet where we can talk?"

Emma scanned for a private corner. "What about over there?" She pointed to an alcove leading to the garage.

Jeremy led the way. One of the bodyguards made to follow her, but she waved him off. Uncle Jeremy wouldn't appreciate an audience.

Jeremy opened the door to the garage. "We better go in here. More privacy."

Emma hesitated. Max wouldn't want her leaving the lobby.

"I have something very urgent to share," said Jeremy.

"Okay, but only for a minute."

Emma stepped through the door.

What—

It took her a moment to process. Otis, on the other side of the door, pointed a gun directly at her.

Emma tried to step back into the lobby. Max and the security men and the police were just six feet away. The cold press of a gun to her temple stopped her.

"Uncle Jeremy?" Her brain wasn't computing why

Detective Warren—her father's friend, the man who was like an uncle to her—held a gun to her head.

"I'm sorry, Emma," he said. "I really and truly am. But I had to help them. I didn't have a choice."

Emma felt like passing out. Two guns pointed at her. The heavy metal door looked soundproof. No one would be able to hear her scream for help.

"Where's her phone?" asked Otis.

The hard, cold muzzle pressed harder into Emma's temple. "Give us your phone."

She had two phones on her, but they didn't know that. Emma made a show of reaching into her legging's thigh pocket and pulling out her work cell from its tight hold. "What do you need my phone for?"

"Drop it now!" demanded Otis.

She did, praying that they wouldn't search her for her personal cell in her other pocket. Thank God for whoever designed the running tights with several concealed pockets tight enough to keep any valuables hidden.

Uncle Jeremy crushed the phone underfoot.

Blood pounding in her ears, Emma barely heard the dull *crunch*.

"Okay, let's go. We need you alive a bit longer," said Otis, and Uncle Jeremy shoved something sharp into her upper arm.

Chapter 51

The hair on the back of his neck stood as Emma and the cop disappeared toward the garage door. Emma trusted her father's friend. Max trusted no one.

He extricated himself from the two FBI agents and strode after Emma, swinging open the thick door.

Something on the ground caught his attention.

A smashed phone. *Emma's* smashed phone.

He roared, rushing deeper into the garage. A few minutes behind them at most, he could still get to Emma in time.

The screech of a car peeling out made him sprint, but he was too late. By the time he reached the exit, the car had already gone. He hadn't even glimpsed the color of the car or its set direction. Didn't know whether Emma had been hurt.

Fuck. An agonizing sense of hopelessness dragged him under. He struggled to breathe.

Footsteps closed in on him.

"Max, where's Emma?" demanded Cynthia.

"Gone. That fucking detective took her. Smashed her fucking phone." Realization hit. Max's heart hammered in his throat. "She has two phones on her at all times."

"*Yes*, and I am still tracking them." Cynthia withdrew the laptop she carried under her arm. She sank to the concrete floor and began to search.

"Access the building's security cameras too. What the fuck happened?"

Max lost ten years of his life as Cynthia searched for any trace of Emma.

Finally, Cynthia spoke. "I can track her cell. She's heading north. Smart girl to hold on to her phone. Now let's see what happened." Cynthia pulled up footage from the building security cameras. "Here's a good angle of the garage." They watched as Otis and Warren shoved Emma's prostrate body into a small red car.

"Fucking bastards."

"Let's see where they're heading." Cynthia pulled up traffic camera after traffic camera, the footage appearing and disappearing on screen in a dizzying array of movement as she cross-checked it against Emma's phone location. "Car's heading toward… wait, I know where. The house off Route 46. It's one of the properties that Milo owns. I remember thinking it was an odd piece of property to have. They're heading there, I guarantee it. I'll keep watching, but navigate here. I just texted you."

His phone pinged as an address populated in his messages.

"I'll call you if his route changes. I'll go grab the cops and the FBI."

Max ran.

Chapter 52

The sun had set by the time Max pulled into the crumbled driveway of the remote home, set deep in a thicket of trees on the New Jersey side of the Delaware River. Max drove straight up to the house. No use creeping in undetected. The security cameras, set up to encompass every angle around the home, had long seen him coming.

Warm, yellow light peeked through the torn curtains of the ground floor, even as the windows upstairs reflected darkness. Someone had left the porch light on, and it cast shadows across the overgrown patch of grass leading up to the house.

There was only one car in the driveway. Otis's sedan, the window of which he'd blown out yesterday.

Cynthia had called earlier to let him know that she and Trevor were heading toward the house. The FBI and the police were also on the way. They should be there soon, she'd told him. But soon wasn't fast enough. He needed to get to Emma now.

The scent of sulfur smacked him in the face as he sprang out of the car. *Gas leak.*

Was this the plan? Get the house to blow, have Emma die in a terrible accident? Almost his own MO.

"Milo!" he shouted. "I know she's here."

The front door swung open, letting dim light escape from the house. Out came Otis.

"Why can't you leave it alone, boy?" his bio father hissed as he trained a shotgun on Max.

Max drew his own weapon. "It's over. The cops and the FBI are almost here."

"Get in the house." His bio dad motioned with the barrel.

Max knew he couldn't shoot Otis, even if he wanted to do so. With this much gas in the air, firing would risk Emma being blown to smithereens.

"Where is she?" he demanded.

"She won't feel a thing. It'll be a painless death."

"Being blown up in a gas leak?"

"I gave her a strong tranq. She won't even know it happened. But you will. You've been a pain in my ass for weeks. Get inside the house."

Max never thought he'd think this, but he wished law enforcement were here by now.

"Otis! What the hell are you doing waving that thing around? You trying to kill us?"

A woman exited the house, marching straight for Otis. In person, the recognition was instant.

"Mom."

***

I feel weird... where am I?

The blinds had been tightly shut against the night, but moon rays managed to sneak through, bathing the room in a pale-gray glow. Emma blinked through the haze. Small room, no furniture except for the bed she lay on. She tried to roll off the bed. Her body felt impossibly heavy.

Oops, that didn't work.

Try two—

Oof.

She flipped herself off the bed, hitting the floor with a loud thud. Her body barely registered the impact.

Can't... breathe...

Emma remembered being confronted by Gimpy in the stairwell to the garage... Uncle Jeremy had a gun to her... she remembered a prick... being moved... another voice at some point...

She tried to shake the haze from her brain.

I have to get out of here. It feels and smells funny in here... Emma peeled herself off the floor.

Must get to the window.

She managed a wobbly walk across the carpeted room until she reached the windows.

Blinds... lift the blinds...

Her fingers weren't quite closing around them.

Okay, never mind.

She slid her body between the cheap plastic blinds, still pulled shut, and the window.

Open the window. Lock... up... down... no, up... pull the window left.

The movements exhausted her, and she sank to the ground to breathe, feeling dizzy.

No. Move it, Emma. Move it. Open the window.

She pushed herself off the carpet once more. This time, she managed to slide the windowpane all the way to the left, leaving one dirty screen between herself and the outside.

The fresh evening air bathed her face. A quick scan told her she was on the second floor of the house. She pushed at the screen with all her might and popped it free. By sheer will, she grabbed it before it clattered down the steep rooftop and slid it into the room.

Okay. Now leave.

The window was low enough for her to climb through if she could just lift her leg. The simple movement took her a few tries, but the fresh air had already started to clear her fuzzy mind.

She climbed through the dormer window and ended up perched on the slanted roof.

Don't fall, don't fall, don't fall.

Where the heck to from here? It's a long way down.

Just below her, she heard voices. *Max.*

Max was here… but he had his gun trained on someone and that was a bad idea. This house smelled like a gas leak ready to blow.

She had to warn him somehow.

But how? Yelling out would distract him and would alert her captors to her escape.

No… yelling out wasn't an option.

Crouching close to the window, she tried to get her still-fuzzy brain to think when she heard Max's voice.

"Mom."

***

Max watched his mother, the woman he hadn't seen in decades. Almost every part of her was different—wide, blue eyes now, arched blonde brows, a sharp chin. Whereas she'd always been slim, she had gained a cartoonlike hourglass shape. Her now-blonde hair was pulled back, revealing the familiar curve of the head, her same hairline, and new pinned-back ears.

Despite the changes, he recognized the woman who'd read him bedtime stories and told him they'd be okay. The one who had scraped and saved to buy him a bicycle, the only thing he had wanted at that age. The one who had never fought to get custody of him after CPS took him away. The one who'd missed the court appearances, the court-mandated family therapy sessions, weekly visits. The one he had thought dead yesterday. Love, bitterness, resentment, relief churned as memories of their time together and time apart slammed into him.

"Maximilian," his mother breathed.

Same voice he'd remembered from childhood.

"You're here." Her eyes settled on his gun. "Put that away. You'll turn the neighborhood into a crater. Otis, put down the shotgun. You're not going to shoot our son."

"Where's Milo?" Max kept the barrel of his gun trained on both of his parents. He suspected he already knew the answer.

"Milo has nothing to do with this. He's a good boy. I didn't want him around this insanity until everything settled down. He will be so excited to meet you."

"You killed yourself," said Max.

She waved off his comment with a laugh. "I needed a way to disappear. Figured death is a pretty final way to do it. It's amazing what a few connections can get you. But you know that better than anyone, Maximilian."

"What does that mean?"

"You had died too. When I heard about the caves… a part of me died with you. When I saw you with Trevor Martin at a gala a few weeks ago, my heart nearly stopped. You were alive."

"You saw me. Why didn't you approach me?"

She laughed. "And tell you what? I wasn't ready for you yet. And you weren't ready for me."

The last event he'd attended with Trevor was the fundraiser for the Calvin Martin Foundation. "What were you doing there?"

"Getting a better look at Martin. He tried to take my son away from me."

"Milo? How? He doesn't even know him."

Anger flashed across her sculpted face. "Years ago, Emma had sent my baby links to scholarships, internships, everything meant to tear him away from me. I had thought she was on my side, but I was wrong. Got him to apply to the Calvin Martin Foundation for a college scholarship. Without asking me, he almost took it. But my baby listens… at least, he listened then. He declined the scholarship when I told him to, but… after Larry—" She swallowed. "We dealt with a lot of change. Turned out, my baby wanted more change. He left his laptop open, and I chanced a peek."

Max kept his gun trained on his mother. "At his email?"

"At all the emails. I saw the message he'd drafted to Emma, thanking her for all the links she'd sent him all those years ago. He told her he'd reapplied and received the Calvin Martin Foundation scholarship again, and got into NYU. I was livid. Furious. Was I not enough for him? We had new names, a new home. I had just lost my husband. And now he wanted to leave me too? Influenced by that bitch I once thought was so sweet. I didn't let him send that email, deleted his account. But I couldn't let the whole thing repeat again. Had to keep Emma from my kid. Her and Martin and that fucking NYU counselor."

"Clifford Reuben. The man from the East River."

"Fuck him. Did you know he met with my son and helped him with his application? Fucking bastard. Never even asked me for permission to speak to my child. I saw the emails they'd exchanged. No one takes my baby away from me. Ever. Again."

"So you killed him."

His mother's head jerked toward Otis. "He did, for a fee. My only regret is that I never saw his face. So I decided to meet Martin, the man financing my son's self-discovery journey. Went to his gala. Then I saw you. You were dead, and yet there you were. Xander Martin. The adopted son of the sniveling recluse giving Milo money to leave me? He had taken you away and now wanted Milo too? It was only fair that I took you away from him instead."

"How'd you plan on doing that, Mother?" Max asked, though he already knew.

Her lips lifted in a self-satisfied smirk. "I had heard a rumor long ago, a rumor from Rose Falls, about how you earn your money. I had dismissed it. After all, you were dead. When I saw you alive, I knew the rumor was true. My son, an elite assassin. I was so proud. So I put a hit out on Trevor Martin with Milo's full name. I knew that the listing would get your attention. I thought the amount may even entice you to do it yourself."

"You are the one behind MiloAugustus."

"I hoped the name would be a bat signal to you, that your family—me and your little brother—is out there. Just waiting for you, once you eliminate Martin."

His mother wanted him to kill for her. To dispatch the man he considered family in exchange for a twisted blood-relative reunion.

"Milo hadn't been himself after Larry died," she continued. "Started questioning me about our new names, about why we keep moving. Had to nip that in the bud. Figured with the counselor dead, Otis would eliminate Emma, you'd take care of Martin, and we'd be good. A family again. Besides, it's not like it was a reach—you'd already killed Larry."

Max froze. *How did she know that?* "Did you know what Bief did when you married him?"

"Ah. Cutting to the chase, are we? Yes, of course I knew. He and I met on Mercury Marketplace. His entrepreneurial spirit matched mine. He wasn't into that stuff himself. He was into the profits, and the profits were great. I'd never have remarried a fifth time, but he came along and it was love at first sight. I've never felt like that for anyone before.

"I hadn't known it was you who killed him at first, but I knew that, for a while now, someone's been killing my vendors. I was concerned that whoever it was might come for me too, after Larry died. So I faked my death. Changed our names. I was devastated, but I had to move on. For Milo. But the deaths and account takedowns continued. I didn't suspect it was you, but I was determined to find the person responsible for the deaths of my vendors, for Larry's death.

"So I leaked Derek Harbor's identity to see who'd find him, and I waited… When you showed up at the Crescent, I understood then. My baby is just as messed up as me. Don't worry, I had Otis take care of the witness you left behind. I had to protect you, even if you killed the love of my life. Destroyed the legacy he had built."

Her vendors. He tasted bile. "You and Otis are the ones running Mercury Marketplace."

His mother laughed. "Me and Otis? You have to be kidding. Otis is barely sober enough to be here. *I am running the site.*"

"Why?"

"*Why?*" She stood taller. "I have thousands of vendors, millions of buyers. The power, Maximilian… the power is unreal." She took a step forward, eyes gleaming. "I've failed at everything my entire life. I've failed at my jobs, failed as your parent, failed in college, failed to make a decent living. But I'm not failing now. I'm *queen*."

"You gave Milo up for adoption. How is he with you again?"

"The family who adopted him rehomed him. Too many issues, they said, like he was some dog from the pound. Rich people. They can do anything. An attorney helped me get him back."

"Clarence Elrod."

"Yes, Clarence. I repaid the favor. Got him a sweet little gig through my site."

"Selling children."

"To parents who want them."

"To the highest bidder," he corrected her. "How in the hell did you manage to even set this whole site up?"

"I've always been good with computers, great with code. I almost got a degree in it, after all, if I'd have graduated. You may remember that. Once I had the time and money to take more classes, it was easy when I set my mind to it. I owed it to Milo. I failed you, but I couldn't also fail him, my little baby. At first, I thought that I couldn't raise him alone… met some asshole who beat us."

"That's how you met Emma."

"She's a nice girl, I thought. Eager to help. Not going to lie—she did a lot to get me out of that shit situation. Then she overstepped. Put too many ideas in Milo's poor little head. I couldn't lose him. Told Otis to take someone she loved away from her too… so she knew what it felt like."

Janie. His parents were behind Emma's niece almost dying.

"When did you start the site?" he asked his mother.

Pride glimmered in her fake blue eyes. "I didn't start it for anything bad. Just an anonymous marketplace. When I saw the things people were selling—the kiddie porn, the sick little videotapes, I was horrified. Sickened."

"Until you weren't."

"Don't you see? I finally found something I *excel* in. I have millions of clients from across the entire globe. They *worship* me—they'll do anything for me. I told Elrod that Emma had to die, and he went along like a little sheep. She tried to take my son from me, got stupid ideas into his head. She had to pay."

Max hated that his mother spoke of Emma in the past tense. It physically pained him.

He turned to his dad. "How are you involved?"

The old man shrugged. "Needed the cash."

"To protect his own son, *he wanted to get paid*. That's your dad for you."

"Money is money," grumbled his birth father.

"When he failed and refused to try again, Elrod sent him a message."

"He burned down his house."

"And all his drugs he was tasked to sell. A good incentive to try again. I told him he can sell through Mercury if he's successful with Emma. But your father fails at everything. Clarence had to step in."

"Elrod found us in Vegas. How'd he know we were there?"

"You, my dear. I tracked your jet to Vegas. Then Ross called. And we knew exactly where you two were."

"He one of your vendors too?"

"Small-town medicine doesn't pay."

"Where is she?"

"Inside. Sleeping soundly. This won't hurt her. He dosed her good."

"Designer tranq," Otis added.

"The cops know everything now. About you. About Milo. I told them about every one of your identities."

"Well…" His mother smiled. "That's unfortunate, but not unsolvable. After all, I'm technically dead. We can start our lives over. Emma will die in a gas explosion. A terrible accident. We'll finish off Martin. And we'll move on. With your skill set and my business acumen, we will be unstoppable. Max, join me. The power… oh, it is unbelievable. Just a taste, and you'll be hooked."

Nausea seized him. His mother ran the biggest illegal marketplace on the dark web. His mother. The one person he thought had been—even with all her flaws—*good* was the founder.

She wanted him to join her—to let her kill the only woman he'd ever loved and the only real father figure he'd ever known—and rule the cesspool she had created for money and power with her.

His mother. Every single seed he came from was evil.

How could he ever think he could be anything but a monster?

His parents disgusted him. He had to stop them. But first, he had to get to Emma.

He had been eyeing the house, trying to figure out a way in. His father would have to be immobilized first. His mother was too smart to let a weapon be set off in the vicinity of so much leaking gas, but Otis was stupid enough to attempt it.

He'd bring him down, then his mother. The mother he hadn't seen in over twenty years, who turned out to be the worst monster of all.

Movement on the sloping roof behind his parents alerted him. His heart sped up as he recognized Emma, crouched above them, illuminated by the pale glow of moonlight. She was quiet as a mouse, watching. He couldn't draw attention to her. Had to figure out a way to get her down before the whole place blew to bits.

Otis lifted his weapon. "What do you say, son? Money's good."

Max took a step forward as Emma shifted on the roof, sliding herself closer to the edge. He could hear her move. If he could hear her, then so would his birth parents as soon as they stopped talking.

A shingle crashed to the ground.

Otis's shotgun arced in the air, seeking the source of the sound.

With a thunderous roar, Emma leaped—her body crashing on top of Ramona. Bull's-eye.

Now or never.

Max dove for Otis, tackling him to the ground, the shotgun between them. Otis fell on his bad leg, shrieking at the impact. Max punched the man—once, twice. Every ounce of his blood screamed to keep punching, to not stop, to hit the man again and again until his face turned to pulp…

Max fought his instincts.

Tried to regain the control he had lost.

Emma and Ramona were locked in a wrestle, with Emma appearing to have the upper hand. Max caught the dull glint of metal as Ramona drew out a gun—

Otis's fist slammed into the side of his face—

Max turned with the blow. Regained his bearings. And punched out his old man.

He spun toward Emma.

She saw the gun too. Balling her fist, she hit Ramona

square in the jaw with so much strength that Ramona's head bounced.

Max lunged for the gun.

His mother kicked and spat and cursed as he and Emma fought to contain her. The sound of sirens in the background grew stronger. Law enforcement arrived.

A parade of police cars, fire trucks, and ambulances arrived first, their bright lights splitting the nightfall, followed by a few unmarked sedans with tinted windows. Cynthia and Trevor arrived in Trevor's SUV, sans the army of hired guns.

Max didn't have to warn anyone that there was a gas leak. They smelled it as soon as they got out of the cars and activated quickly, seeking the source of the leak.

The police handcuffed his parents and led them away. The EMTs hustled Emma into one of the ambulances. She had inhaled a lot of the carbon monoxide. He watched as one of them administered oxygen before another closed the ambulance doors and the vehicle set off. The siren—and the flashing lights—slowly faded as they turned the corner.

He didn't go with her.

He couldn't.

If he went, he'd never be able to let her go. And he had to let her go. She deserved so much better than him—a monster born of two monsters. He'd always known his bio father was vile, but he'd thought that at least his mother was good. Now he knew better.

There was not a single decent member in his family.

Emma deserved better than him.

So he stayed, addressed the questions as best he could, and silently mourned, finally accepting that genetic evil ran through his veins.

Chapter 53

The next day, Emma sat alone at Max's gargantuan kitchen island, Dusty on her lap and a cup of tea in her hand. It'd been an hour since she was released from the hospital, where she had spent the entire night and a good chunk of that morning. They had put her on pure oxygen for hours and had given her a prolonged neuro exam.

Max hadn't made an appearance.

Cynthia and Trevor had arrived at the hospital shortly after she did. They had stayed with her the entire time, made sure that she was given top-notch treatment.

They had shared that Uncle Jeremy had been found, but he had put an end to his own life before he could be taken into custody. Apparently, he had been buying child abuse materials on Mercury Marketplace, and Max's mother had threatened to expose him unless he helped her grab Emma. Now that Ramona/Carmela/Cara was arrested, Jeremy must have known that it was only a matter of time.

Emma hadn't processed his death yet, or his involvement in her kidnapping. He had always been like an uncle to her, and it was a lot to work through.

Her family had descended on the hospital like a tornado within an hour of her arrival. Emma was certain that the only reason they had been allowed to stay was because Trevor had pulled some strings. They had made themselves comfortable around her spacious, private room until the doctors deemed her well enough to be released that morning. She was given an extensive instruction list should she develop delayed complications, and advised to return in two weeks for a follow-up.

Every time the door to her hospital room had opened, her heart had sped up, expecting Max, but he never showed.

When she was released, her parents insisted that they take her to Cold Spring with them, but she stood her ground. She wasn't going anywhere until she spoke with Max.

What he must be going through...

His own mother ran the site he had been infiltrating.

She had the NYU counselor killed—maybe even also her abusive fourth husband.

His parents tried to kill her—almost killed him.

She wished she could find Max and comfort him, to tell him that they would work through what he was feeling together.

Yet she had absolutely no idea where he was. To this day, she didn't even have his cell phone number.

She had asked Trevor and Cynthia to take her back to Max's apartment. Thankfully, Cynthia had a key. She needed to talk to Max, to make sure he was okay. Had she gone to her own place, she had a feeling she might never see him again.

Last night, back in that remote home in New Jersey, his expression had shuttered completely as they heard the sirens approach. Whatever shock and anger and disgust he had been feeling had been completely locked down by the time law enforcement arrived. Max had gone back into his emotionless world. Emma didn't know how she'd pull him back out of it.

She froze as she heard the front door of the apartment open and shut, then familiar footsteps.

Her heart sped up. *Max.*

Yet when he walked into the kitchen, it both was Max and it wasn't. His eyes were as cold and hard as permafrost. He glanced at her but didn't acknowledge her presence in any way.

"Max…"

He avoided eye contact. "You need to go."

"Go where?"

"My family isn't trying to kill you anymore. You're safe. Go back to your life. Forget everything for the dark chapter that it was."

She stood, setting Dusty to the floor. "I don't want to forget. Max, I don't want to go back to my old life. I—"

"I don't care what you do. I just need you gone."

She didn't recognize him as he was now, so emotionless and detached.

"I don't understand."

"Don't you see? I not only have my father's bad blood inside me, I also have my mother's. My mother is the one who was running that site. My mother is allowing people to capitalize on abuse… you need to go. I've sullied you with my darkness."

"No, you haven't."

"You want to fuck a monster? Is that why I can't get rid of you?" The cruel words hurt like a hailstorm. "Fine. On your knees."

"What?"

"I said… on your knees."

The command, given in that hard-edged tone, should have scared Emma. But when he strolled to the living room and came back with a throw pillow that he tossed on the floor at his feet, she knew she had nothing to fear. This was her Max. No cruel monster would be concerned about her comfort, about her knees being on the hard floor surface.

Emma accepted his challenge.

She took a step forward.

Got on her knees on the cushion in front of him, reached for his zipper, and freed his ready erection.

He watched her from beneath hooded lids, the need in his eyes burning her. His voice gentled as he tilted up her chin. "You want this?"

"Yes," she breathed.

Not breaking eye contact, she tightened her hand around him and ducked her head. His body jerked. She took it as a good sign as she slowly sucked him into the cavern of her mouth.

His hands fisted at his sides as he groaned.

Encouraged, holding his length steady with her hand while the other rested on his powerful thigh for balance, she explored him with a teasing skim of her tongue.

His dark eyes bonded to her face, as if unable to look away. She worked her mouth over him, the nails of her free hand digging into his thigh as she picked up speed. He threw his head back with a loud moan, closing his eyes against the onslaught, his fists releasing, clasping again. Suddenly, he dragged her up his body.

Disoriented, Emma tried to form a coherent question. "What—"

He pulled her the few steps to the counter and bent her over it. Face down, ass out.

The hard marble felt cool through the thin material of her dress. Her nipples, already hard, puckered further at the new sensation.

Max didn't give her much time to react. He pulled

up her dress, tugged her thong to the side, and entered her in one powerful glide. He was moving instantly.

Emma couldn't catch her breath as sharp pleasure spiraled through her.

One hand released her hip to find her clit. The sensations were too much, too overwhelming; she lost all sense of awareness, of time, and then she exploded. The scream he wrenched from her didn't even sound like her own voice.

He moved away from her too quickly. Her knees were wobbly, and she needed the counter for support. When she turned toward him, she realized that they were both still fully clothed, and that he was still hard.

"Wow," she exhaled. "That was—" Before she could find the right word, Max's mouth was on hers, kissing her with a desperation she couldn't mistake. She let him plunder her mouth, let him take what he needed, and kissed him back with all the love and emotion she felt for this frustrating man.

He tore off her thong in one move, entering her on a desperate groan. His mouth plundered hers as his body found her again and again. He kept pumping until he, too, found release with a thunderous roar, emptying himself deep inside her.

"I'm sorry, I'm sorry," he whispered, and it took Emma a second to catch the words he kept exhaling against her skin like a mantra.

"What for?" she asked, trying to follow his trail of thought.

"For not being strong enough to let you go. I can't."

Emma framed his face with her hands, forced him to look at her. "I'm not asking you to. Your parents are really fucked up, Max. Majorly fucked up. But you're not them. You're you, and I love you."

A shudder racked his body. "Say it again."

"I love you, Max. I don't want you to let me go."

"I love you so much, I can't breathe when you're not near me," he confessed against her mouth.

"It's a good thing I'm not going anywhere then."

He covered her mouth with his. "Marry me," he declared, pulling back to look at her.

Her gray eyes rounded in surprise. "What?"

"I know I should propose somewhere romantic and memorable, but I'm an impatient son of a bitch. I don't have a ring, but we can go pick it out together today."

"Max…"

"I am the wrong person for you. You deserve someone so much better than I can ever be. But marry me, and I'll spend the rest of my life making sure you never regret the decision."

Her eyes burned with emotion. A tear leaked out. "Of course I'll marry you." She laughed. "I'm shocked and surprised and I'm so happy. I love you, Maximilian Clark—Xander Martin."

She could see the relief and excitement that danced through him. His arms closed around her as his mouth found hers again. "I love you. I can't imagine my life without you in it."

"Good. Because neither can I." She pulled back. "Looks like you're going to have to join me at my parents' barbecue tomorrow after all."

His lips pressed to her cheek. "Wouldn't miss it for the world."

Chapter 54

One week later

"I don't think I can do this." Max anxiously paced around Emma on the sidewalk next to his building.

"Of course you can. He's your brother. He wants to meet you."

"He knows nothing about me. He doesn't even remember me. How could he possibly want to meet me?"

"Because you're siblings."

They had learned a lot about Milo in the last week. He had been born with fetal alcohol syndrome, and had development and speech delays as a child. The failed adoption must have been a wake-up call for Max's mother, who had worked diligently with Milo to help overcome his learning challenges after she had gotten him back. She had done an incredible job with early interventions. Trevor and Cynthia had briefly met Milo— who went by Ryan now—earlier in the week. They had shared that he seemed like a well-adjusted, though sheltered and shy, twenty-two-year-old.

He'd been homeschooled his whole life, knew nothing about his mother's or stepfather's dark web activities. Learning that his mother was going to prison had nearly broken him.

But his mother had used his little brother. She'd linked most of her illegal activities to his accounts—she said she wanted to protect him, but it appeared that she was trying to protect herself. Even the house off Route 46 that belonged to him on paper had been rented out by her for filming to a couple of her Mercury Marketplace vendors.

Ryan would have to deal with a lot: his mother's arrest and upcoming trial, learning that his birth father lived within miles of him this entire time and would soon be tried too. Max wanted to be there for his sibling in whatever capacity was needed, but he was scared. He'd never been a real big brother before.

As minutes ticked by and his brother had yet to join them, Max fought to hold his clawing anxiety at bay.

Trevor, who came for moral support but stood off to the side, joined them. He must have noticed Max's increasingly agitated pacing. He placed his hand on Max's shoulder, his touch reassuring. "Can I talk to you for a minute?"

Emma squeezed his hand before stepping away to give them privacy.

Max's father looked at him for a long time before he spoke. "I've known you a long time. Hell, I've been your legal father for years. Something occurred to me when you ran off to New Jersey last week to get your girl." Trevor hesitated.

Max had never seen the man nervous before.

Trevor continued. "It never occurred to me to tell you that... that I love you. I know, I know, it's not something you want to hear. But I want you to know. I'm very proud of you, Max. Of the man you've become. You coming into my life made me want to live again—and I am grateful for you every single day. I pray every night, thanking God that you're in my life. You're…" He cleared his throat. "You're the son of my heart. I wanted you to know that. How…" He cleared his throat again, his eyes shining. "How much I love you. Like my very own son. I only wish you could have met Calvin. He'd have loved having you as his brother. He'd have looked up to you. Now you have a chance to meet your biological brother. And he's the luckiest guy in the world. Because he has you for a big brother."

His own eyes burned with tears. Trevor had been in his life for so long, had been his legal parent for so long, had been his mentor for so long, but Max had been too terrified to tell the man how much he meant to him. He had feared that Trevor would scoff, would tell him that Max was nothing more to him than a coworker with the same mission in life. Even worse, what if Trevor secretly feared him, or was disgusted by him, and wanted nothing to do with him?

It took Max several moments to find his voice through the tears that clogged his throat. "I love you, Dad. You've always been… thank you for… thank you for being a great father."

As his dad's arms tightened around him, Max felt a deep sense of gratitude to have Trevor in his life.

Emma approached the two men quietly, and Max pulled her into his side. "I think I'm ready to meet my brother now."

"Good." Emma waved to the young man walking toward them. "I know he's ready to meet you."

Epilogue

One year later

Max was going to freak. Emma left her doctor's office, unsure how she'd break the news to her husband. She'd taken three tests at home—they were all positive—and the doctor confirmed. She and Max were going to have a baby.

A little baby boy or a little baby girl due this spring. Emma could hardly believe it.

She knew Max just might pass out.

Although they'd broached the subject of kids a few months back, he was hesitant. He didn't want to screw up his kid as badly as his parents had screwed him up. She had tried to tell him that he'd be an incredible father, but she knew her words sounded like syrupy platitudes to his ears.

She had no idea how he would react now that a hypothetical situation had become a reality.

They'd been married almost a year. In that time, the FBI had partnered with the Justice Department and Homeland Security Investigations to fully shut down Mercury Marketplace. Gaining access to Ramona's account had allowed them to pinpoint where her servers were being hosted—the Netherlands. Dutch law enforcement had worked with the courts to shut them down, seizing $30M in cryptocurrency linked to the site. Investigators were now tracking down each vendor, in partnership with Trevor, Max, Cynthia, and their team, to bring them to justice.

The high-profile case allowed Trevor, Max, and Cynthia to officially launch their Cyber Clarity Taskforce, which worked across all countries, offering their services to investigate and shut down dark net activities pro bono to local law enforcement agencies. They still tunneled into the darkest recesses of the web to ferret out the scumbags, but they now partnered with law enforcement to bring them to justice legally. Max had a direct line to Homeland Security, the FBI, Interpol, and innumerable law enforcement organizations across an ever-growing list of countries. He no longer dealt with the criminals himself, leaving wet work behind once and for all.

Trevor Martin made sure that the Cyber Clarity Taskforce would always have generous funding to make their work possible.

Max's biological parents had both been sentenced to life in prison. Emma and Max never thought or talked about them.

Max had seamlessly integrated into her family. Her parents treated him as another son, and Max and Emma drove up to Cold Spring every other Sunday to have dinner with her parents, siblings, and niece and nephew. They all called him Xander, but it didn't bother Emma. It was his official name, after all.

Trevor had become part of the family as well, joining them for many occasions. Janie and Finn called him Grandpa Trevor, and the old man's face would shine in joy every time they did. He'd have his very own grandbaby now.

Riley had recently shared with Emma that she was ready to date again. Emma was thrilled. It had been a difficult journey to recovery for her sister. She was giving it a few more months and then she'd set up her sister with one of her colleagues at work. Her gut was telling her that the two would hit it off, and she'd learned to trust her gut again.

Max's brother had become a key member of the family as well, moving in with Max and Emma last year. The two brothers needed each other to process what their parents had done. Ryan had absolutely no idea what his mother was involved in, and was tired of the constant name changes. Ramona had told him that his abusive father was looking for them, and that was why they had to constantly hide their true identities. The kid had to absorb and adjust to a lot of information at once, but Max was helping him through it, like the great big brother that he was. Ryan was now officially enrolled in college and would soon be moving into NYU housing, but Max and she insisted that he come home for dinner at least a few times a week.

Emma had made up with Leslie Pepper, who attended their Cold Spring wedding, and if she were having a girl, she'd like to name her daughter Matilda, after Max's childhood friend who had meant so much to him.

When she arrived at their apartment, Emma found Max in his home office, studying something on his computer screen. Dusty sat on his desk, his eyes focused on the same screen. The Himalayan considered himself a key partner to Max in his work.

Max looked up at her approach and smiled widely. He was smiling a lot more now. Emma loved it.

He stood up from the desk, coming around to meet her halfway across the room. His arms tightened around her. "You're never home this early from work. To what do I owe this surprise?"

Emma hesitated. She was thrilled about their soon-to-be new addition to the family, but what if he had the opposite reaction?

"Sweetheart?" he asked, suddenly alert. "Everything okay?"

Emma could hardly speak from the excitement bubbling inside her. "Everything is perfect. I just came from the doctor. I'm pregnant."

Max's face exploded in joy. "We're having a baby?"

"Yes. And before you get all moody and say you don't know how to be a dad or that this baby will have your bad genes, know that you're wrong. You'll be a wonderful father. You've been an incredible uncle to Janie and Finn and a great older brother. This baby is going to have the best dad in the world, and he's going to grow up to be a good person, like his daddy."

Max pressed Emma close and kissed her with barely contained excitement. "Of course this baby is going to be perfect. She has you for a mother. You're pure goodness in human form, and she has your blood in her veins."

"So you're not freaking out?"

"I'm freaking out a little," he admitted. "But I'm so happy, Emma. You've given me a family. It's more than I ever thought I'd have."

"I love you."

"I love you. Since you seem to be done with work early today, let me remind you how much."

He scooped her up in his arms, and carried her to their bedroom.

About the Author

Anya London resides in California. When she's not writing, she enjoys running, hiking, reading, and traveling. Please contact her at www.anya-london.com/.

Also by Anya London

A Very French Scandal
Once Upon a New York Summer
A Very Italian Scandal